T0354518

SPIRIT WALKER

SPIRIT WALKER

Jeff Miner

SPIRIT WALKER

iUniverse books may be ordered through booksellers or by contacting:

iUniverse
1663 Liberty Drive
Bloomington, IN 47403
www.iuniverse.com
1-800-Authors (1-800-288-4677)

ISBN: 978-1-5320-4625-4 (sc)
ISBN: 978-1-5320-3918-8 (e)

Library of Congress Control Number: 2018904188

Print information available on the last page.

iUniverse rev. date: 04/03/2018

CHAPTER 1

The morning cry of a rooster woke Helaku from a deep, restful slumber. He moved aside the warm animal hides he slept beneath and steadily got to his feet. Walking to the entrance of the tepee, he stretched slowly, hearing the popping from his joints and feeling the aches and pains he had become all too accustomed to each morning. At sixty-one years old, it was certainly more difficult than it had been in his forties and fifties.

After dressing, he began the daily ritual of braiding his long white hair into two ponytails. Glancing at his reflection, he could see his years in the wrinkles and creases on his face like so many roads on a map. From the neck down, however, he was a totally different man. His body was still lean and toned, and he could easily be mistaken for someone in his thirties or forties if not for his snow-white mane. That was not the case three years earlier, before his wife, Saswanna, had passed. They were a couple in their late fifties, but they acted like love-struck teenagers. They hiked in the mountains, ran on the beach, and held hands everywhere they went. Several of her older family members had their hearts fail on them as well, but she had always assumed that her active lifestyle would protect her from their fate. Tragically, it did not, and at only fifty-seven, she was struck down in the prime of her life. Helaku was devastated. He fell into a deep depression and began drinking again after going more than twenty years without a drop. In only a year, he appeared to age a decade, and his family feared that they would lose him too—to a broken heart.

Ultimately, the love and support of his grandson Richard turned Helaku around. He and Richard were truly kindred souls, filled with life. They both loved nature and running along the beach until their lungs burned and their legs ached. In the end, Richard was able to bring Helaku back from the darkness, and the older man chose life over despair.

Looking over his shoulder, Helaku could see Richard sleeping in the tepee. He lived with his parents and younger sister, but he loved going to stay with his grandfather. On their long walks in the woods, Helaku would teach Richard about the different birds and woodland creatures and share fantastical stories of their people that had been passed down for countless generations.

Stepping outside of the canvas and feeling the cool dew-covered grass on his bare feet, he could immediately see that it would be a beautiful day. The sky was crystal clear, and the hills around them were green and majestic as they had been for as long as anyone could remember. Redwoods outlined the crest of the ridge like gigantic soldiers standing proudly at attention, and a large brown hawk flew overhead, looking for its next meal.

Closing his eyes, Helaku could just pick up the faint sound of the ocean only half a mile away. With a deep inhale through his nostrils, he took in the sweet smells of ocean breezes and all things in his mind that represented nature. The sensation invigorated him, as it did every morning, and he felt truly good to be alive.

Ping. The soft but distinct sound was coming from the back of the tepee.

Ping. There it was again. With his moment with nature now officially interrupted, Helaku turned with annoyance and walked back inside.

"Your phone is chirping again," he said.

"Huh?" a muffled voice came from beneath the heavy animal skin.

"Your phone—that thing you are so utterly consumed with—is chirping again at you."

Throwing back the animal skin to reveal a torrent of flowing black hair, almost completely covering the face of the young teen, the boy answered. "It's called a tweet, not a chirp."

"Then your phone is tweeting at you. Do you need to call someone?"

The young man slumped back under the covers. "It's just an IM."

"You are what?" Helaku asked.

Realizing he was not going to be sleeping any longer, Richard slowly sat up. "What are you talking about?"

"You said 'I am,' but then you didn't continue. Are you hungry or thirsty?"

Shaking his head in disbelief, the boy said, "No, Grandpa. IM is short for 'instant message.' It means that someone sent me a note or something. Might also be a Facebook update."

"A what-book update?" Helaku asked. "That's another one of those computer things that you spend all of your time on, right?"

Richard smiled and pulled his shoulder-length jet-back hair into a ponytail. "Yeah, Grandpa. It's one of those computer things. You really should get a cell phone now that they put up that tower at the top of the hill last year. That way, I can actually get a hold of you when I need something. I can show you how to use it. We'll just get you a really basic one."

"Why would I need another phone when I have the one at the house?"

"Oh, that one with the answering machine that you only check once every couple of weeks? I was thinking of something a bit more reliable. What if something important came up and we really needed to get a hold of you?"

"If you call and I don't pick up, you can also call my neighbor. Your mother has his number, and he never leaves the house. And if it's all that important, you're only a twenty-minute drive away."

Realizing that it was pointless to continue this topic of conversation, Richard changed the subject. "So are we running this morning?"

Helaku's entire disposition changed as he smiled with pure joy and pride. "Of course. Your cross-country practices start next week, right? We need to make sure you're in good condition. Let me use the restroom, and we can leave in a few minutes. Work up a good appetite for breakfast."

Richard smiled as his grandfather walked through his yard toward the mobile home where he lived when he was not being at one with the spirits of his ancestors in the traditional tepee he had erected in his backyard. Richard loved running with his grandfather almost as much as he did talking with him about nature and all the different legends of their tribe.

Richard came from a long line of runners, and Helaku actually translated to "Running Bear." He had been jogging the trails along the reservation his entire life, and two years back, at the suggestion of Richard's father, Eneyto, he entered a 10K race. Helaku came in first for his age group, and he broke the California record for men over fifty by more than a minute! To make the accomplishment all the more amazing, he ran the entire race barefoot! The barefoot part especially attracted everyone's attention, and the local news made a pretty big deal about it. He actually became a bit famous in their little corner of the world for several weeks, and that notoriety really got Richard excited about the sport.

Helaku was eventually persuaded to buy a pair of actual running shoes, and he started competing in longer and longer races, eventually completing his first marathon about eighteen months earlier. He ended up placing fourth for his over-fifty age group, even though he was one of the oldest competitors in that bracket. Once he turned sixty and he was racing in the sixty-to-seventy-year-old division, he was nearly unstoppable. Over the next year and a half, he ran twelve marathons and was currently ranked seventh in the nation for men over sixty.

After their usual stretching session, the two headed out through town, toward the entrance to Ridge Trail at the far end. Running through the reservation, the roads were mostly empty at this hour, save a few older folks enjoying their morning coffee on their front porches. It never failed to amuse Richard when they consistently gave Helaku the same stares of utter disbelief as he ran past them. Many of his neighbors were his age or younger, but they were old, stiff, and broken down from a life of poverty and hardship. How in the world was this man striding past them with the grace of a gazelle, seemingly immune to Father Time?

Once on the trail, the road began to incline as it branched to the north. Richard felt the sweat dripping down his forehead and into his eyes as they passed the one-mile mark. His grandfather was only a few paces ahead of him, but Richard knew he was holding back. If he had wanted to go full-steam ahead, he would have already left him in the dust. Richard kept reminding himself that his grandfather was a highly accomplished distance runner, but when you're getting thoroughly schooled by someone more than four times your age, it's hard not to beat yourself up a bit. The incline increased significantly, and Richard's legs began to burn fiercely as the lactic acid started to build up in his quadriceps. Finally, after another mile, they reached the high point of the ridge and began the long, winding trail back to the ocean. They would run the last two miles on the beach.

Richard sighed with relief when they started the gradual downhill section of the trail. It was the most beautiful section of the run. Between the moss-covered redwoods and coastal cypress trees, he could see the ocean in the distance. His lungs filled with the cool sea mist in the air, and a renewed strength returned to his legs. After another fifteen minutes, they finally made it to the beach, which was his favorite part of the run.

As usual, once making it to the cold, firm sand at the water's edge, Richard and his grandfather removed their shoes and ran the last section barefoot, carrying a shoe in each hand. For the final stretch, both picked up the pace and gradually built up speed until it was practically an all-out sprint for the last two hundred yards. The run culminated in the same way that it did every time. Helaku kept it close, but in the end, he always beat Richard by at least a few strides.

The two quickly slowed into a walk, holding their sides in pain as they regained their breath.

Visibly winded, Helaku turned to Richard. "That was a good run, Grandson. You get faster and faster every time we run together. It will not be long before I will be chasing you. Let's take a swim to cool down. There's no better time for a swim in the ocean than after a good run."

A look of terror immediately swept across Richard's face as he turned to his grandfather. "No! I'm good. I learned my lesson last time."

Smiling warmly, Helaku said. "Are you still making a big fuss about that? I really don't see what you could be so upset about."

Red with embarrassment, Richard said, "What I should be upset about? The last time we had this conversation, I was just about to jump into the water. I looked over, and you were butt naked! You have any idea how weird it is to go swimming naked with your grandfather? I'm surprised that I'm not in therapy as we speak!"

Helaku chuckled to himself. "I just don't understand why someone would intentionally jump into the ocean in their clothes, getting them soaking wet, when they can simply take them off and then have nice dry clothes to put on once they get out. Our people have run along this stretch and beach and swam naked in the ocean for a thousand years. There could be nothing more natural that this."

Realizing that Richard was not going to come around on his position that morning, the old man said, "Very well. Perhaps next time. Come on. Let's go make some breakfast."

After walking half a mile back to the mobile home, Helaku showered so he could prepare breakfast while Richard got cleaned up.

By the time Richard was out of the shower, the meal was ready. They sat down for a delicious plate of mutton, eggs, and freshly baked biscuits with butter and honey.

After finishing breakfast and helping his grandfather with the dishes, Richard made his way to the large recreation center at the center of the reservation. Helaku had to prepare for a meeting with the tribe elders that afternoon, and Richard hoped to meet up with his cousin and other reservation friends for pool, Ping-Pong, or some movies on the big-screen TV. Most of the people who lived on the reservation were quite poor and had few amenities that most people took for granted. The rec center provided them a place to relax, play, and have fun. There was also a section with toys, and mothers would often drop off their kids on the way to work or the store and leave them for hours on end. It was all one big family there, and everyone looked out for everybody for the most part.

Once inside, Richard saw his cousin Chenowa playing an old Space Invaders arcade game. Smiling wickedly, he snuck over and surprised Chenowa. "So you got the high score on that thing yet?"

Startled, Chenowa turned around and was quickly killed by the flashing pixilated aliens on the screen. Realizing who it was, he smiled and jokingly punched his cousin's shoulder. "You jerk! You made me die. Why did you have to sneak up on me like that?"

"For exactly this reaction," Richard said.

"How much longer are you here?" Chenowa asked.

"Till tomorrow afternoon. I wouldn't want to miss the harvest celebration tonight."

"Bitchin'! I'm sure we'll have a blast, bro. The whole tribe will be there. It's just not the same since you guys moved into the burbs. Elania will be there!"

"That's okay," Richard said. "She's cool and all, but I guess I'm just not that into her. Besides, I thought she was seeing your brother."

"Screw Ahote! He's just a big a-hole-e!" Chenowa said. "He's nothing but a big jerk who thinks he can always get his way. Elania doesn't even really like him. She only hangs out with him because she knows that he'd go ape poop if she told him where to stick it. I'm telling you... she likes you, bro!"

Richard's cousins fought like cats and dogs, and they had done so for most of their lives. Chenowa was ten when he first figured out that Ahote sounded a lot like a-hole-e, and from that moment forward, he proceeded to use the phrase at every possible opportunity. Chenowa was fourteen like Richard, and the two had always been as close as brothers. They spent countless hours playing together at the reservation, right up until Richard's family had moved away three years earlier. Ahote was two years older and got his size earlier than most, which only exaggerated the age difference. He had always razzed both of them, but he had gotten outright cruel about two years ago.

Richard's father, Enyto—or Ernie, as he liked to be called—was born and raised on the reservation. Growing up quite poor, he was a particularly driven young man. During high school and college, he worked construction for a company where he learned the ins and outs of the industry. After college, he passed the exam to earn his contractor license, and shortly after, he started his own construction company. The early years of the business were tough, and Richard had a somewhat limited memory of his father, who was almost always at a job site. Ernie eventually learned that with a minority-owned business he had an inside track on a number of government jobs. After fifteen years of hard work, he employed twenty full-time workers, and he had at least a dozen more contractors working for him at any given time. Richard's family bought a 2,500-square-foot home in Bentleyville, a suburb of Laguna Hills, about fifteen miles from the reservation.

One of Ernie's employees was Chenowa and Ahote's father, Senawa. His construction skills were tolerable, but his work ethic was horrible. He was habitually late, many times hungover, and he took more sick days than any two of Ernie's other employees put together. Being the brother-in-law of the owner, he assumed that Ernie would always let him off with a stern warning. After several months, Ernie finally had no choice but to fire him. Unfortunately, that's where things really started to spiral downward for Ahote and their entire family. After being out of work for nearly six months, Senawa finally got a job driving a truck throughout the Pacific Northwest. After several months, he met a waitress in Portland, and after a brief affair, he had the audacity to handwrite a letter for his wife and sons, telling them that he was leaving the family and moving to Portland.

As one might expect, this turn of events had a profound impact on the two families. Richard's mother, Ayiana, horrified by her brother's behavior, cut off all communications with him and became exceptionally close with her sister-in-law, Lisana. Richard's parents did what they could to help them financially, but the family still struggled greatly. Thankfully for Richard, his relationship with Chenowa was not damaged by the turn of events. His cousin obviously loved his father greatly, but he understood that it was ultimately his father's actions that led him to make the decisions that put their family in the predicament they were in.

Ahote saw this entire sequence of events as a series of dominos, initiated by his father getting fired at the hands of Ernie. He figured that if he had only given his dad one more chance, none of this would have happened. Unfortunately for Richard, he quickly became the primary object of Ahote's anger and frustration. To add fuel to the fire, he once overheard Richard making a comment to his dad about Senawa being sick a lot. In reality, he was a ten-year-old kid mimicking the same complaint he'd heard his father say countless times before. To Ahote, that one statement ultimately led to his father getting fired. It really made no sense logically, but fury and frustration often cloud one's capacity for rational thinking.

Ahote made great efforts to turn his brother against Richard, but in the end, his lifelong friendship with Richard won out over the irrational ramblings of an older brother who'd picked on him for as long as he could remember. In a way, it made things even worse for Chenowa since he had to live with Ahote 24-7, while Richard only ran into him occasionally during his time on the reservation. Their mother did what she could to try to keep the peace, but it was a constant struggle. The dynamic made the time Richard spent with Chenowa all the more special. Chenowa had literally chosen Richard over his own sibling, and in his mind, that truly made them brothers.

After a few minutes of small talk, the two headed over to the pool table. After they racked the balls and did a quick rock-paper-scissors, Richard made the initial break. It was a clean shot that hit just to the right of the yellow one ball, sending the group of spheres cascading across the faded green table. He was especially pleased to see the burgundy five ball sink into one of the corner pockets.

"Oh, yeah! Solids. Eat my shorts, Chedderman!" Richard exclaimed.

The friendly nickname materialized several years earlier at a large potluck on the reservation. One of the attendees brought a huge cheese plate. At that time, Chenowa was a fanatic about cheese, specifically cheddar, and proceeded to eat about thirty of the small cubes of yellow goodness. All was well until about an hour later, when the ceremonial dances took place. After apparently overexerting himself, he proceeded to puke up the orange sludge all over the dancing area, bringing the entire event to a screeching halt! He had been Chedderman ever since.

"Go ahead and take your next shot, Blockhead," Chenowa said. "You'll need all the help you can get. You forget that while you're down in the burbs gaming online with your other friends, I'm here practicing!"

The Blockhead moniker had a similarly traumatic origin. When Richard was ten, his father, who had kept his hair short for years, took Richard to the barber in town to get him a proper haircut. Before he knew what was happening, he had a crew cut with the hair clipped nearly to his scalp on the sides and back and leaving only an inch on top. With the little remaining hair standing straight up, it gave his head a somewhat squared appearance. Upon seeing the new hairdo, it only took Chenowa seconds to shout, "What the hell happened to your hair? Your head looks just like a block of wood!"

Even though it was four years ago, and Richard's hair had grown back to his much-preferred shoulder-length style, the nickname still made him wince.

The two of them continued playing for another ten minutes, and Chenowa took the lead with his last shot.

"Well, if it isn't Peppermint Patty and the traitor."

The words were like daggers. With a feeling of dread, both turned toward the door of the rec center.

Ahote was staring at them with a look of sheer malevolence. He had his own nicknames for Chenowa and Richard, but they were used with absolutely no goodwill or fun spirits. Since moving to the suburbs, Richard was no longer a real Indian because he was now living like the white man. He was only brown on the outside and all white on the inside: Peppermint Patty. For Chenowa, there was not even an attempt to be clever or witty at all. He had been given the opportunity to take the side of his brother, or Richard, and he chose the latter. From that moment on, he was always going to be considered a traitor.

"What are you two numb nuts up to?" Ahote said. "Nothing good I'm sure. Patty, shouldn't you be going home to your white-guy house to hang out with your white-guy friends? Or do you like slumming it here with the rest of your *former* people so you can gloat about how much richer you are than the rest of us?"

"What the hell are you talking about?" Richard said. "First of all, I don't have any more money than you have. My parents do, and it wasn't even my idea to move out. I would have just as soon stay here. And as far as my white-guy friends are concerned, my three best friends—other than those here on the reservation—are Mexican, black, and Chinese. You just need to chill the hell out and get over yourself."

Ahote had a fire in his eyes as he shot stares of pure rage at Richard. His response to his earlier statement had aggravated the situation. Ahote quickly marched toward Richard.

Realizing the imminent peril he was in, Richard glanced over to the main office and observed the volunteer on the phone at the front desk. Quickly scanning the rest of the room, the only other people were younger kids. There was no one who could to do a damn thing if things got physical.

Had Richard not taken those precious moments looking for help, he might have been able to make a run for it, but by the time his eyes made it back Ahote, his cousin was already on top of him. His right hand struck out like a viper, grasping Richard's neck and pushing his body against the wall behind him.

Richard grabbed at his hand and tried to loosen the grip at his throat, but his opponent was two years older, two inches taller, and close to fifty pounds heavier!

Chenowa did what he could to help, but his efforts were met with a quick punch to the chest from Ahote's free left hand, stunning his brother with pain and fear. Terror shot through Richard's mind as the lack of oxygen took hold. There was a ringing in his ears, and all the sounds around him were muffled and distorted. His vision started getting blurry and going black all around him. Terror overwhelmed him, and his strength drained out of him like a deflating balloon. Richard was just about to lose unconscious when he heard a sharp crack followed by the sudden release of pressure from his windpipe. Slumping to the ground and backing away from his opponent, Richard took several deep breaths.

Ahote screamed, "You little bastard! You're gonna pay for this big-time!"

Glancing past Ahote, whose back was now toward him, he could see Chenowa standing a few feet away with a pool cue still grasped tightly in his hands. Examining a bright-red mark at the back of Ahote's neck, Richard realized that Chenowa must have struck him with the cue to get him to release his chokehold. Chenowa had just saved his life, and now Richard was frozen in fear as Ahote mercilessly took his revenge. The smaller brother took a second strike, but Ahote, seeing the blow coming, grabbed the stick and tore it out of his hands.

Now disarmed, Chenowa could only stand powerless as his brother grasped the front of his T-shirt with his left hand and landed three quick, stinging punches to the side of his brother's face. Following the vicious attack, he mercifully released his brother, only to turn back to Richard on the floor. "So what you gonna do now, Patty?" Ahote sneered. "I just beat the crap outta your best friend! You gonna take a swing at me? Come on. I'll even let you take the first punch. I won't even try to stop you." He stared on with a look of utter disgust and sheer exhilaration. Richard was absolutely terrified of him, and he loved every second of the torment.

"You going do something, or you just gonna sit there and piss yourself?"

Every fiber of Richard's body wanted to jump up and hit this bully harder than he had ever hit anything. Nevertheless, despite his best intentions, he just couldn't will his arms and legs to move. He simply sat there motionless.

An adult voice shouted, "What the hell is going on here? Look what you did to your brother, you big bully. I'm gonna tell your mother what happened. You get outta here now!" The man working the front desk had finally managed to pull himself away from his phone call.

Better late than never, Richard thought.

Ahote offered one last hateful sneer before casually walking out of the rec center.

Finally able to move again, Richard rushed over to where Chenowa was sitting on the ground, hands covering his red and quickly swelling face.

"Are you okay?" Richard yelled. It was an utterly stupid thing to say, and he knew it, but it was the only thing he could think of in his mentally frazzled state. "That bastard can't get away with this. I'm sorry I couldn't do more to help. I should have taken a shot at him when I had the chance, but I just couldn't get myself to do it."

"It's okay," Chenowa said, fighting off the tears that streamed down his face. "If you had taken a swing at him, he would have just come back and beaten the hell out of you too. At least with me, he stopped after three punches. I'm pretty sure that if it was you, he wouldn't have stopped swinging."

The man working at the rec center brought a plastic storage bag filled with ice from the kitchen. The initial contact stung sharply, but the coolness that followed was a welcome change. Within a few minutes, Chenowa began to feel better.

Suddenly, Lisana walked through the entrance with Ahote. "And just what the hell have the two of you been up to?" she yelled. "Fighting again I see. Why can't you guys just get along?"

"We had nothing to do with it!" Chenowa said. "He just came in here, and out of nowhere, he nearly choked Richard to death, and then he punched me in the face three times!"

"It wasn't like that at all," Ahote said. "We were just horsing around, and all of a sudden, Richard started really throwing punches. While I was distracted with him, this little jerk whacked me with a pool cue! I'm lucky he didn't damage my spine. I admit that I kinda lost it for a second and slugged him in the face, but it was only one time."

Lisana looked to the man at the desk. "Did you see what happened here?"

"I only caught the end of it," the man replied. "I was on the phone and was interrupted by the sound of the older one getting hit with the pool cue. When I finally got here, the older one was yelling at the third one who was sitting on the ground."

"See?" Ahote said. "Just like I said it went down."

"Are you friggin' nuts!" Chenowa said. "All the guy said was that he was on the phone and basically missed the whole thing. Look at my face—and look at Richard's neck!"

"Enough!" Lisana shouted. "The three of you are all family and should not be fighting. Now learn to get along—and no more of this. Period! If I hear about any more fighting, both of you will be grounded for a month. And I'll strongly recommend the same to your mother, Richard."

"What the hell?" Richard said. "The two of us are almost dead and a-hole-e gets away scot-free?"

"I said enough! From all of you. That's it!" Lisana turned and stormed out of the door.

Ahote was grinning like the Cheshire cat. His eyes oozed a malice that they could almost taste in the air. He had successfully outsmarted everyone, and as he casually walked back toward the exit, he stopped and took a bow like a sadistic ringmaster. Just before leaving, he gave one last sinister look to Richard and whispered, "See you at the celebration tonight."

After gathering the strength to thank Chenowa again for saving his life, Richard slowly walked back to his grandfather's mobile home. The flood of feelings that swept over him were overwhelming. Rage, humiliation, terror, and self-doubt swirled through his mind like a tornado. He kept replaying that moment when he could have taken a shot at his foe but was too afraid to do so. Over and over, he went through those few seconds, trying desperately to replay them with a different outcome in his mind. And what would he tell Grandpa? He certainly couldn't tell him the truth. He froze while Chenowa was getting his face smashed in. Should he tell him anything? Even though Richard came within seconds from his death, he had virtually no visible marks to show for it besides some redness around his neck. With his grandfather's eyesight, Richard doubted if he'd even notice it.

At the stairs leading the door of the mobile home, he paused and glanced up woefully. Still not sure what he was going to say, he dragged his steps, each foot feeling like it weighed twenty pounds. At the top, he took a deep breath and entered the living room.

"Welcome back," Running Bear said. "You were gone for a while. Must have run into some of your friends."

"I was with Chenowa," Richard answered.

"Excellent! I'm sure that you kids had a great time. It does my heart good to know that you guys always remained so close. When his father left, I prayed that it would not harm your friendship given the circumstances—and thankfully it did not. I only hope that one day his brother will come around as well. So I take it you had a good time?"

A cold sweat came over Richard as the tremendous weight of the moment burdened him greatly. It was his chance to fess up to his grandfather about what happened. *You may not have had the courage to trade blows with Ahote, but at least you can come clean now.* Richard knew that his grandfather would be disappointed, but he would be reassuring.

"Yeah, it was fun." Richard felt the life draining out of him as the words escaped his mouth.

"Great!" The old man was chipper as ever. "Tonight will be a great celebration for our people. I'm so glad that you will be here with us."

"Yeah, about that," Richard whispered. "I'm actually not feeling very good. I ate some food from the vending machine, and I think it was past its expiration date or something. My stomach is all in knots."

A look of sadness and disappointment washed over Helaku as his grandson spoke. He gave Richard a once-over and said, "Yes. Now that I take a look at you, something does seem a little off. I'll ask your mother to come and pick you up. Hope you'll be okay for school on Monday. At least, you'll have tomorrow to rest up… first day of high school, right?"

Richard didn't reply, and he slowly eased down into the La-Z-Boy in the living room and reached for the remote to the TV. He flipped through a couple of channels and finally stopped on a rerun of a *Seinfeld* episode he'd seen at least four times. It didn't matter since he was not really watching; he was hopelessly lost in his thoughts. He heard his grandfather on the phone with his mom, but he couldn't make out the words. Everything seemed muffled and blurred again, just like it had earlier.

It was about an hour before his mom arrived. During that time, Richard gathered up all the belongings he'd brought with him, and when she finally got there, he nearly sprinted to the car. Ayiana actually had to stop and remind him to say thank you and goodbye to his grandfather before leaving. As with most of their partings, Richard gave him a hug, but this time, he held on a little tighter and for a bit longer than normal. Making his way to his mom's 4Runner, he prayed that his mom would just get into the car and start driving without her typical game of fifty questions, but as soon as she sat down, the inquisition began.

"Sorry you're not feeling well. Is it your head or your tummy? Did you have a good time otherwise? I heard you had a good run this morning. Are there any other clothes we need to buy you for school this week?"

CIA interrogators could not keep up with his mom's sheer endurance and persistence when it came to asking questions. Thankfully, after half a dozen one-word responses, she finally clued in that he was not in a talking mood and mercifully stopped her inquiry.

As they drove off the reservation, they passed the center square where the autumn celebration would be starting in a few hours. Richard looked on solemnly at the large bonfire; the ceremonial lighting would occur shortly. He could smell roasting pork and deer in the air and saw several children—already dressed in their traditional clothes—running and playing, the same way he remembered doing not so many years earlier. There was also was a raised stage where his grandfather and the rest of the elders would speak to the entire tribe about their people's history and the pride they should all be feeling during traditional events.

Richard's mood was starting to cheer up a bit, until he stopped and locked in on a solitary figure leaning against a tree toward the back of the crowd.

Ahote was looking as smug and condescending as ever. As Richard looked on—still fuming at the day's occurrences—their eyes met.

Ahote's self-righteous, satanic smile grew even bigger than before. He scared Richard completely off the reservation. He was so traumatized by his beating that he had to call his mommy to come and take him home. And to add one final insult to injury, he waved goodbye as the truck turned to leave the reservation.

Overwhelmed with embarrassment and anger, Richard cursed for not having the guts to stand up for himself or Chenowa. At that moment, he was not sure if he could ever bring himself to come back to the reservation. During the entire ride home, Richard was silent, using every ounce of free will to fight off the tears that were welling up in his eyes.

CHAPTER 2

The alarm clock sounded at six thirty, and Richard slowly woke from his slumber and proceeded to grope around for a few seconds before hitting the snooze button and retreating under the comfort of his warm covers. Much to his surprise, he did not immediately fall back asleep. After the alarm went off a second time five minutes later, he made his way to the bathroom. It was a Monday morning— the first day of a new school year. Normally, that particular event would have been met with utter melancholy and despair, but this time was different. It was the first day of high school! Unlike the awkward years of junior high—filled with changing voices, acne, and boys who hadn't figured out that they needed to start wearing deodorant—high school was the place where boys became men, girls became girls, and you started developing into the person that will ultimately determine the overall course of your life.

The events on the reservation two days earlier still bothered him, but having had all day Sunday to think about it gave him some perspective. Ahote was two years older, way bigger, and would have no doubt beaten the holy heck out of him if he had been brave and stupid enough to take a swing at the big jerk. And despite his near-fatal experience, he was clearly not dead and would need to deal with all the teenage trials and tribulations of high school just like everybody else. At least, he would not have to do it alone.

Following a quick shower—he managed to beat his little sister to the bathroom—Richard headed downstairs. His mother was standing at the stove, and his father was eating breakfast and reading the *San Francisco Chronicle*. They received a local paper as well, but Ernie ordered the *Chronicle* to make sure that he was fully up to

19

speed on all the real news going on out there. Noticing Richard as he entered the kitchen, he smirked sarcastically. "So first day of high school? Pretty big stuff. You know, grades actually start counting now with regard to college, so you may want to consider cutting back a bit on the time you spend on the computer playing Overwork. You know your Mom and I aren't made of money, so it's not too early to start thinking about some sort of scholarship."

"For Christ's sake, dear," Richard's mom said. "He's not even made it to his first day of high school, and you're already getting him stressed out over his SAT scores! Let the boy just enjoy his time there. He knows that school is important."

"I'm just saying, if his grades as are good as they are, and he's still playing on the computer three hours a night, just think about how great they'd be if he spent some more time studying!"

"I get it. I get it," Richard said. "Work hard and get good grades so I can get into a reputable college and make something of myself like you did. I know. And by the way, the game we play is *Overwatch*—not overwork."

"So, in that case, I guess you better *overwatch* your grades so you don't end up being *overworked* on some dead-end job because you didn't get into a good college," Ernie said with a smirk.

Both Richard and his mother groaned at the sheer corniness of the pun, but deep down, even he had to chuckle at the comment. "You know I also have track and cross-country going for me. Maybe I'll get an athletic scholarship."

"Athletics is good too," Ernie replied. "But it's no excuse for slacking off with respect to your grades. At any rate, enough talk about school. Sit down and eat some breakfast."

Lake many growing teenagers, Richard was nearly always famished, and he devoured his food like a starving animal. He was just reaching for two more pieces of bacon when his sister walked in and sat down directly across the table from him. Milene had recently turned eleven, and she was starting sixth grade. With an identical complexion and straight black hair even longer than

Richard's, the two siblings looked eerily alike, though both would deny it vehemently if you dared to mention it. Their personalities were as different as night and day. While Richard was relatively soft-spoken, easygoing, and friendly, Milene was feisty, opinionated, and even a bit snarky at times. She was the more naturally aggressive of the two, which was apparent on the basketball team she had played on for the past two years. If she ended up taking after their father with respect to her height, she'd likely be the one to end up with the athletic scholarship.

"Don't you dare try to grab the last of the bacon, Buckwheat!" she shouted with the authority of a pint-sized dictator. "You already had your share, and you're not eating my pieces!"

"Good morning to you too." Richard smiled. "I was actually just grabbing it for you to make sure Dad didn't accidentally eat it."

"Don't get me in the middle of this!" Ernie said. "I know better than to get on her bad side."

Going over and seizing the last three pieces of bacon off Richard's plate and putting them onto hers plate, she hugged their dad vigorously. "Don't worry, Daddy. I know that you would never steal the last of my bacon. Richard is just trying to start some crap."

"Language!" Mom said. "And you kiss me with that mouth?"

"I didn't use the bad word, Mom," Milene said. "People use crap all the time at school. They actually use a lot worse ones. The s-word, the f-word—you name it. It's a wonder I don't go around swearing like a sailor all day."

"Well, just because you hear it at school does not mean that you can use it in this house. And exactly when did you ever meet a sailor?"

Richard was completely entertained by this entire conversation and was reminded of how lucky he was to have a little sister who was actually somewhat interesting and entertaining—in contrast to being annoying like all her friends who came over to the house. The lively debate also had the added benefit of changing the topic of him already slacking off in high school before he'd even started his first day.

After breakfast, Richard grabbed his backpack and gave his mom a hug and a kiss on the cheek. "Bye, Mom. Love you."

"Love you too, sweetheart. Have a great time at high school!"

Before he even got to the door, Richard sent a text to Hector: "Hey, dude. Ready to jet?"

Once outside the door, he briskly headed east toward the school. The front door opened three houses down, and Hector Ramirez met Richard at the bottom of his driveway.

"S'up, *ese*?" Hector gave Richard with a fist bump, which was immediately followed by a small explosion sound after the two sets of knuckles met. It was a silly, childish thing to do, but they had been doing it for nearly the entire three years they knew each other.

"You ready for high school, bro? We're in the big-time now, eh?"

"Yeah, I suppose," Richard replied. "More homework, more responsibility, and now we're on the bottom of the food chain again."

"Cheer up, man. The work won't be that much harder, and you're pretty smart. Plus, what are you worried about? Your old-man owns a big-ass construction company. You could be a total screwup and still end up running your dad's company when he retires!"

"Are you kidding? Not a chance he's gonna let me run his company. I'll be lucky if he gives me a job over the summer. Pretty sure his plan is to sell the thing off after another twenty years. Sis and I better get our act together so we can support ourselves. At least that's what he keeps implying."

"Damn. That's rough, homes. I guess you'll end up being a working stiff just like the rest of us, eh? All the more reason to really enjoy these next four years! Especially the girls—or should I say *women*! They are really starting to develop—if you know what I mean."

"Yeah. I think I got it," Richard said. "All the more opportunity to accidentally hit on some senior's girlfriend and end up getting pummeled."

Hector said, "Man, you're way too consumed with pissing people off all the time. You didn't used to be like that. Just don't go picking fights—and you'll be fine. Plus, I'll be looking out for you!"

"I feel totally at ease now," Richard said.

Hector Ramirez was a good three inches shorter than Richard and probably fifteen or twenty pounds lighter, but the way that he carried himself, you would think that he was a six-foot-four linebacker with the 49ers. Richard had met Hector four days after his family moved to the neighborhood, and after a ten-minute conversation, Hector suggested a one-on-one game using the basketball hoop Richard's dad had erected over their garage. Due to Richard's height advantage and natural athleticism, he could beat Hector fairly easily, but Hector's smack-talking was so biting and completely hilarious that Richard was barely able to keep a straight face, which actually made it a much closer game. From that day forward, the two were as thick as thieves. Richard always assumed that Hector's sense of humor was developed as some sort of a defense mechanism to offset his small stature. Wherever his wit came from, it along with his don't-take-crap-from-anyone attitude made him a blast to be around.

After walking half a mile, they arrived at James A. Garfield High School. Like most suburban high schools, it was comprised of half a dozen reasonably well-kept buildings, surrounding a large center quad area where the majority of the student body would hang out between classes. The centerpiece of the area was a gigantic oak tree and multiple wooden benches. It was always assumed that the tree, which easily predated the school, was the inspiration for their incredibly unoriginal school mascot—an acorn—but no one really knew for sure. Like just about every other high school, Garfield has its various cliques, including the brainiacs, the gamers, the sci-fi nerds, and the jocks. The only way they knew any of that was through Hector's older sister. Susana was a junior.

They headed to their respective first-period classes. For Richard, it was Algebra 1 with Mrs. Wexler, which thrilled him about as much as a root canal. It was easily his least-favorite subject, and to have it first thing in the morning when he was still waking up seemed just short of criminal to him. He could understand the basic concepts, but despite his best efforts, the numbers would always come out wrong. The one bright point of this ongoing lesson in frustration was that Jenny Lee would be in the class with him.

Jenny walked into class with her straight black hair intermixed with streaks of hot pink and neon green and an equally colorful outfit to complete the look. Being a first-generation American, her image and personality were in stark contrast to her parents, who were a pretty straitlaced Chinese family. It was a long, hard-fought battle to get the okay from her parents to allow this change of her appearance, but in the end, they picked their battles—and hair color was not worth putting a foot down. Her personality was exactly like her look: bright, bubbly, and charmingly corny.

Richard met Jenny about two years ago at a party at Hector's house. Jenny's sister was good friends with Hector's sister, and her whole family came for the event. After a few minutes of uncomfortable small talk, Richard learned that she was also a big *Overwatch* online gamer. He and Hector invited her to join them the next time they played. Little did they realize what they had done. She proceeded to annihilate both of them only a few minutes into the game. Fortunately, she was kind enough to share some of her strategies, tips, and gaming techniques, and their playing improved significantly.

Since they were only twelve, they were not at the age when boys typically liked girls and vice versa, so their friendship developed the same as it did with Hector and his other friends. They would online game together and hang out, usually with Hector and other friends at the mall. Romance was the furthest thing from their minds. For Richard, it changed about a year later. He was at Hector's house for a Memorial Day party. His family had a pool, and the two of them were just goofing around in the water when feelings started coming over Richard. He was too afraid to act on them, but it lit a spark that only grew steadily over time. Having already established a good-friend relationship, he did not want to jeopardize it by sharing his feelings and possibly making things weird between them. He decided to just play along like nothing was different. His conscious efforts to suppress his feelings enabled him to keep his infatuation completely secret from everyone except Hector, who figured it out after a few months. As a loyal friend, he kept Richard's secret well. However, when the two of them were alone, Hector would razz him mercilessly, inquiring as to when he was going to make his big move and let her know how he really felt.

Jenny also struggled in math, and the two found solace in their mutual aversion for the subject.

"Richie!" she squealed as she shuffled across the room to give Richard a big hug.

"S'up, crazy girl," Richard replied. "I like the color scheme you got going on. How long did it take you to convince your mom to let you do that to your hair?"

"Just had to promise her straight As and at least three grandchildren after I get married," she replied. "Still on for gaming at five?"

"Oh, yeah. Pretty sure they won't be assigning any homework the first day back, so it will likely be the last time we'll have a free weekday evening for who knows how long."

"Please be seated class and take out a notebook," The teacher said, quickly ending the conversation.

The two took seats next to each other. They would most likely be moved due to their witty in-class banter, which was almost certain to begin within the first week, but they'd enjoy it for as long as they could.

The rest of class was spent discussing the objectives of the class and outlining some best practices to follow to end up with the highest grade possible—the typical, boring-as-hell, first-day mumbo jumbo.

After the bell, Jenny smiled and said, "See ya at lunch."

For Richard, second period was English, which was just as uneventful as math, followed by Spanish in third period. Fortunately, Hector was in that class, so he would have someone to goof around with when the opportunity presented itself. Fourth period was science, which was slightly more interesting that his other subjects, immediately followed by lunch.

Making his way to the cafeteria, Richard looked around and eventually found Hector. He had already met up with Jenny, and they were both scoping out a table to eat. Hector jumped up and down and waved. "Tommy, over here!"

Glancing back to the entrance, Richard saw Tommy Parker meeting eyes with Hector and starting to make his way over to the group. At first, he needed to take a second look to confirm that it was Tommy because he *almost* blended in with the other students. Standing nearly six feet tall and weighing about two hundred pounds, he was practically a giant compared to the other eighth graders last spring, but now here with kids who were two and three years older, he was just another kid. He was still very big for a freshman, but if you didn't know any better, you wouldn't necessarily give him a second look. Tommy got his size from his father, who had played offensive guard for the University of Michigan twenty years earlier. He was very good and would have likely been drafted as a pro if a knee injury hadn't ended his college career.

It was actually a connection through Tommy's father that led to him joining their jolly band of misfits. His dad got a construction job working for Richard's father a little over a year ago, and they met and developed a friendship at a company picnic. Tommy was a whiz at mathematics and had aspirations of becoming a theoretical physicist. On many occasions, he was bribed by Richard's mom to come over for dinner in exchange for helping out Richard with his math homework or to study for an exam. Hector especially liked having him as part of the group since his big mouth had a habit of getting him in trouble from time to time. Having a hulking figure like Tommy around discouraged most physical confrontations. Though he was the newest member to the group, he seemed to fit right in, and the four of them spend countless hours over the summer online gaming and hanging out.

"What's happening, Tommy Boy?" Hector called out as he got within a few feet from the group.

"Who you calling *boy*?" Tommy said.

"Would you prefer *homey*?" Hector said, playing along with the act.

"Oh, so you had to go to the black thing?" Tommy replied.

"Dude, black, brown, yellow—and whatever the hell Richard is—we're all minorities here in a sea of white guys," Hector answered.

Tommy said, "No kidding, eh? I kinda get the feeling that the principal got hit with some sort of diversity quota, and with the four of us, he could check off pretty much the entire list."

They found a table and talked about their classes and which teachers they liked and hated the most so far. Granted, it was only the first day of school, but kids are quick to judge. Everyone was joking around and having a pretty great time when they heard an abrasive voice booming out from behind them.

"Hey, freshies, what are you guys doing at our table?"

They all groaned.

John Sandal was standing a few feet from the table with a couple of his friends and lackeys. John was a sophomore, and two years ago, he had made Richard and Hector's experience a living hell. They were rescued from their torment when he moved up to high school, but now that everyone was back together again, he appeared to want to pick up right where he had left off.

"Oh, hell," Hector said. "You haven't flunked out yet? I was expecting that you'd already have started your promising career at McDonald's by now."

John stared at Hector, initially stunned.

The two friends behind him were starting to snicker when he said, "Those are big words coming from a midget. Don't worry. I'm not going anywhere, Bilbo. You've got three more years of this to look forward to."

"Go with the short joke?" Hector said. "Real original. You couldn't come up with something more obvious like the sky is blue or something? I actually think before opening my mouth, and instead of going after the easy insult about how ugly you are, I decided to comment about the fact that you're also really stupid."

This brought on a series of "oohs" and "damns" along with chuckles from John's friends.

John clenched his teeth, lunged forward, and grabbed the front of Hector's shirt.

Richard's stomach immediately dropped through the floor, and perspiration started forming on his forehead. He was instantly brought back to the moment when he was in nearly the same predicament with Ahote and Chenowa. He would have to stand up to an older and larger opponent and probably get beaten to a pulp or stand by and watch one of his best friends get clobbered.

They outnumbered them four to three, but they were all freshman, and one of them was a girl. Tommy was bigger than all of them, but he was kinda slow and not really physical. They may or may not know this fact, but Richard really didn't want to take the gamble. *Why the hell does Hector keep instigating stuff like this? I love the knucklehead, but he's gonna get the four of us killed one of these days!* Suddenly, by the grace of the spirits his grandfather kept telling him about, fate appeared to defuse the situation.

"What the heck is going on here?" Mr. Hoskins, one of the history teachers, said. "You boys knock it off right now! It's the first day of school for Christ's sake. Want to get suspended before your school year even begins?"

After a few awkward moments of silence, John pushed Hector backward, releasing his T-shirt as he stumbled into the table where the four of them were sitting. "This ain't over, man!" He turned and walked out to the quad to eat with his friends. John's cohorts were still snickering as they left the cafeteria.

"Dude!" Richard said. "Are you actually trying to get us all killed? Why the hell did you egg him on like that? Did you not see the size of those guys?"

"Yeah, that was pretty stupid," Tommy said. "I mean we would have tried to help and all, but you know me. I'm a lover not a fighter."

"You're a pizza-lover that's for sure," Hector said.

"Oh, so now I'm fat too!" Tommy said. "Forget about those guys. I'm gonna squash you myself!"

"Uh-oh. You're gonna sit on me?" Hector said as the two began throwing mock punches at each other.

"Ugh," Jenny said. "I don't know why the hell I hang out with you dweebs. I really need to get some other friends—ones who actually know how to play *Overwatch* correctly."

They returned to their table, finished their lunches, and goofed around for another fifteen minutes.

Richard had history for fifth period. Thankfully, he did not have Mr. Hoskins, which would have been somewhat awkward following the lunch confrontation. He had Mrs. Briar, who Hector's sister also had two years earlier, and was quite fond of. History was kind of a double-edged sword for Richard. He inherently enjoyed the subject; the amazing stories about historical figures reminded him of the tales his grandfather would tell him on their long hikes at the reservation. In his mind, he could easily take himself back to that moment in time and envision what life would have been like in that period. However, having gone through history twice in junior high, he was deeply frustrated that it dealt almost entirely with Western civilization, only briefly mentioning the Native American tribes as a tiny footnote in the chapter about Columbus and the early explorers of North America. Next year, he would take American history, which he hoped would discuss his people in greater detail. Unfortunately,

Hector's sister confirmed that it had very little content on the impact of the Native American peoples and nothing on their history prior to the Europeans discovering North America. This incredible oversight of history angered him greatly. It was bad enough that the Europeans essentially killed off nearly his entire population with war and disease—and now they were trying to erase them from history as well! After fuming for a few more minutes, Richard eventually calmed down and followed along for the rest of the class. As Susana described, she did seem like a nice lady, and it's not like she wrote the curriculum.

At the end of class, Richard gleefully made his way to the physical education building to go find Mr. Ramirez. Hector's father was one of the PE teachers at their high school, and he was the varsity soccer coach. Their team was very good and had almost made it to the regional championships last year.

Hector had played on soccer teams for several years, and his dad fully expected that he would try out for the junior varsity team when their season started in a few months. Hector had confided in Richard over the summer that he'd decided not to try out for the team and wasn't sure how he'd break the news to his dad. In his heart, he knew that he was not really that good, and even with his dad's connections, he was pretty confident that he'd end up making the team, but the whispering behind his back about him playing only because his old man was the varsity coach was something Hector wanted no part of. He certainly didn't need any other potential scenarios, which included physical confrontations.

Richard was heading to the coach's office for a reason that had nothing to do with Hector. Mr. Ramirez knew the head track and cross-country coach quite well and was going to introduce him personally. He made his way to the office and knocked twice on the open door.

"Mr. Ramirez?" Richard asked quietly.

"Richard, it's great to see you. So how do you like high school?"

"Pretty good so far," Richard replied.

"Mr. Hoskins told me at lunch that you guys almost got into some trouble with some other boys."

"Oh, that…"

"Let me guess… Hector opened his big mouth again. I swear that kid is going to be the death of me! I love the little smartass, but sometimes I want to just shake him. I really wish he was more like you. Nice and easygoing—but he's got to be a hothead like his uncle. That got him into a lot of trouble when we were growing up. At any rate, enough about him. Let me go and introduce you to Coach Goldfried."

Walking twenty feet down the hall, they entered another office.

An athletic, slightly balding man sat at his desk, glasses perched halfway down his nose.

Mr. Ramirez said, "Hey, Jed. This is the kid that I was telling you about. One of my son's friends. I hear he's a hell of a runner."

"Is that so?" Coach Goldfried pushed his glasses back up the bridge of his nose. "Distance guy or more of a sprinter?"

"I'm a pretty good sprinter, but I'm really more of a distance runner. I ran six miles in the hills on Saturday with my grandfather,"

"You remember his grandfather—Running Bear Williams? He set that state record for men over fifty a couple years back. Ran the whole 10K barefoot."

"You're Running Bear's grandson?" Mr. Goldfried said. "He's running marathons now, right? He's ranked nationally if I recall."

"Seventh in the nation right now for men over sixty. He turned sixty-one last April."

"Pretty impressive! Let's hope it runs in the family—pun intended. So you as fast as he is?"

"Not yet, but I'm working at it," Richard said confidently.

The coach smiled and reached across to shake Richard's hand. "Good answer. Now let's go meet the rest of the team. If I had my way, I'd have you guys out running today, but since it's the first day of school, the principal just wants us to discuss class expectations and boring crap like that. Don't worry. I'm not going to mention your lineage to any of the other guys on the team. It's up to you to share—or not share—anything you choose to."

Coach Jed even did him the favor of allowing him to enter the gymnasium where the others were gathering about a minute before he did so none of the other students would know they had walked in together. Once everyone was present, he took roll call and spent the next twenty minutes discussing his expectations of the class. "It's not all about winning but putting in the effort and trying your best. You're only competing again yourself."

To Richard's delight, they would be starting with runs of two or three miles, but they would eventually work up to runs of six miles or more. Knowing that he could run six miles without too much difficulty now, it seemed like it would be pretty easy.

After another thirty-five minutes of Q&A and killing time, the last bell of the day rang.

Richard made his way back the front of the school to meet up with Hector. To his pleasant surprise, Jenny was also waiting to walk home with them.

Richard had the nagging feeling that the interaction with John Sandal and his two friends was not over, but that afternoon, the three encountered nothing except a warm late-summer afternoon filled with sunshine and the optimistic hopes of a great school year.

Two blocks from their houses, Jenny turned left on Trinidad toward her place, and the remaining duo walked the last hundred yards or so. Stopping momentarily at Hector's house, the two departed with their ceremonial fist bump and explosion.

Hector grinned. "See you online at five to go kill some stuff, loser."

"Not if I see you first!" Richard said.

Milene was shooting baskets in their driveway.

Richard smiled to himself and stopped to appreciate the moment. After asking his sister how her day was, which he knew would be answered with a snide, yet equally entertaining comeback, he went inside to be met with a big hug from his mom who always did something special for dinner on the first day back to school.

Maybe this will be a pretty great year after all.

CHAPTER 3

Richard awoke unexpectedly to the sound of arguing downstairs. The clock in his room showed 12:18. His mom and dad were having a heated argument. He rarely recalled hearing them fight—and never so late on a school night. He tried to make out the topic of the conversation, but it was too muffled through the walls and doors. Initially, he told himself it was probably nothing all that important, and he should just go back to bed and mind his own business, but after a few minutes, his concern and curiosity got the best of him. He slowly crept out of bed and silently made his way to the top of the staircase. Five steps down, he found a spot where he could make out the conversation clearly.

"So tell me again exactly what you found at the site," his mom said.

"I don't know exactly," his dad replied. "But it appears to be some sort of burial site. We had the backhoe excavating a section of the hillside at the north end of the lot, and all of a sudden, Fred comes across an opening to this cave. He immediately stopped and called me over to check it out. We went through the opening with a couple of flashlights, and about twenty feet in, we come across a hole in the ground. It was about three by six feet and only a couple of feet deep. I initially thought it was a big dog or something, but after taking a closer look, it was just an old animal skin. We pulled back the hide, and a skeleton was looking up at us. It scared the living hell outta me!"

"How long do you think that it had been there?"

"A long time. Hundreds of years probably. It was Native American for sure—I could tell from what was left of the clothing and the jewelry it had around its neck. That's why we need to move the body and not let anyone know about it!"

"Are you crazy? Whoever this man or woman was, she's most likely one of our own people. You know as well as I do that the Tolowa tribe has inhabited these lands for centuries. We need to tell my father about this. It could be a great discovery for our people. If this person was buried in the manner you speak of, he was probably a chieftain or someone of great importance. It would be sacrilege to move the remains."

"That's definitely not an option!" he said. "If we go to your father with this, he'll go to the rest of the elders—and then to straight the governor of California—and he won't stop until he has the entire area identified as some sort of sacred burial ground. That will shut down the project altogether! Our only option is to move the bodies to another site and rebury them."

"It's *bodies* now? Exactly how many are we talking about? Who cares if they stop the project? I know it's a nice job for you, but we've got lots of other jobs. We'll be okay. You just need to do the right thing here!"

"It's only two remains. You don't understand, Ayiana. We won't be okay if this thing goes south. We'll lose everything!"

"How is that possible? How much could we possibly have lost in labor and materials given that you only broke ground a couple weeks ago? You need to go to owners and tell them what happened. I'm sure that they'll be upset, but these are our people we're desecrating!"

"We are the owners!" He caught himself halfway through the words and lowered his voice.

"What?" She stared at him in utter disbelief.

"When the plot of land came up for bid six months ago, I went to the bank and took out a loan. One of my guys has a brother with the city, and he let me know that the land was just about to be rezoned from agricultural to residential. If I played my cards right, I could buy it up before news of it got out. I wouldn't have to compete against all the other big development firms who'd be fighting over it.

I had to include the house, the business, everything for collateral, but they eventually gave me a loan of $3.5 million, which would get me the land and the capital needed for the first ten houses. Once those properties sold, we'd use the proceeds to build the remaining twenty. With the market where it is now, we can easily get $400,000 apiece for them. That's $12 million! Even after paying back the bank, we're up close to $9 million!"

"And you're just telling me all of this now!" she screamed, apparently no longer concerned about waking anyone. "You didn't think making a decision of this magnitude was something that I should have at least been consulted on? If this discovery hadn't happened, when exactly were you planning on letting me in on this?"

He paused for a few moments and finally said, "I was planning on surprising you with it on our anniversary."

"Six months from now?"

"Yeah. I was thinking that, by that time, the first group of houses would have been built and sold. I'd know for sure that we'd be free and clear to complete the rest of the development. I could not think of a better way to celebrate sixteen years of marriage than by telling you that all of our hard work had paid off. We would be able to do practically anything we wanted to do for the rest of our lives! We'd have money to move to a bigger house, cover the cost of college for the kids, travel, and do whatever else we wanted."

Richard's mom was quiet for several seconds. "I suppose that would have been a pretty great surprise. What the hell am I going to do with you? I don't know whether to kiss you or choke you! Are you sure there's no other option? Maybe if we go to my dad and explain, he can meet with the elders, and they can come up with a way to move the bodies properly, but you can still keep the land."

"It doesn't work that way, babe," he answered. "I researched it on the internet all afternoon. Once your dad learns of this, it's all over! The plot will get identified as sacred land, and we'll own a $3.5 million piece of dirt that's not good for a goddamn thing! I know that this is killing you inside. It's hurting me as well, but we just have no other choice here."

A long period of silence followed.

"I suppose you're right. God help us if my father ever gets word of this. We should obviously keep it from the kids as well, especially Richard. You know how close he is to my dad. So what's the plan?"

"Agreed. I'll work out the details tomorrow. There's a storm that's supposed to hit on Wednesday, so it won't be weird to have the crew take the day off. I'll go there with Fred, and the two of us will take care of moving the remains. Obviously, he already knows about everything, and I trust him. I promised him a promotion to foreman for helping me out on this. I promise it will be okay."

They spoke very quietly for a bit longer, but Richard was no longer listening. He was just sitting there on the stairs, trying to comprehend what he had just heard. Ten minutes ago, he was the son of two boring, average, middle-class parents—just like everybody else. Now his parents were high-powered real-estate moguls who were working to cover up an archaeological conspiracy that was centuries in the making! *What the holy hell is going on here?*

Suddenly shaken back into reality, Richard heard his parents making their way to the staircase. Quickly tiptoeing back to his room, he silently closed his door and got into bed before his parents walked past his room. His mind was a torrent of thoughts and emotions, and he didn't fall asleep for another ninety minutes.

After four hours of sleep, he had no problem quickly falling back into unconsciousness. Three snoozes later, his mom went into his room and said, "What are you still doing in bed? You're going to be late to your second day of school!"

Slowly dragging himself down the hall, he was met with a closed door to the bathroom. He heard running water and the high-pitched, out-of-tune voice of an eleven-year-old singing a Katie Perry song.

Crap. Milene is already in the shower. No chance of getting her outta there for at least another twenty minutes. Looking at the hall clock, he groaned. *No shower for me today. Guess I'll just have to put on some extra deodorant and hope for the best.*

After getting dressed, he went downstairs.

His parents were sitting around the kitchen table like the day before, but there was a completely different vibe in the room. The two of them were eerily quiet, and they seemed nervous and unsettled.

Richard needed to play along to make sure that they didn't catch on that anything seemed different. After a quick bowl of cereal, Richard looked at his watch. He needed to get going if he was going to make it on time. Following a brief hug from his mom and a text to Hector, he started making his way to school.

Hector glanced at Richard, and instead of their traditional fist bump, he said, "Dude, you look like hell."

"Yeah. I didn't sleep very well," Richard whispered.

Having missed out on several hours of sleep and being denied his morning shower, which he all but depended on to wake up in the morning, he found first period particularly brutal. Even the quirky comments of Jenny could not shake him out of his stupor, and he moaned and groaned through nearly the entire hour.

Second period was a little better, and by his third class, he was starting to feel like his old self again. He did his best to stay focused on the topics at hand, but his mind kept going back to what his father said about the job site and the ancient Indian burial grounds he had uncovered. He wondered if those bodies could really be his ancestors from centuries earlier. It would make sense if they were. Richard agreed with his mother that his grandfather would be terribly disappointed in the whole family if he ever found out what had happened, but at the same time, he was really torn. He didn't want to see their family devastated financially, and the idea of them being rich in a couple of years excited him quite a bit. He was confident that they would do a lot with their wealth to help Chenowa's family and the whole reservation. Even a million dollars would have a tremendous impact on the tribe. Maybe even Ahote would finally come around? If everything that his dad described went as planned, he could end up doing whatever he wanted to. Sure, he'd still need go to college and get a job, but he could pick a career he was passionate about and not have to worry about whether or not he'd make a lot of money doing it. It was all very liberating, the more he thought about it, and if his grandfather ever did find out what happened, he could just deny knowing anything about it. Grandpa would be pissed as hell at his parents, but he'd still be in the clear.

Despite his best efforts, he could not get the thought of the burial site out of his mind for the rest of the afternoon. Finally, in sixth period, during the first official workout for cross-country, an idea occurred to him. He knew exactly where the site was because his dad had pointed it out to him while driving around a few weeks earlier. It was only about four miles from the house, a relatively easy bike ride away. What if he snuck out tonight and took a look at the ancient burial site? They were not going to move the body until the next day, so it was the only night he could actually do it. The idea of riding his bike several miles after midnight to go look at centuries-old human remains terrified and exhilarated him simultaneously. Granted, he would be really tired tomorrow, but this was a once-in-a-lifetime experience. What choice did he have?

That evening, Richard did his best to act as if everything was normal, but it was an ongoing struggle to keep up his poker face. When he got home from school, Richard went to the garage, found a large flashlight and a small hand shovel, and snuck them up to his room. After removing his school books from his backpack, he put in the flashlight and shovel, and shoved the bag under his bed.

After an unusually small dinner for him of only one helping of lasagna, he retired to his room to do some homework before going to bed—or at least that's what he told his parents. After watching a dozen YouTube videos on his laptop, Richard crawled into bed in the hope of getting a couple of hours of sleep before the alarm on his phone went off at twelve thirty. It was much quieter than the primary alarm clock he used, and it would be unlikely that his parents would hear anything.

Despite his best efforts, he tossed and turned for two and a half hours before the alarm went off. Confident that everyone in the house was fast asleep, Richard carefully snuck downstairs, grabbed his jacket from the closet, and tiptoed to the garage. With the precision of a brain surgeon, he cautiously navigated his bike out through the side gate. He was so paranoid about making any unnecessary noise that he even walked his bike two houses away before finally pedaling down the street.

For late August, it was not terribly cold—even in the middle of the night—and within a few minutes, he was starting to perspire. Fortunately, Richard knew a back way to the site that was made up almost entirely of residential streets. As he grew closer to the site, his anxiety level grew exponentially.

After a twenty-minute ride, he arrived at the site and hid the bike behind a backhoe. Richard hoped he would not have to use the flashlight until he found the cave since a strange guy waving a flashlight around a construction site at one o'clock in the morning might draw some attention. Unfortunately, the moon was little more than a sliver in the sky, and there were no streetlights. After a few minutes of fumbling around in the darkness, he eventually had no choice but to take out the flashlight. After a couple of minutes, he finally found the entrance to the opening. There were a couple of cones across the entrance, and some plastic film was stretched between the two.

Carefully ducking under the tape, the full weight of the situation hit him like a ton of bricks. Shivers shot up his spine, and the perspiration running down his forehead was icy cold.

This was a mistake. Fear continued the fight to overwhelm him, and he unconsciously turned a full ninety degrees to head back out of the cave. *Stop it, Richie! You stayed up half the night and rode your bike all the way out here—and you're not going to chicken out now!*

He took several steps forward, alternating the beam of light from the roof of the low cavern to make sure he didn't hit his head and back down to the ground so he could actually see what he was looking for. After a few more terrifying steps, he finally came across a shallow hole in the ground.

His flashlight slowly dipped into the shallow grave and illuminated a mass of animal hair, which shocked Richard, causing him to jump and hit his head on the top of the cave. Swearing violently, he went down to one knee for a few moments to compose himself. The top of his head stung fiercely, and he was quite relived when his hand returned without any blood after touching the impact point with his fingers. Cautiously turning the light back into the hole, he could see that the animal the hide originally belonged to had been dead for as long as whoever was beneath it.

After a few minutes of gathering his nerves, Richard carefully reached down, grabbed the animal skin with both hands, lifted the skin off whatever it was covering, and put it on the left side of the hole. He had to temporarily put down his flashlight, and the light ended up being covered by the animal skin, leaving him in complete darkness. Panic shot through him like a jolt of electricity, and he quickly scrambled around with the fur-covered hide to retrieve the light.

After a few seconds, he heard the sound of moving plastic. Suddenly, the light shot straight into his eyes, momentarily blinding him. The flashlight fell into the shallow grave and positioned itself so that the beam shot from the foot of the hole up straight toward the top. A perfectly intact skeleton was staring back up at him. With the angle of the light on the bones, he could have sworn that the creature was coming to life right in front of him!

Shrieking in terror, Richard jumped up again and whacked his head again. Cursing profusely for the second time in two minutes and holding his throbbing head, it occurred to him that he had a perfectly good bicycle helmet hanging from the handlebars of his mountain bike. The realization helped calm him, and his eyes slowly moved back to the skeleton, which was still nightmarishly illuminated by the flashlight. Richard grabbed the light and repositioned it to get a better look at the remains. The person appeared to have received a multitude of injuries before death. Strangely, nearly all the fractures and injuries were along the left side of the body, including breaks in both of the left leg bones, a cracked left hip, several broken ribs, and multiple breaks on the arm. Moving the light back to the head, he saw a large indentation on its left temple. Richard guessed that it was the injury that killed this person.

During his inspection of the skull, something caught Richard's eye. Its clothing had all but disintegrated, but around its neck, he saw something truly amazing. It was a primitive necklace, and other than a good amount of dust, it appeared to be perfectly intact. It was held together by a strand of leather and strung along its front were four clearly identifiable items. The first one to catch Richard's eye was what appeared to be the claw of a large grizzly bear. It was at least four inches long and looked as if it could have torn a deer clean in half with one swing. The next thing to catch his eye was a large tooth. At first, Richard assumed it was another relic from a bear, but the shape of it was somehow not right. From its curvature and razor-sharp point, it seemed to be more feline. A mountain lion was the only large cat that would have been present in the area hundreds of years ago. To the right of the tooth was a piece of wood or bone. Upon closer inspection, he realized that it was actually a piece of antler, most likely a deer antler based upon the shape and diameter. Having seen a thousand deer on hikes with his grandfather, Richard had a lot to compare it to. The last notable item on the necklace was a brown feather that was about six inches long. Not being a bird expert, he could only guess, but based upon the color and proportions, he believed it was either an eagle or a hawk feather. The feather grabbed his attention.

How the hell can this feather look like it was plucked from a bird yesterday? Claws and teeth are bone and can last a long time, but a feather should have long since disintegrated. And yet here it is?

Richard noticed the spacers that separated the items. At first, he assumed they were just a collection of smaller and larger beads, but after taking a second look, he could see that the larger ones were actually small stones that had been carefully drilled through so they could be added to the necklace. He guessed they were quartz since it was readily available in the area and came in different colors. There were four stones—two in the center and two small black beads on either side. The bear claw and lion tooth were to the left and right, and the two remaining colored rocks with beads were on either side. The feather on the far left of the necklace, and the deer antler was on the far right.

Though the item was nothing more than a piece of leather intermixed with some old rocks and animal parts, it absolutely memorized Richard as he gazed upon it. *Could I take this home with me?* Slightly adjusting the flashlight, he saw a small knot in the leather in the area that would have been positioned at the back of the neck. Just as Richard was about to reach down to see if he could carefully untie the knot, he stopped. *What am I doing? I'm desecrating the grave of one of my own people. Grandpa would kill me if he ever found out about this! I should just cover this guy back up and get the hell outta here before I get caught.*

He paused a second time. *Of course. Come tomorrow afternoon, my dad is going scoop this dude up and take him who knows where and rebury him where he may never be found again. This might be the only chance to save something from this individual, and it will represent his time on this planet. Perhaps I'll take it to Grandpa at some point and tell him I found it on a hike or something so it can get a proper burial back on the reservation.* It felt like the right thing to do.

Carefully positioning the light so that it illuminated the area while freeing up both of his hands, he reached down to untie the knot. Given how long the connection had been in place, it did not loosen easily. After a few seconds, Richard began tugging with a little more force—and a little less caution. After several more attempts, he jerked with a bit too much gusto and accidentally whacked the side of the skull with his right hand. The impact knocked the skeleton's head clean off his spine, causing it to roll right toward him. The unexpected shock of this action caused Richard's hands to instinctually jerk away from the corpse. Unfortunately, as his left hand moved up rapidly, part of the necklace slid between his middle and ring fingers and was pulled up. At the same time, the lion's tooth on the necklace managed to hook under the jawbone, launching the skull from its grave and hitting Richard right between the eyes! Shrieking like a schoolgirl, he stumbled back and hit his head on the ceiling for the third time. Terrified, blinded by pain, and swearing like he never had before, Richard scrambled out of the cave.

He was just about to make a bee line for his bike when he remembered the flashlight. *Crap, crap, crap, crap!* It was his dad's light, and it even had their last name written on it. If he left it in the cave, his dad would know for sure that he had been there. Intense feelings of dread overtook him as he realized what he needed to do. Hands shaking and head throbbing, he ducked especially low to avoid any further head trauma and shuffled back into the cave. Reaching down to grab the flashlight, out of the corner of his eye, he noticed something slightly illuminated. Turning to his right, he could see that it was the lion tooth. *Oh, hell. I've gone through this much misery—I might as well come away from it with something!* He grabbed the ancient necklace and walked out of the cavern.

Outside, he stretched his back, which had cramped up considerably inside the cave. His head still pounded, and he was pretty sure that he'd given himself a concussion during this half-brained endeavor. In the night air, the sweat covering his body rapidly grew cold. Shivering with a combination of chill and fear, he quickly put the flashlight and his newly found prize into his backpack and jogged over to his bike. Glancing down at the bicycle helmet hanging on the handlebars, he could only shake his head in irritation. Carefully putting it on his bruised skull, he fastened the chin strap, hopped on, and started the long ride home. *This is definitely the stupidest thing that I've ever done!* He slowly came to the realization that he had faced and overcome a situation that had absolutely terrified him. *I suppose that's worth something.*

CHAPTER 4

If Richard thought that getting up day before was difficult, that was like Christmas morning compared to what it felt like waking up today. His head still throbbed with pain following the repeated assaults he managed to self-inflict. That, along with approximately three hours of sleep, made him feel only slightly better than the time he was sick with the stomach flu and a 102 temperature. He reached for the snooze button, but something stopped him. Since he hadn't had time to take a shower the day before, he really needed to take one today; without his usual routine to wake him up, there was no way that he'd make it through the school day. He seriously considered telling his mom that he was sick and taking the day off, but it was only the third day of the school year, and he didn't want to bring any suspicion that something was different than it should be. Fortunately, he made it to the bathroom before his sister. Stepping under the hot water made him feel a hundred times better. Shampooing his long black hair, he could feel three distinct knots at the top of his head, which stung sharply when even the slightest amount of pressure was put on them. With the shower now full of steam, he took several deep breaths and started to come around. It would still be a really long day, but he'd somehow have to get through it.

Once out of the shower and dressed, he refilled his backpack with his school books and binder and then remembered the necklace that he had put into one of the smaller zippered sections. He unzipped the pocket and was just about to take it out when he stopped himself. If he was going to leave it in his room, he'd need to find somewhere to hide it, and in his current skull-battered, sleep-deprived state, he couldn't think of a good spot to save his life. He certainly couldn't risk his mom finding it. He decided—just for today—to take it with him. He'd have his backpack with him the entire day except for cross-county practice when it would be secured in the locker room. Tonight, when he was feeling better, he'd figure out a good place to keep it.

Breakfast was another game of poker, and Richard made every effort not to show anything on his face to imply that he knew anything that he was not supposed to. He was not letting on that he had done anything out of the ordinary the night before. He was definitely hungrier than the day before, and after four frozen waffles and two cups of coffee, he headed out for school.

With Hector, Richard was even quieter than before. There was some small talk about whether or not the 49ers had any shot at the playoffs, but Richard was not really paying attention. The remainder of the day proceeded in a similar haze until he realized that he had completely forgotten to do his homework the night before. Tonight, he'd have to complete that homework and any other work he got today. Only three days into his high school career, and he was already screwing it up! He could hear his dad yelling at him in his head. Lunch couldn't come fast enough, and once in the quad, Richard found Tommy. The two of them found Hector, and the three picked out a spot in the cafeteria to eat their lunches. Jenny had told him in first period that she would not be able to join them for lunch because she needed to meet up with a couple of people in her science class to discuss a group project.

"You don't look so good, dude," Tommy said as they settled on the lawn.

Richard said, "Yeah. I didn't really sleep all that well. And I got a killer headache."

"You're not getting sick, are you?" Hector said. "You looked rough yesterday too, and you look ever worse today. You better not be getting me sick, bro. I got too many girls I need to be putting the moves on to waste any time being home coughing and stuff."

"Don't worry. I'm not getting sick. I'm just really tired."

"Why do you think you're not sleeping?" Tommy asked. "Stressed out about something?"

"It's a long story."

Hector said, "So we got another thirty-five minutes of lunch to kill. What's up? Now you've piqued my curiosity."

Crap, Richard thought. The whole thing was supposed to be a secret, and barely twelve hours later, he was already in a situation where he'd either have to outright lie to two of his best friends or not tell them anything and come off like some sort of arrogant a-hole. He also had to admit that, on a selfish level, he wanted to share the tales of his midnight adventure. It was unquestionably the coolest thing he'd ever done, and if he couldn't share it with two of his best friends, who the heck could he trust? He weighed the pros and cons of both scenarios and whispered, "Can the two of you keep a secret?"

Tommy and Hector looked at each other curiously and then said, "Sure."

"I'm serious. This is a big deal, and I need you guys to swear that neither of you will speak a word of this to anyone!"

"Dude, we said that were solid. You can trust us, man," Hector said.

"Okay. I'll tell you. The other night, I overheard my parents talking about one of my dad's job sites. Apparently they were cutting away at the side of this hill when they uncovered the entrance of a cave that had been covered up for centuries. He looked inside and ended up finding a burial site!"

Tommy and Hector were completely riveted as they ate their PB&Js and sipped their sodas.

"So I heard him say that the remains are probably from one of our ancient ancestors based on the age and the way it was dressed. I get the idea that I'm gonna ride my bike down to the site to check it out while everyone's asleep. So last night I set my alarm for twelve thirty, and when it went off, I snuck down to the garage, got on my bike, and went to check out the bones. By the time I got back home it was after two, and that's why I look like hell today."

"You're full of crap, dude," Hector said. "I don't buy for a second that you got on your bike in the middle of the night and rode who knows how far to go look at a dead guy. No offense, bro, but you don't exactly have a reputation for being the courageous type. He was probably up all night looking at YouTube videos or something."

Let it go, Richard thought. *You shared your story, and they didn't buy it. Now they're changing the topic. Just don't say another word, and it will likely never come up again. Your secret will stay safe. Who the hell cares what Hector says? It's not like he isn't going to be your friend anymore. Just don't say one more word.*

"If I'm such a scaredy-cat, then where the hell did I get this?" Richard had a minor out-of-body experience as the words were leaving his mouth. It was almost as if they were said by a totally different person, who somehow had temporarily taken over his face. *What the hell are you doing?* The small zippered pouch on his backpack was open, and he had reached in and slowly removed the ancient necklace.

"What the heck is that?" Hector asked.

"What does it look like, Einstein?" Richard said. "It's a necklace I took off of the dead guy."

"Let me see that." Tommy reached out toward the ancient item. "You said that this thing was hundreds of years old, right?"

Richard said, "Yeah. I'm pretty sure it must be by looking at it. No way to tell for sure, but I'd guess two hundred or three hundred years old at least."

"It's a fake," Tommy said.

"What do you mean? Since when are you some sort of an expert of ancient artifacts?" Richard said.

Tommy said, "Don't need to be an expert on artifacts to know that a feather left buried in the ground for hundreds of years would disintegrate like everything else. Pretty sure the leather strap would be gone too. You might find the tooth and the claw, but that's about it. Sorry, bro, but it's basic science."

Richard was furious and speechless. He'd had the same thought about the feather, but with Tommy, who was clearly smarter than him confirming his suspicion, he had to admit that it did seem very odd. But what else could it be? The only other possibility was that his father staged the whole thing, but why the hell would he do that? None of it made any sense. "Listen, I don't know about decomposition rates. I just know what I saw, and I can tell you that I took this necklace off of a skeleton buried about five miles from here."

Tommy and Hector looked at each other with a mixture of confusion and suspicion. This was followed by an incredibly awkward period of silence for the next few minutes before the bell for fifth period. *This entire thing went completely wrong.* He should have never even opened up his mouth in the first place. In an attempt to look cool in front of his friends, he told them everything. Instead of coming off as a badass who goes exploring grave sites in the middle of the night, he just came off as a mega-dweeb who created some ridiculous story about a made-up artifact.

With a mixture of embarrassment and anger, Richard made his way back to class. Following the events at lunch, his fatigue and lack of sleep were really kicking in and his headache, which had subsided a bit in the past couple of hours, came back with a pounding vengeance.

Fifth period was particularly brutal—and then came cross-country practice. Though it was only three miles, which would have normally been a fairly easy run, it felt like his feet were made of cement. Every stride was a struggle, and practice seemed to drag on forever. He thought about quitting several times in the first mile, but something kept him going. To his amazement, it was actually his grandfather's reputation. Coach Jed knew of his lineage, and if he was to puss out on the second day of practice, it would in some way forever tarnish the family reputation. Somehow, someway, he just had to get through the run. He'd get plenty of sleep tonight, and tomorrow would be better. During the last couple of miles, he actually started to feel a little less miserable—physically and psychologically. What the hell did he care what Hector and Tommy thought of the necklace? He knew that it was genuine despite what Tommy said, and that's really all that mattered.

Following the run, Richard made his way back to the locker room and started changing back into his regular clothes. As he grabbed his backpack, a bizarre thought occurred to him. It was the necklace. Just a few hours ago, he was actually ashamed of it and how it led to embarrassment in front of his friends. This was a piece of his people's lineage, and he should be proud—not embarrassed by it!

Setting his backpack on the bench, he unzipped the pouch and sat down. There were no other students near him, and he could work on the ancient knot in the leather with relative privacy. To his great surprise, after a couple of minutes of pulling and prodding, he was able to untie the knot. Once loosened, he carefully pulled the ends back behind his head until the necklace hung at the level of his collarbone and tied it again. With surprising ease, he secured the knot, which left the necklace just below the collar of his T-shirt. Once the item was in place, a bizarre feeling swept over him. It was difficult to explain, but he quickly noticed that the overwhelming fatigue he had been fighting all day disappeared. He almost felt energized. Richard assumed that it must be some kind of psychological effect and gave it little attention. Now in better spirits, he grabbed his backpack and started walking home.

Assuming that his improved mood was some sort of adrenaline rush brought about by the excitement of wearing the ancient artifact, Richard fully expected it to quickly dissipate. Instead, the feeling actually improved as he walked. After a surprisingly brisk trip, he turned onto his street saw his sister shooting baskets in their driveway. She was wearing her wireless headset so she could listen to music while working on her layups. Richard was about four houses away from home when he saw Milene make a shot that hit the rim at a particular angle, causing it to bounce over her head and down toward the street. Ever the competitor, even against no one, she instantly pivoted and sprinted toward the ball at the bottom of the driveway.

Richard immediately noticed a minivan driving straight toward them. Mrs. Marks was driving, and her head was turned toward the seats behind her. Her two-year-old twin boys had a reputation for being only slightly less destructive than a herd of wind elephants.

Milene was at the bottom of the driveway, and within a second, she would be in the street. One of their dad's work trucks was parked at the edge of the driveway and was completely blocking his sister's view.

Richard's blood turned ice cold, and time seemed to stand still. He could try yelling to his sister, but she would likely not hear anything due to her headphones. He had to do something. He somehow had to get to her before the van did. There was not a chance that he could make it in time. He was a good 150 feet away, and within a second or two, she would sprint out from behind that truck. The distracted driver might not see her until it was too late! He had to try!

Dropping his backpack, Richard lunged toward her. Time was moving incredibly slowly, yet he experienced a strange feeling of acceleration within his body. Somehow, someway, he appeared to be closing the distance. Glancing back at Mrs. Marks, her attention was still on her children. She was not going to see his sister in time to stop! Milene passed the truck, and with tremendous effort, she reached out to grasp the basketball, leaving her off balance and standing right in the middle of the street! Suddenly realizing her peril, she glanced up at the minivan racing toward her. Frozen with fear and unable to scream, she could only stare in terror as the vehicle approached.

I'm not going to make it! Richard thought. With every millisecond, he was getting closer to her. He appeared to be approaching her faster than the van. With one last straining effort, Richard grasped under her arms, and using all of his momentum, he lunged to the side and threw their bodies out of the path of the automobile! Richard hit the pavement hard, and his left shoulder took the majority of the impact. His shirt ripped at the sleeve, and he could feel his skin scraping and tearing along the asphalt. Milene fell on top of Richard, which cushioned her impact but added all the more damage to his injuries.

Mrs. Marks stopped in the middle of the street and ran around to the front of the van. "Oh my god! Oh my god! Are you too all right? Did I hit you? Should I call 911?"

Wincing in pain, Richard slowly got into a sitting position on the street, and after giving Milene a quick once-over, he replied, "No. We're okay. It was a close call, but I got there in time to pull her out of the way."

"I am so sorry! I just don't know what happened. I must have been distracted by the boys."

One of the twins was repeatedly whacking his brother over the head with a stuffed giraffe.

"For Christ's sake, would the two of you stop fighting! I just nearly ran over our neighbors because the two of you were distracting me!"

The twins started screaming their heads off.

Mrs. Marks turned back to Richard and Milene. "So sorry again. Glad to see that you two are okay. I guess I better get the boys back home to calm them down. Christ, I need a drink."

She staggered to the driver's side of the van and slowly continued along the street.

Milene looked around and said, "Holy cow! What the hell just happened? Did I really almost get run over?"

Richard whispered, "Yeah. You were almost pancake city. Guess you need to be more careful shooting hoops in the driveway, eh?"

"Yeah, I guess so," she replied. "So you pulled me out of the way of that car, didn't you? Damn. I guess this means I'm gonna have to start being nice to you now."

Richard smiled at his sister and slowly got back to his feet. "That would be cool, I guess. But just don't be too nice—or it will look suspicious to Mom and Dad."

"Oh, crap!" she said. "Are you gonna tell Mom and Dad what happened? They've yelled at me a dozen times about being careful of cars when I'm practicing in the front yard. If you tell them, Dad will pull down the basketball hoop in a second! You can't tell them okay. Please!"

"Okay. It will be our secret."

"Oh, thank you, thank you, thank you! I promise I'll be more careful from now on."

Milene grabbed her basketball, looked in both directions, and walked across the street to their driveway. Once she was safely on the other side, Milene looked back warmly and quietly added, "I gotta say, big brother, that was pretty cool! Thanks again. But don't let it go to your head or anything. It wasn't that spectacular." She smirked and jogged toward the front door.

Richard stood up straight, and despite the aches and pains throughout his body, he felt an amazing sensation of satisfaction. He closed his eyes and took a deep breath, feeling the warm sun on his face and taking in the smells of fall, which was rapidly approaching.

He looked for his backpack and saw it in front of the Petersens' house. Curious as to exactly how far away it was, he purposely took measured strides, walking back as close as he could estimate to a yard per stride. He counted them off to himself. Twenty yards, thirty yards, forty yards—finally at fifty-six yards, he made it to his backpack. Glancing back, he scratched his head in confusion. *How the hell did I run fifty-six yards in a few seconds? It must have taken longer than that. Maybe the van was moving a lot slower than it appeared? Oh, well. I guess stuff happens.* Richard picked up his pack and walked home. At the front door, he met his mom as she was on her way to the stairs.

"Hey, sweetie, how was your day today? Anything interesting happen?"

He tried not to smile. "No, Mom. It was a pretty run-of-the-mill afternoon."

CHAPTER 5

Following the events of the past forty-eight hours, Richard made the wise decision of going to bed at nine thirty that night. After eight and a half hours of sleep, his alarm at six thirty the following morning was met with significantly improved spirits and attitude. Making his way to the bathroom, he closed the door and quickly surveyed the series of scrapes on his back, shoulder, and arm caused by the impact with the pavement. To his surprise, the injuries actually looked a lot better than he had expected. He realized he was still wearing the necklace. He'd actually had it on all night. Given all the miscellaneous items hanging from it, one might expect it to be rather uncomfortable to sleep with. Why didn't he notice it? *I must have been really tired!*

After carefully removing it, he took an invigorating hot shower to give everything a good cleaning. After drying off, he applied half a dozen Band-Aids to the worst scrapes and cuts. After getting dressed, he intended to stash the artifact in his room for safekeeping. A strange feeling came over him to take the necklace back to school again. After mulling it over for a few moments, he eventually gave into his gut reaction and stashed the item into his backpack.

During breakfast, Milene looked awkward and uncomfortable. She had not told anyone about her near-death experience. Richard would come off as the hero of the family if he shared the tale of how he bravely risked his life to save his stupid little sister. Throughout the meal, Richard smiled to himself and didn't say a word about it.

Hector and Jenny both commented about how much better Richard looked that morning and how he must be feeling back to his old self again. Actually, it was better than normal, now that he really thought about it. His back and shoulder were still pretty sore, but otherwise, he felt really good. More energized and alert. *It's amazing what a good night's sleep can do for you.*

He and Jenny joked around during first period until their teacher intervened and made her first comment that she would need to break them up if they weren't able to get there goofing around under control. The rest of the morning went on without any great excitement, and when the bell for lunch went off, Richard gleefully walked, almost skipping, toward the cafeteria. It was Taco Thursday! For the most part, they would generally try to avoid cafeteria food whenever possible, but Thursdays were different. The head cook, Maria Santos, used to run a small Mexican restaurant in town with her husband. From what Richard had heard, the food was delicious, but since neither of them had any formal business acumen, it eventually went out of business. She was forced to take a job in the school cafeteria. Though strict financial constraints prevented her from making the quality of authentic food that she was capable of, she had figured out a way to make her signature tacos and still somehow work within her budget of $1.10 per meal. Though Richard had never experienced Taco Thursday, Hector's sister had raved about it for the past two years.

Fortunately for Richard, his fourth period class was fairly close to the cafeteria. He secured a place in line close to the front. Even though the cafeteria staff was supposed to have everything ready to go as soon as the lunch bell rang, Mrs. Santos always waited an extra five minutes on Taco Thursday to build additional anticipation.

As the line continued to form, John Sandal and his posse of goons got in line about twenty people behind Richard.

John shot Richard a nasty look as he walked past. Just as the line was starting to move, Hector, Jenny, and Tommy showed up and cut in line behind him. Richard glanced around nervously, hoping that no one would say anything. No such luck.

"Hey, what the hell is up with these losers cutting in line up there?" John was trying to draw as much attention as possible.

Nonchalantly looking back, Hector said. "Chill out, dude. There will still be plenty of tacos left for you *pendejos*."

John did not speak Spanish, but he glared furiously and was ready to leave his place in line to go over and have it out with Hector when one of the teachers walked by. His friends wisely pulled him back into line.

Richard and his friends got their meals, found a spot at one of the few tables in the quad with direct sunlight, and sat down to enjoy their tacos, refried beans, and tortilla chips. Prior to jumping in line, Hector and Tommy had bought four ice-cold Cokes from the vending machine.

Richard cracked one open, grabbed a taco, and took a large bite. The shell crunched loudly when he chomped down. Even though the shell was the typical store-bought variety, the meat inside was absolutely delicious! It had just the right amount of spice and flavor, and the cool lettuce and tomatoes on top were the perfect contrast. Richard couldn't help but appreciate the moment. He was enjoying a sunny day with four of his best friends and having a great meal. *It doesn't get much better than this!*

"I've just about had it with you buttheads!" John was walking toward them with three of his friends.

Tommy had a very nervous look upon his face, but Hector seemed completely oblivious to the situation. He continued to enjoy his meal as they approached.

Now standing directly in front of their table, John said, "You dickwads really stepped in it now. You thought that junior high was bad. That's nothing compared to the amount of crap we're going to give the four of you for the next three years! The teachers won't always be around to save your butts!"

Casually glancing over, Hector said, "Dude, what the heck is your problem? I see that you got your tacos, so why don't you go sit down, have a coke and a smile, and shut the hell up!"

John said, "Aren't you supposed to be in a field picking strawberries somewhere?"

Hector carefully placed his taco back on his plate and stared at John. "Listen, man. This strong-arm intimidation crap is not going to work on us. You may be bigger and stronger than us, and you very well might kick our asses, but every time you knock us down, we'll keep getting back up—every time!"

"Bring it on, losers!" John said. After an uncomfortable silence, he motioned to his friends to find their own places to sit. Just as they were about to walk away, John whacked Richard in the back of his head with his elbow. It wasn't a hard blow. It was just meant to insult and degrade.

Richard shot him an angry gaze, but he could only see the back of John's head. He thought about standing up or saying something, but before he could do or say anything, Hector's foot quickly shot out from under the table—right in front of John's leg as he walked past. As Hector's foot caught John's, Richard could only sit and watch. It was the greatest thing he had ever seen in his life! With the dexterity of a giraffe with two broken legs, John jerked violently, stumbled, tried to catch his balance on his other leg, and ended the futile struggle with a climatic swan dive onto the pavement. As his lunch tray impacted the ground, fireworks of tacos and chips shot up from the earth and scattered across the courtyard. It was a truly magnificent thing to witness.

Richard felt an odd sense of disappointment that Hector, who was facing toward him on the other side of the table, was not able to actually see this amazing catastrophe that he had so brilliantly created. Richard was almost certain that both would quickly be beaten senseless, but it would still be worth it to have witnessed such an event.

Quickly getting onto his feet, John turned back to the group, grabbed Hector by his T-shirt, and pulled him out of his seat.

Other students were gathering around the group. "Fight! Fight! Fight! Fight!"

John smiled wickedly, raised his fists, and lunged for the first strike.

Jeff Miner

Hector was fast and agile, and he managed to duck out of the path of the blow. He took a few steps back, and when John lunged forward with a second swing, he was barely able to avoid that one as well.

Richard could feel the crowd starting to get behind the smaller opponent, but it was only a matter of time before Hector's luck would run out. One of the punches would connect, likely with devastating results.

"Break it up! Break it up!" Principal Bell barged his way through the students, and the fight came to an abrupt halt. Mr. Bell was six foot four and weighed at least 240 pounds.

The crowd quickly dispersed, and the principal said, "The two of you want a suspension? Then knock it off!"

Seething in anger, John glared at Hector. "Your days are numbered, dude! You better grow eyes in the back of your head!"

John motioned to his friends, and they walked toward another part of the quad.

Hector casually sat down and started eating again as if nothing had happened.

Richard said, "Dude, are you friggin' nuts tripping him up like that? You know that he's not gonna stop till he beats the tar outta you. I'll admit that it was a pretty awesome thing to watch, but, man, that was not a bright move."

"Richard's got a point," Tommy said. "You just escalated the situation from mere torment to outright physical confrontation. This is not going end well. I can just feel it."

"You need to tell your dad what's going on," Jenny said. "Just stay late after school and go home with him. It's too risky for you to be walking home alone."

"And for exactly how long am I supposed to hide behind daddy?" Hector said. "A day? A week? A month? I got myself into this mess, and I need get myself out of it. If it means that I get beat up on my way home from school today, so be it!"

The rest of their lunch was eerily silent and incredibly uncomfortable. Richard had always admired Hector's overall attitude toward life, but he was truly in awe at the courage—or perhaps stupidity—that he showed. Richard knew he also would likely be impacted in some way by this turn of events, but at that moment, he made an oath to himself to do everything possible to help and protect his friend.

During fifth period, Richard could barely focus on the topics being covered. His mind kept racing through different scenarios of how and when this imminent confrontation would go down. Should he fight fair or try to kick out their knees or something? One could hardly blame them for pulling out all the stops given that fact that these boys were older and larger. They would very possibly be outnumbered. Then again, a knee kick could also go very wrong. It had been years since he had practiced any of his martial arts, and he was terribly rusty. Attempting to make a dirty move like that could further antagonize them and up the stakes from delivering a generic beatdown to really wanting to hurt them! It was all very confusing, and he found himself terribly fatigued.

Cross-country practice was a welcome change following the turmoil of the previous hour. Running was better than any therapy since it cleared his head and completely changed his physical state. Today was a bit longer run than the previous days—four miles. Whether it was finally having a good night's sleep or the relief of not having to focus upon the interaction at lunch, it was one of his best runs ever! He seemed to stride easily by all the other freshman and sophomore runners and soon found himself with the varsity squad. He noticed several surprised glances from the older runners as he caught up to and even passed a few of them. His mood was completely different. He felt fast and strong. Perhaps everything would be okay after all. He did have a way of being overly negative from time to time. As he got back to school and finished his run, Coach Jed was there with his stopwatch. "Nice time!"

Richard tried to catch his breath.

"Guess you picked up some of those running genes from your grandpa after all?"

Even though the coach had said he would make a point not to compare him to his grandfather, Richard didn't mind the comment. He was pretty sure that none of the other runners heard it, and he deeply appreciated the compliment. Making his way back to the locker room, Richard quickly changed and grabbed his backpack.

"Dude, I ended up staying late with some school stuff. I figured maybe we could walk home together?" Hector said. On his face was something that he had never seen before in all the time they had been friends. It was actual concern and possibly even fear!

My god. He is human after all! Richard thought. Apparently, the consequences of his actions had finally sunk in, and the seriousness of his predicament was becoming a reality. If Hector was looking nervous, things must really be bad. Richard thought about bringing up the idea that Jenny had mentioned earlier about trying to find his dad and getting a ride home with him. He stopped himself before saying a word. It would only meet with the same response. Just because he was now scared did not mean that he didn't firmly believe the words he had said before. He was still walking home as he did every day and facing whatever fate had in store for him, but he just wanted a friend along for moral support. Who could blame him? Richard was aware that he was likely to end up involved in any confrontation that might occur, whether it was today or some other day, but he had made a promise to himself and fully intended to keep it.

Slinging his backpack onto one shoulder, he thought of the necklace. He felt a strange impulse to put it on. For some reason, he felt better when wearing it. Wearing something owned by an ancient Indian brave helped him feel more like a warrior himself. If something did happen, they would need all the help they could get! Setting down his backpack, Richard unzipped the pocket and pulled out the necklace.

"You still screwing around with that fake-ass thing?" Hector asked, sarcasm creeping back into his voice.

"Don't give me crap, man," Richard said. "You got me into this fine mess, and it makes me feel better, okay."

"Whatever you say, Kemosobe. Let's get out of here."

After securing the pendant around his neck, the two made their way to the edge of campus. As they officially stepped off school grounds, Richard noticed a heavy, foreboding feeling coming over him. He thought about suggesting they try jogging home to speed up the trip and reduce the chances of running into John and his cohorts, but that would somehow defeat the whole purpose. No, they were in this together. They would walk home as usual; whatever happened to them would be dealt with to the best of their ability.

The first few blocks were painfully slow. Richard unconsciously kept increasing his pace, finding himself a dozen or more feet in front of Hector and having to stop to let him catch up. Step by step, Richard's anxiety and anticipation grew. As they passed the halfway mark, he started to believe they might just make it home unscathed after all. This after-school ambush required John and the others to stay after school for more than an hour. *They probably just got tired of waiting and went home.*

They were only a couple of streets from home when they heard the ominous sound of bicycles approaching from behind. They froze for two or three seconds and turned around slowly to face the noise.

Richard's heart dropped as John Sandal and three of his friends rode their mountain bikes toward them. The thought of making a run for it certainly occurred to him, but he knew Hector would have no part of it—and he was certainly not going to leave him behind. They dropped their backpacks and moved closer to each other until they were standing shoulder to shoulder.

The four bikes screeched to a halt just in front of them.

"Here we thought that we'd have to chase you guys down," John shouted. "You made it too easy for us."

"We ain't gonna run from you, man," Hector said. "If we're going to do this, then let's do it!"

"So you're stupid as well as ugly," John replied. "Oh, this is happening it all right, and no one is here to save you this time—just you and me, amigo."

"*Amigo* means friend, you racially challenged moron!" Hector said. "I'll call you a lot of things, but *friend* is definitely not one of them."

John and the three others got off their bikes and quickly surrounded them.

"I thought you said it was just gonna be you and me, asshole. What's with all these other guys?"

"They're just here for moral support," John said. "You got a friend here too—so it's all good."

Richard said, "Yeah, but there's only two of us and four of you guys."

John sneered. "Oh, yeah. I suppose you're right. Guess life's a bitch, eh?"

Stepping forward, Hector put up his fists in a protective stance and rose up on his toes to provide quicker movement.

John grinned sinisterly and raised his hands as he approached.

The two maneuvered around each other, sizing up their opponent and planning their first moves.

With the patience of a two-year-old, John initiated the battle with a wide-arching right cross.

Hector's reflexes came through again, and he skillfully ducked out of the path and jumped behind him. Immediately turning around to face his opponent, he swung wildly again.

For the fourth time that day, Hector managed to avoid his blow.

"Stop running away and fight me, you little turd!" John shouted.

John's friend Bill approached Hector from behind.

"Hector, look out behind you!"

It was too late. Bill threw his arms around Hector, putting him in a bear-hug. He was at least thirty pounds heavier than his friend, and Hector would most likely not be able to break out of the hold, leaving him helpless to John's impending blows.

"Hey, let him go!" Richard shouted as he lunged toward the two. As his eyes locked with those of Hector, he could now clearly see the fear as he realized the seriousness of the situation. He also saw the acknowledgement that even in the face of significant danger and overwhelming odds, Richard was running to help him. Whatever would be the result of the following minutes, they would always have this moment that would represent an important juncture in their friendship.

Before Richard could reach them, John stepped up and landed a powerful blow to Hector's abdomen. He winced in pain as his body curled up, reacting to the impact.

Richard noticed a quick blur from his peripheral vision. Within a moment, an arm flew across his face and under his neck, putting him in a headlock. Within a moment, he was completely immobilized. He grasped at the arm, trying to loosen its grip.

Looking back at Richard, John sneered. "Oh, don't worry, In-Jin Joe. You'll have your turn too once I'm done with bigmouth here. Wonder how big a talker he'll be without any teeth!"

He followed this statement with a right cross to the side of Hector's face just above the jawline.

Tears welled up in Hector's eyes, but he refused to cry out.

Richard was absolutely terrified at the reality of what was happening to his friend and his own dire situation. As the squeeze of the chokehold tightened, he started to relive the events on the reservation several days earlier. As the oxygen was being deprived from his brain, panic set in. Just before it turned into complete hysterics, Richard's fear transformed into rage. A wild, primal feeling welled up inside of him. It was as if some strange and powerful beast was taking over his body. Inhaling a deep breath, he let out a roar that shocked him as much as everybody else. The thundering cry was unlike he had ever heard a human make. With this beastly call, an overwhelming feeling of strength flowed through him. Digging his fingers along the arm that was securely around his neck, he easily pulled it away from his throat. With the arm still in his grasp, he swung it around, pulling the boy completely off his feet and throwing him a good six feet away. Crashing to the ground, the boy cowered and held his injured arm.

Pete, the only one not yet involved in the skirmish, lunged forward and swung at Richard with an overhead roundhouse. Apparently retaining some of his old martial arts training, Richard countered the blow with a side block, which—to his amazement—easily batted away the blow as if it were thrown by a five-year-old. Pete's eyes grew like saucers as the pain shot through his mind like a dagger.

With primal rage coursing through his veins, Richard grasped Pete's shirt and pulled him completely off the ground. Pete weighed at least 140 pounds, but he felt nearly weightless to Richard. Turning slightly to adjust his trajectory, Richard shoved as hard as he could and released his grasp on Pete's shirt. The force behind the movement was so powerful that the boy's body flew five feet through the air before smashing straight into John, knocking both to the ground.

Overcome with shock and disbelief, Pete and John could only sit and stare at Richard.

Bill promptly released his grasp on Hector and stepped backward.

Hector was standing by himself and looking at Richard with complete awe and amazement.

Richard took a step in their direction, and the four of them scrambled like rats toward their bikes and awkwardly pedaled away.

Hector's face was bright red and starting to swell, yet it appeared not to bother him in the least. "What the hell was that?" Hector exclaimed.

"I don't know?" Richard said. "Something just sort of came over me. All of a sudden, I was throwing those guys around like rag dolls. Pretty crazy, eh?"

"Crazy? You mean pretty crazy-friggin' awesome!" Hector shouted. "I don't know how the hell you did that, but it was without question the coolest thing I've ever seen!"

Suddenly, an epiphany came over him. "The necklace!" Richard shouted. "The necklace must have done something to me. And I think it makes me fast too."

"What?" Hector asked.

"When I was walking home from school yesterday, my sister almost got run over by a van. I was able to run really fast and pull her out of the way."

"How fast?" Hector asked.

"Not sure," Richard answered. "Pretty fast, I guess. So now what do we do?"

A sly grin came across Hector's face as he looked back at his friend. "Don't sweat it, homey. I got a plan!"

CHAPTER 6

On Friday, Richard could scarcely believe that he was still in his first week of high school. With all the ridiculous and amazing events of the past four days, it seemed like summer vacation was months ago. It was like he was a totally different person, and nothing would ever be the same again.

On the way to school, Hector said something about having a big plan. "We'll go back to the high school on Saturday morning, and I'll take care of the rest."

They agreed that they needed to keep the magical necklace secret from everybody! The fewer people who knew about it, the better. Their most obvious concern was John Sandal and his three moronic friends. They had witnessed Richard using his abilities firsthand, and they could easily blow his cover. Would they? They might tell everybody what happened, hoping enough attention would be brought to them that someone would get to the bottom of things. This would require him telling everybody that he and three of his sophomore friends got the hell beaten out of them by a scrawny freshman. It could very well result in no one believing their crazy story and become a total embarrassment for all four of them.

As luck would have it, no one said a single thing to either of them for the entire day. During lunch, Richard did catch John speaking with another student and pointing in Hector's direction, clearly bragging about the beating he gave him. Richard could have walked over there and completely blown his entire fabrication, but it was better for both of them that everyone bought into John's story and left it at that. Richard was fairly confident that his issues with John and his friends were over. At one point, Richard made a point to lock eyes with John. Within an instant, the fear was back in his eyes. John was a bully, but he was not a complete idiot. He was in a no-win situation if he tried anything now.

Pretending as if nothing unusual happened was no problem for Richard, but for Hector, it was absolute torture! Keeping his mouth shut was the best course of action. The topic of whether or not Tommy and Jenny would be included in this cone of secrecy came up in their conversation, and Richard was adamant that Tommy and Jenny not know what was going on. If Richard was going to express his feelings toward her, he wanted her reaction to be the result of how she felt about him—not some kid with superpowers or whatever the heck he could now apparently do.

Saturday was the first morning that Richard could sleep in all week, but he somehow managed to get himself up at seven thirty. He had agreed to meet up with Hector at nine to go to the high school for the big plan. He told his mom that he was going to meet some guys down at the school for a friendly game of touch football. Though it was unusual, it was not unprecedented. She seemed to buy into it without much hesitation.

During their walk to school, Hector was eerily quiet, but he had a perpetual grin. His only instruction to Richard was to be sure to bring the "item" and some good running shoes. At school, Hector led them to the track.

Richard was shocked to see Tommy waiting for them. "What the heck is Tommy doing here? I thought we were trying to keep this thing secret?"

"Yeah, about that… I thought about it a lot, and we got something pretty amazing here. Before we get too deep into this, we've got to do some testing on this sucker… just so we know exactly what we're dealing with. So that's where Tommy comes in. He's the scientific one of the gang. Plus, I just gotta tell someone—and you know he can keep a secret."

Richard looked back at him cautiously. He also was dying to tell someone about this incredible turn of events, and if there was one person out there who he could trust outside of Hector, it was Tommy. "Okay, man. I guess he's in."

"He's in what?" Tommy called out as he approached them, having apparently overheard the last part of their conversation. "I'm not sure what I'm now supposed to be a part of, but the two of you better have a damn good reason for me to get my butt outta bed and drag it down to school at nine o'clock on a Saturday morning!"

"Oh, it's good all right!" Hector said. "But before we go any further, you got to promise that whatever you see here today must stay between the three of us—no exceptions!"

"So, by no exceptions, you mean that you don't tell anybody, right?" Richard replied.

"I get it," Hector said. "I know we said the same thing yesterday, but it's Tommy! He's cool."

"He's still totally confused if anyone gives a hoot," Tommy said.

"Oh, yeah, right," Hector said. "So check it out. This is some crazy stuff that's gonna blow your mind, dude!"

"Let me take over from here," Richard interrupted. "It's my deal, and I'll explain it. So you remember that old Indian necklace I showed you guys the other day?"

"Yeah," Tommy replied.

Richard said, "Well, I really can't explain it, but it somehow seems to give me certain… abilities."

"Exactly what are you referring to?" Tommy asked, looking more suspicious than ever.

"Well, for one, I can get really strong if I get upset enough."

"Do you turn green too? There better be a friggin' hilarious punchline coming up ASAP, or I'm going off on the two of you big-time!"

"I know that it sounds unbelievable, but Hector witnessed it firsthand and can vouch that we aren't pulling your leg."

"Dude, it's all true, man. Richie whooped the hell out of John and all three of his stooges yesterday afternoon like they were nothing!" Hector said.

Tommy said, "So what are we doing on a track?"

"I'm pretty sure that I can also run really fast," Richard replied. "My sister was almost run over the other day, and I was able to run hella fast to pull her out of the way."

"What kind of speed are we talking about?" Tommy asked.

"That's why we have this!" Hector held up a stopwatch. "My old man's got several of these he uses for practice. I borrowed one. We'll have Richie run a hundred-meter dash and time him to see how fast his is! That would give us a good baseline of data to work with."

Tommy said, "I still think the two of you are totally delusional, but since we're here, we might as well give it a shot. One thing though. I'll be the one holding the stopwatch. Hector's clearly too invested in this fantasy to be trusted to give an accurate reading."

Richard and Hector walked to one end of the track, positioning themselves at the start, and Tommy took the stopwatch down to the finish line.

Richard began to feel nervous. There was no guarantee that it would work at all. He was pretty sure he ran really fast to save his sister, but he didn't have any proof. *I guess there's only one way to find out.* He walked up to the starting line and positioned himself. Though he was a mostly a distance runner, he'd done some sprint work before. He knew the stance required for the fastest acceleration possible. He didn't have track spikes, but his running shoes would provide effective traction on the newly resurfaced track.

"Come on, Richie. You can do this, brother!" Hector said.

Reaching the finish line, Tommy called out, "Okay, Hector. You give Richard a ready, set, and go. Once you say go, I'll start the stopwatch, and we'll see what happens."

With nerves racing faster than ever, Richard took his stance at the starting line. For the life of him, he could not remember exactly what happened when he had to save his sister. Did he think some fast thoughts or something? Now that there was no real emergency, perhaps the necklace wouldn't do anything. It would be really embarrassing if this thing turned out to be a gigantic bust!

"Ready!" Hector shouted.

Richard's anxiety faded, and an overwhelming feeling of alertness and focus came over him.

"Set!"

Glancing down the runway, a tree at the end of the track caught Richard's attention. He locked in on it. That would be the focal point of his run. Get to that tree fast as humanly possible. His body felt exceptionally light, and his muscles tightened up like a tripwire ready to spring.

"Go!"

Before the last sound left Hector's mouth, Richard could feel himself rocketing forward like he had been shot out of a cannon. He could feel the acceleration in his body like when he was running to save his sister. It almost felt like he was moving in slow motion, but in his peripheral vision, the bleachers were a blur as they flew by. His focus remained on the tree. At first, it didn't seem to be getting much closer, but then Richard realized that he needed to start slowing down or he'd end up smashing right into it. Putting on the brakes, he managed to decelerate just in time to slow to a quick jog before reaching the trunk.

Richard turned back to see that he was actually a good thirty yards from Tommy.

Tommy was staring at the stopwatch, completely motionless.

Richard and Hector jogged over, arriving within a couple of seconds of each other.

Tommy continued to stare at the watch.

"Dude, what's wrong, man?" Richard asked.

"It can't be right. I must have done something wrong," Tommy whispered. "You just ran the hundred-meter dash in 8.54 seconds. That's more than a second faster than the current world record! You're the fastest human who ever lived!"

The three boys just stood and stared at each other.

Finally, Hector said, "Man, that's friggin' awesome! You gotta let me try that thing out!"

The comment caught Richard completely off guard. It was *his* necklace. He went through absolute hell to get it. Could he really let Hector just try it out? A mixture of suspicion and trepidation went through his mind. What if Hector could do the same thing with the necklace that he could? What if he ran off and decided to keep it for himself? Could he ever get over the betrayal? Richard caught himself. Hector was one of his closest friends. If he couldn't trust him, then he couldn't trust anybody. As much as it hurt for the words to leave his mouth, he said, "I guess you can give it a try."

It was a complete toss-up as to who was more shocked at the response. Hector and Tommy stood there with their mouths open.

Following a few awkward moments, Richard slowly untied the necklace, and then with great care, he walked over to Hector and fastened it around his neck. He quickly jogged back to the starting line and took his position. Richard opted to stay at the finish line with Tommy and see the result of this unplanned experiment for himself.

Tommy reset the stopwatch. "Ready… set… go!"

When Hector took off, the effort and strain were apparent on his face. It looked like he was about to pass out, but he finally he crossed the finish line. After taking several seconds to catch his breath, he hobbled over to Richard and Tommy.

"So how fast was it?" Hector asked.

"It was 15.87 seconds" Tommy answered.

Hector's excitement drained out of his face. "That's not that fast, is it?"

"Not especially," Tommy replied. "But look on the bright side— at least you the second-fastest person on this track right now."

"I don't get it. What the heck do you think I did wrong?"

"I don't think that's it," Tommy replied. "Rich, you said you were pretty sure that the necklace you found was around the neck of an ancient Native American who you thought came from the same tribe as yours, right?"

"Yeah. I think so. As far as I know, they were the only tribe that inhabited this area for centuries."

"That must be it," Tommy said. "The necklace only works on you because you're a member of the same tribe as the ancient warrior who you took it off of. I mean there's no scientific rationale as to why any of this is happening, but it makes as much sense as anything else at this point."

"Aw, man! That sucks!" Hector said.

Though he did his best not to show it, Richard was secretly thrilled that the necklace did not work on Hector. He was the special one after all. Once Hector returned the artifact, Richard secured it around his neck.

Hector said. "Wait, guys! That was just round one!"

Following a series of uneasy looks between Richard and Tommy, the three made their way to the weight room. As expected, it was locked.

After Tommy pulled at the door, Hector produced a series of keys from his pocket. "I swiped them from the old man's dresser this morning. I'm in deep doo-doo if he ever finds out."

Once they were inside, Hector locked the door behind them. "So we know that you're really fast. Now we need to test just how strong you are. What's the best lift to figure that out?"

Grinning widely, Tommy and Richard looked at each other and then back to Hector. "Bench press!"

Deadlifts, squats, or cleans would have been a better overall evaluator of total body strength, but as every red-blooded teenage boy knows instinctively, if you want to impress people with how strong, you are, you tell them how much you can bench press. That's what they were going with.

At one of the flat benches, Richard put two twenty-five-pound plates on a standard forty-five-pound bar before positioning himself under it.

"That's it?" Hector barked.

"Relax, Arnold," Richard replied. "Before I had this thing, this is how much I could bench… once… with a lot of effort. Let me just see how this feels."

Hector sighed with a bit of disappointment, but he did not argue with the logic.

Once properly positioned, Richard grasped the bar in both hands. Before attempting to lift it, he closed his eyes and thought back to the fight two days earlier. He focused on how angry he was and tried to put himself back into that state. As he did so, he felt the strength welling up in him again. With the smallest amount of effort, he lifted the bar off of the rack and completed ten repetitions in rapid succession. The bar felt practically weightless in his hands. If he didn't know better, he would have sworn that he was lifting nine pounds instead of ninety-five pounds! Quickly placing the bar back on the rack, Richard sat up and said, "Okay. Now let's make this interesting. Put two plates on each side!"

They placed two forty-five-pound weights on each side of the bar. The four plates and the bar added up to 225 pounds. It was not exactly superhuman, but it was a good next step. It was also more than a hundred pounds more than he had ever lifted in his entire life. Richard could feel the excitement building in the room as he positioned himself under the bar. After taking a moment to focus, he lifted the bar off the rack and slowly brought it down to his chest. After a momentary pause, he drove the weight up again until he could rack the bar. The rep was not exactly weightless, but it was manageable. "Okay, guys. Two more plates!"

Giggling with excitement, Hector and Tommy added two more forty-five-pound plates to the bar, bringing the total weight to 315. It was approaching three times his body weight, and despite how easily the last one went up, Richard still felt a bit nervous. He opted to have Hector and Tommy help him lift the weight off the bench and get it into position.

After a few seconds of focusing and a three, two, one count, the bar was lifted off the rack. With steely determination, Richard lowered the bar once again, and as soon as it touched his chest, he felt a primal roar from within. With a bit more effort, he drove the bar up and racked the weight with a loud clang that echoed off the walls.

Once the weight was back in place, Richard looked up at Tommy and Hector. They looked anxious and excited. Knowing that neither of them would suggest it, Richard grinned mischievously and said, "Two more plates,"

It was difficult to say if the three of them were more amazed, excited, or terrified as the plates clanged loudly, impacting the other weights on the bar. It was 405 pounds—more than 300 percent of his body weight! His nerves were on fire, and his mind raced as he mentally forced himself to focus. The last lift did not really feel that heavy. *You can do this! Summon the rage. Summon the strength!*

After a few seconds, he shouted, "Okay, guys. On three… one… two… three!"

With a combined effort by Hector and Tommy on opposite sides of the bar, and Richard pushing from the middle, the bar slowly lifted off the rack. All three steadied it directly above Richard's chest. The bar bowed slightly as the weight at the ends pulled downward. As the two carefully released their hands from the ends of the bar, Richard could feel the full weight pressing down on him. A streak of panic shot through his mind like a lightning bolt. For a moment, he thought about racking the weight, but then he caught himself and refocused. *You've got this!*

After taking a deep breath, he lowered the bar to his chest, and with a surge of energy even more powerful than before, he grunted angrily and drove the weight back up to full extension. Once he reached the end of the lift, he felt so exhilarated that he casually let the bar slam into the rack with such force that it nearly toppled the bench over backward!

Tommy and Hector managed to jump in at the last second to avoid certain disaster!

"Dude, careful with that thing!" Hector shrieked. "You could have crushed both of us! Though I gotta say, bro, that was awesome!"

Still on an adrenaline high from the previous lift, Richard glanced around and over at Tommy and Hector. He could see the panic in their eyes as they realized what he was about to say. "I dunno, guys. I'm still feeling pretty good. I think I still got one more lift in me!"

After an audible gulp, Hector and Tommy looked at each other nervously. Without a word, they removed two more plates from a stand and placed them on the bar. It would bring the total amount to a crushing 495 pounds!

If anything went wrong during this lift, Hector and Tommy could do little to help Richard out. It was a do-or-die situation, and he fought hard to quell the nerves welling up inside. He somehow managed to get up 405 with power to spare, and this was just another lift. The magical forces at work needed to come through one more time!

Before positioning himself under the bar, Richard jumped up and down several times and pounded his chest like a gorilla to get his adrenaline pumping. He went back the fight again in his mind, feeling the anger and trying to remember the sensation of the power coursing through his limbs. Richard gazed at his friends with a look of absolute confidence. "It's go time!"

He grasped the bar tightly and called out, "Three... two... one... go!" With assistance from Hector and Tommy, Richard lifted the bar off the rack and steadied it directly above his chest.

Once in place, the two spotters nervously let go of the bar, which bent noticeably on either side of Richard's grip.

Taking a deep breath, Richard let the bar descend toward his chest—faster than with the previous lifts but still in control. Tommy and Hector could only stand and watch as their friend either lifted this ridiculous weight or was crushed to death in front of them!

As the bar finally hit his chest, Richard pushed with everything he had. For a split second, the bar didn't move. Then, just as his friends were about to jump in to see if they could do something to help, Richard let out a roar like the one he let out during the fight with John. It was the call of some sort of wild beast, and the power flowed through Richard's arms and chest as he drove the bar all the way up to full extension.

The spotters immediately jumped in and helped him rack the weight safely before loosening his grip on the bar.

"Holy cow!" Richard called out, still catching his breath. "That was pretty intense! I think we're good for now as far as the bench press is concerned."

"Yeah... totally," Hector replied. "Safe to say you're strong as hell—as well as superfast! I'd say that our testing session today was a complete success."

"What about the other two items on the necklace?" Tommy said.

"Huh?" Richard grunted.

"The necklace has four distinct items on it, right? That thing on the far left is a piece of deer antler, correct?"

"Yeah, it's definitely some sort of antler. Almost positive it's a type of deer," Richard answered.

"Deer are superfast, so it makes sense that this crazy contraption is making you fast with some assistance from that piece of deer antler. Then there's the bear claw. Bears are really strong, so it's logical that your strength is somehow coming from the bear claw. That still leaves the tooth and the feather. Since the bear is already represented by the claw, I'm guessing that it's not a bear tooth. Given that this is a Native American artifact, and there were only a select number of predators in North America hundreds of years ago, my guess would be a mountain lion."

"Yeah, I would have guessed that as well," Richard added. "So what does that mean?"

"Lions are cats, and cats are well known for being incredibly agile. So maybe you've got super dexterity as well?"

"So how are we supposed to test for that?" Richard asked.

"I've got keys to the gymnastics room," Hector said.

Once inside, Richard looked around and was initially at a loss for exactly what to do to try out this potential ability. Looking over at the tumbling mat, he remembered some tumbling and gymnastics maneuvers he had to learn when he was testing for his black belt in Tae Kwon Do a few years back.

This is as good as any place to start I guess. After removing his shoes and socks, he walked onto the mat and took a horse stance like he was starting a martial arts maneuver. He closed his eyes and focused on the necklace. Unlike speed and strength, he had never used this ability before. If it was going to be there at all, he had no idea how to activate it. In his mind, he pictured himself as a large cat, moving silently and effortlessly through a thick forest. After a few moments, he began to notice a lightness to his body and an enhanced feeling of awareness throughout his muscles. Now feeling fully in the zone, he began.

He started with some basic kicks—side kick, front kick, back kick, axe kick—and then a jump kick and a spinning back kick. It had been years since he'd tried any of the maneuvers, but his kicks were faster, more powerful, and more precise than they had ever been. He launched into a jump-split kick that ended with his legs completely parallel to the floor and a full six feet off the ground. Now getting excited, he took several steps toward the center of the mat and launched into two hand-over-feet somersaults followed by a jumping front-flip that nearly took him off the mat. Sticking the landing, Richard looked at Hector and Tommy.

They both stared back in amazement.

Glancing over toward the balance beam, Richard sprinted toward it. When he was fifteen feet from the apparatus, he jumped through the air with tremendous height and agility and came down with only his right foot hitting the top of the beam. The momentum should have pulled him over the other side of it, but with inhuman coordination, he quickly regained his balance and completed two standing front flips and two standing backflips on top of the beam!

After several seconds of silence, Richard turned back to his friends and grinned. "I guess we can check super dexterity off the list too, eh?"

"I guess that just leaves the feather," Hector said.

Richard said, "So you think I'm supposed to be able to fly with this thing?"

Richard and Hector looked to Tommy for some sort of confirmation. "Don't look at me! None of this stuff makes any sense from a scientific perspective. I've got no clue what the hell a magic feather is supposed to do? Only one way to find out."

The three made their way out to the practice soccer field for a dry run. It was the remotest part of the campus and contained a large grassy area. If Richard actually did take flight, they definitely did not want anyone else seeing it. Once on the grass, the three looked at each other in hopes that someone would have an idea about what to do next.

After a few seconds, Richard said, "I guess I'll just take a few steps and jump?"

"It's as good a plan as any, I suppose," Tommy answered.

After an approving nod from Hector, Richard closed his eyes and thought about the necklace, specifically the feather. He tried to picture himself soaring through the air, far above the school. Some sort of feelings did come over him, and he started to get a light feeling again. *I guess this is it.*

Taking a deep breath, Richard ran across the field. After about twenty yards, he planted his right foot firmly and jumped up with everything he had. Once airborne, he spread his arms out as wide as he could and looked toward the end of the field and the fence about two hundred yards away. For a moment, Richard could have sworn that he was hovering in midair, perhaps even gaining altitude. The feeling left him, and a second later, he awkwardly crashed onto the ground with a tremendous thud that completely knocked the wind out of him.

He rolled over onto his back and was trying to catch his breath when Tommy and Hector ran up to him.

"Dude, that was harsh, man! You okay?"

"I think I'll live," Richard said.

"I wonder what went wrong," Tommy said. "Perhaps you need to be at a greater height before it kicks in?"

"I've got a key that can get us to the roof of the gym!" Hector said.

Still reeling in pain, Richard shot Hector a stare of disbelief. "Yeah. That's okay. I think we're done here. That's enough testing for one day."

CHAPTER 7

The following week flew by almost overnight for Richard. His spirits were through the roof—and why shouldn't they be? He was catching up on his schoolwork, he would likely be the top cross-country runner on his school's frosh-soph team, and he had several great friends to share his high school experience with. Oh, and he was apparently some sort of a superhero!

Three of his teachers even commented on how he seemed different this week. *Confident* and *energetic* were some of the adjectives used. Everything was pretty great overall. John Sandal and the others would not even look at them anymore, and Richard was only too happy to keep his distance as well.

Tommy and Hector were thoroughly enjoying their special secret and were in pretty great moods as well. The one slight wrinkle in the plan was Jenny. She quickly noticed that John and his goon squad had immediately stopped messing with the four of them, and she found it very odd. Richard and Hector told her that they had it out after school, and Hector still had the bruises to provide evidence. After the confrontation, John had declared them even. As long as Hector kept his mouth shut, they would lay off the four of them.

The story made sense logically, but Richard could tell that she wasn't completely buying it. She was smart, and everything seemed a little too neat and clean to be all hunky-dory. When she asked Richard about it, he came close to breaking down and telling her everything, but he caught himself. He was determined to express his feelings toward her sometime that year, and he did not want her judgments clouded by the strange abilities he now possessed.

Hector and Tommy stuck to their story, and after a couple of days, Jenny stopped asking about it. Things seemed to get back to normal—or as ordinary as they could be, given the circumstances.

On Wednesday afternoon after cross-country practice, Richard was met by his mom in the kitchen. "Honey, I hope you had a great day at school today. I spoke with Grandpa this morning, and he asked if you would like to come out the reservation this weekend. He felt really bad that you were not feeling good last time and missed the autumn celebration."

As soon as his mom mentioned the reservation, Richard's mind immediately went to Ahote. A smug grin crept across his face. He certainly had some unfinished business that needed to be addressed. He'd already put one bully in his place, and another one definitely needed a good talking-to. "Yeah, that would be great. Can you drive me over on Saturday morning?"

"Yeah, that will work. I'll run you over as soon as I get back from the gym. Is ten okay?"

"That'll be fine. Thanks, Mom."

The remainder of the week flew by. His run at cross-country practice on Friday afternoon was so strong that Coach Jed even dropped a hint that he might consider having him run varsity, which was almost unheard of for a freshman. As excited as he was at the possibility, he felt some degree of guilt with his recent running accomplishments. Though he never actually wore the necklace during practice, it did appear that just having it on him as much as he did had some ongoing effects on his running abilities. It bothered him for a bit, but in the end, there was nothing he could really do about it. Since he was not trying to cheat, it must be okay. At least that was the rationalization he used.

On Friday night, he spent the evening as he usually did: online gaming *Overwatch* with the gang. He was distracted, and it showed.

"Dude, get it together, man. You're playing like a schoolgirl," Hector said over the computer headset.

"Hello, losers. I am a schoolgirl, and I can play better than all of you," Jenny said.

"You know what I mean, girlfriend. Rich is our support player. We need his healing to get through this level, and he's slacking big-time!" Hector said.

The banter went on as it always did throughout the game, and Richard started to play a little better. His mind was still elsewhere. How would it go down this weekend? Would he actually go and seek out Ahote or just wait for him to make the first move? What if he didn't do or say anything. Should he actually instigate something? That would probably be wrong. No. He would just go and pretend that everything was great and see if anything happened. Granted, he would not go out of his way to avoid a confrontation, but if Ahote wanted to start something, he was more than happy to finish it!

The next morning, Richard arrived at the reservation at ten thirty. He greeted his grandfather with a big bear-hug.

"Oh, geez. Easy there, Hercules!" Grandfather said. "I'm not as young as I used to be, and you've obviously been working out. You don't want to break me in half!"

"Sorry, Grandpa. It's good to see you again."

"It's only been two weeks."

"Seems like a lot longer."

"You do look much better, I have to say. Like a new man. So how's cross-country practice going?"

"Awesome! The coach is even toying around with the idea of having me run varsity if my times keep improving."

"Okay, you two. I gotta run, but you be good, okay?"

"Sure thing, Mom. Love you," Richard answered.

Following goodbye hugs and kisses with both Richard and her dad, Ayiana went home, leaving Richard and his grandfather to catch up on things. He continued on about his running accomplishments, school, and home. He didn't mention anything about the necklace and the stories surrounding it, and he found it much more difficult that he thought not to say anything. His grandpa was still his closest friend, and it killed him to omit the amazing thing that was happening. He almost slipped up a couple of times, but he caught himself, and in the end, he managed to keep everything under wraps.

After another twenty minutes of chitchat, Richard suggested that they head to the beach for a quick swim to work up an appetite for lunch. After quickly changing, the two made their way to ocean. After a brief warm-up run, they dove into the surf. The cold water was completely invigorating. Richard and his grandfather swam two hundred yards to a buoy that was anchored near the coast. They looked back at the beach, contemplated the amazing beauty of nature in all of its forms, and headed to shore. The swim served its purpose, and by the time they got back to the mobile home, Richard was famished. They had a large salad made of vegetables grown right on the reservation, and to provide some more substance to the meal, they added leftover chicken to the greens. They ate it with some crusty bread that a neighbor had baked a few hours earlier.

Following lunch, Richard helped clean up the kitchen and headed over to the rec center.

Chenowa was one of the only kids in North America who still didn't have a cell phone, so texting ahead to let him know that he was coming to the reservation was out of the question. He could have just called the house phone, but he decided to surprise him. Though he was certainly not looking for a fight, he would at least be prepared. Just before heading over, he rummaged through his bag and grabbed the necklace that he had hidden in one of the pockets. Outside his grandfather's place, he quickly tied it around his neck and hid it under his T-shirt.

Inside the building, Chenowa was playing pool with one of the other kids from the reservation. Richard knew Stephen fairly well, and aside from being a bit annoying whenever the topic of baseball came up, he was nice enough. Aside from Richard, he was one of the only other kids on the reservation with an Americanized first name, so they had that in common.

When Richard was about thirty feet from the table, Chenowa said, "Rich? What's going on, man? I didn't know that you were coming down this weekend. You'll be here tonight, right?"

"Wouldn't miss it," Richard answered.

"I was just afraid that you might steer clear of this place after what went down last time. I know that you were pretty upset," Chenowa said. "I mean who could blame you after Ahote nearly choked you out!"

Chenowa's face still had signs of the black eye from two weeks earlier.

"How are you doing? That looks like it must have been pretty nasty last week?"

"Yeah. The first week, it hurt like hell, but over the last several days, it felt fine. It will probably be a bit longer for the rest of the discoloring to go away. On the positive side, those first couple of days, when it really looked bad, my mom went off on Ahote big-time! Made him promise that he'd lay off us from here on out."

Though it would have been great news in any other situation, Richard experienced a strange feeling of frustration and almost disappointment as he heard the words. The whole point of the trip was to stand up to that bully and let him know that it was not okay to pick on smaller people. If Ahote stayed on good behavior all weekend, there would be no opportunity to confront him. Richard could sense that Chenowa saw that something was off with his reaction, so he quickly changed his mood and went back to playing pool. For the next three hours, they played pool, video games, and air hockey without a peep from Ahote. Eventually Richard sort of forgot about him altogether and enjoyed the rest of the afternoon.

Richard finally made his way back to his grandfather's place to help prepare for the potluck dinner the tribe would have in a couple of hours. The main course would be a delicious venison chili that one of the members of the tribe had perfected after many years of practice and tinkering. The cornbread was made from scratch in the "old-world way" as Grandpa described it. I was not as sweet as the packaged stuff at the store, and it tasted more rustic and authentic. Everyone else brought whatever they wanted in terms of salads, side dishes, and desserts. Richard's grandpa's contribution was always his famous Chinese chicken salad. It was not an authentic Native American dish by any stretch of the imagination, but it was quite good. He used cabbage instead of lettuce, so it held up much better than most other salads, and the homemade dressing was delicious. The two of them worked on the salad for nearly an hour, and at five thirty, they headed over to the main meeting area where the large group meals always occurred.

More than twenty park benches were set up near and around the large fire pit in the center of the area. Most of them were for the various families to sit and dine, but four of them were arranged end to end for all the different dishes.

Making his way to the table where he and his grandfather would be eating, Richard immediately noticed his aunt, Chenowa, and Ahote sitting there. He knew it was his grandfather's plan all along. Learning of the incident between the three boys, Richard was certain that he intended for the meal to resolve any remaining issues between the kids once and for all.

Ahote looked at Richard smugly and said, "Hey, Richie. How have you been?" There was a hint of pompousness to his tone. He could not make it too obvious, but Richard picked up on it right away.

"Hey, Ahote. Been really good, actually," Richard replied as confidently as he could.

Chenowa looked back and forth between them for a few seconds. "Hey, guys. I'm starving. Let's eat!"

The group all got up from the table and got in line behind about a dozen others who were waiting to fill their plates. The food was delicious, but Richard could hardly pay attention to the meal. He was completely focused on Ahote.

Helaku finally said, "How is school going so far? I hear that cross-country is going well for you."

The topic had already been discussed in great detail, but the opening gave him a chance to boast a bit about his accomplishments in front of his cousins. He then recapped the story he had told his grandfather earlier, making a point to look at Ahote as much as possible—without appearing obvious—and to smile as wide as he could. With each word, he could see the anger welling up behind his eyes and on his forehead.

Chenowa looked concerned as well.

Richard was pressing Ahote's buttons, and nothing good could possibly come from it. The rest of the meal continued with discussions ranging from tribe gossip to the standings in the NFL.

After dinner, Richard and Chenowa walked fifty yards or so to an open area and threw a football around. After several throws, Richard noticed that Ahote had walked off toward some tall redwoods. He was talking to Elania, but she appeared not to be very interested in the conversation.

After a few more tosses of the pigskin, his aunt said, "Ahote, can you do me a favor and run back to the house? I forgot the peach pie I baked. Can you please get it for me?"

Ahote sneered at her, but she shot a look right back at him to clarify who the boss of the house was. Ahote finally answered, "Yeah Mom. I'll get it."

As soon as Ahote started to jog toward his house, Richard said, "Hector, going deep!"

Richard started running a long pattern that conveniently happened to be in Elania's general direction. Seeing that he'd need to throw the football as hard as he could to catch up with his cousin, Chenowa took three big strides and heaved the ball with everything he had. Richard saw the arc on the ball and quickly determined where he'd need to be to reach it in time. Normally, he wouldn't have had a shot in hell at reaching it as it veered to the right, but by applying just a bit of his super speed, he covered the distance and ended up completing a jumping catch that would have made Jerry Rice proud.

Chenowa started whooping and hollering as if they had just won the Super Bowl, but Richard was not even looking in his direction. After covering the distance to reach the ball, he was now only about twenty yards from Elania. She had also witnessed the catch and was fighting hard to hide her grin.

Sensing his opportunity, Richard jogged the last few yards toward her. "Elania, it's good to see you. It's been a while since we talked. How's school going?"

"Oh, pretty good, I guess. It's high school, so that's cool, but we're freshmen, so everyone gives us a hard time. Is it the same with you?"

Smirking to himself, Richard said. "No too bad actually. I had one little thing, but I'm pretty sure that no one will be messing with us for the rest of the year."

Elaina said, "So did you end up using some of your Kung Fu on someone?"

"Actually, it was Tae Kwon Do—and you could say it was something like that." He did his best to answer as nonchalantly as possible. Glancing back in the direction of Chenowa's house, he could just make out Ahote returning with the pie about two hundred yards away. If this plan was going to work, he'd need to move fast. "So there's something that I've been meaning to tell you for a while."

"What's that? Elania replied.

"Even though we've been friends for a long time, I always thought that you were kinda cute. I was thinking that maybe we could sit together at the bonfire tonight?" Richard asked in the coolest voice he could muster.

She blushed. "Wow. That's super nice of you to say, Richie. I always thought you were pretty cute too. I'm just afraid that Ahote might get really angry with you. He's been asking me out for a while now. I tried to let him know that I'm really not that into him, but he just won't take a hint. Fortunately, with him being two years older, my mom hasn't approved of me dating anyone, so I've been able to keep him from pushing the issue too hard for now."

"I wouldn't worry about Ahote," Richard answered. "I'll have a talk with him about it. We're family after all. He'll listen to me."

A look of confusion and disbelief came across Elania's face.

From across the field, Ahote yelled, "Hey, what the hell are you doing talking with my girl, ya big creep!"

Richard estimated from the sound that he was still a good hundred yards behind them. He only had seconds to act. "Hey, do you trust me?"

"Yeah. I guess so. What do you have planned?"

"Okay. Don't freak out." Richard reached his hand around Elania's waist and pulled her closer. As their bodies met, Richard turned his head slightly, planted a kiss on her lips, and held it for a good two to three seconds.

"Oh, you're friggin' dead, traitor!" Ahote sprinted toward the two of them after placing the pie on a nearby table. Finally breaking his momentary make-out session, Richard could see Elania's eyes big as saucers with a mixture of excitement, fear, and confusion. Richard spun around, and Ahote was charging toward him like a crazed bull.

Richard sprinted into the forest through a small clearing to his left.

Ahote immediately changed course and followed in close pursuit.

It was playing out exactly how Richard had planned. He knew he could not go all superhero on his butt right out in the open where everyone could see, and he needed to take it to a more secluded place. Fortunately, he had an entire forest at his disposal. It surrounded the reservation on nearly all sides. Richard could have easily outrun Ahote, leaving him in the dust, but that was not the objective. He would kick in the extra juice just enough to keep out of his grasp but still make it seem like he'd eventually catch him. Finally running into a clearing a good 150 yards from where the others were, Richard stopped and faced his opponent,

Ahote tried to catch his breath. "I don't know what the hell is wrong with you, but you're going to pay for it big-time! I was ready to just leave you alone for my mom's sake, but you just had to make a play for my girlfriend. Well, let's see how she likes you when your face looks like a catcher's mitt!"

Richard stared back at him—not the least out of breath and without the slightest hint of fear or intimidation. "She's not your girlfriend, man. She tolerates you being around because she knows it would be awkward and difficult if she told you to get lost like she wishes she could."

Ahote lunged forward and swung wildly with a flailing right cross.

Richard easily moved to the side, and the blow missed completely.

Grinding his teeth and grunting loudly with each attempt, Ahote swung three more times, each one missing worse than the one before it. "Come on, coward! Stop dodging around and fight me!" Ahote threw a haymaker, but Richard reached up and caught the blow with his left hand. It hurt like hell when it hit, but focusing his strength, he clamped down his fingers and locked Ahote's fist in his hand like a bear trap.

Unable to pull his hand away, Ahote swung hard with his left hand.

Richard batted it aside.

The expression on Ahote's face immediately changed from hatred and contempt to disbelief and legitimate concern.

Richard applied greater pressure to Ahote's fist.

"Let me go, you freak bastard! You're gonna pay for this—I swear! Either you, or someone you care for, will suffer!"

A thought occurred to Richard. Sure, the necklace could protect him from this colossal jerk, but what about Chenowa? Would Ahote target someone else? His sister or one of his friends in town? The thought enraged Richard, and the force on Ahote's hand increased accordingly. He could hear the snapping and crunching of bones, and Ahote finally dropped to his knees. "Stop it! I'll do whatever you say. Just let me go!"

"So here's what's going happen," Richard said. "You'll go back and tell everybody that after you saw me kiss Elania, you chased me into the forest, but when you went to punch me, you missed and accidentally hit a tree, breaking your hand. And if I ever hear about you taking any sort of action in retaliation on me—or anyone I know—what I just did to your hand will be the least of your problems! Do you understand?"

Eyes filled with tears, pain, and hatred, Ahote said, "Yeah. I get it. Now let me go!"

From the edge of the clearing, Chenowa said, "Richard! What the hell, man?" He was looking at them with a mixture of confusion, anger, and disbelief.

Richard released his grasp, and Ahote pulled back, cradling his battered right hand. A panic shot through Richard like an electric shock. *Crap! He must have followed us after we ran into the forest. How much did he see and hear?* "Chenowa, let me explain. It was in self-defense. He took a swing at me. I was just defending myself."

"Who are you kidding, bro?" Chenowa said. "You baited him by putting the moves on a girl he liked, then ran out into the forest, and after showing that you could simply dodge his punches all day, you crush his hand as some sort of revenge for the other week. I agree that he can be a real jerk a lot of the time, and he probably had this coming to him, but what you just did was cold-blooded, man."

As the realization of what had happened swept over Richard, the life started to drain out of him. He had just become what he hated the most in life: a bully. He was no better than Ahote. He was actually worse. Even at his most brutal, Ahote only left them with some bumps and bruises. Richard could have just permanently injured his dominant hand, which could affect him for the rest of his life. Chenowa was right. He didn't need to do this. His safety was never in any danger. He could have just tossed him around a bit and accomplished the same thing. This was straight-up revenge, and Richard felt terribly ashamed of himself for giving in to his childish impulses.

Richard was shaking and overcome with emotions. Looking up, he realized that he was now alone in the clearing. Ahote and

Chenowa were gone, and he was only there with his thoughts. What would the two of them say when they got back to the others? Had he completely blown his cover? Did he destroy everything? He was paralyzed by indecision for several minutes before he finally made his way back to the reservation.

In the main area, he was surprised to see that everything seemed pretty much as he had left it. Some of the tribe members were starting a bonfire, and the smaller children were still running around and playing. Making his way back to the picnic tables, he saw his grandpa with a somewhat worried look upon his face. Richard had no idea what he might have been told, and he thought about darting back into the forest. Their eyes met, and he knew that he needed to speak with him. A hollow pit formed him his stomach as he walked to Helaku's table. "Hey, Grandpa," he whispered.

"Richard? Are you okay? Chenowa and Ahote came back and said that there was some sort of a fight again, but he hit a tree or something? Lisana just left with the boys to drive Ahote to the hospital. Were you hurt at all?"

Richard felt worse than ever, and he couldn't even bring himself to look his grandfather in the eye. "No, Grandpa. I'm okay."

The rest of the evening was utter torture. He did his best to go through the motions like everything was fine, but they were not. At one point, he sat by himself and stared into the campfire.

Elania sat next to him and said, "Are you okay? When I saw you two run into the forest, I thought for sure that Ahote was going to tear you in half! I was really glad to see that you're okay. Lucky break him hitting that tree, eh?"

Richard stared silently into the flames. He was lost in his thoughts.

"So I was wondering if you wanted to go see a movie or something next weekend?" she continued.

Oh, hell. Now she thinks we're dating. And why wouldn't she think that? I did kiss her after all. In fact, it was his first kiss, and he didn't even like her that way. He liked Jenny—even if he might never have the courage to tell her. He used this girl and played with her emotions for the sole purpose of instigating the fight. *What the hell's wrong with me? I'm a walking train wreck!* "Yeah, about the kiss earlier, I'm really sorry about that. I just sort of did that out of the blue without asking, and that was wrong of me. I've got a lot going on right now, and I don't know if I'm in a place where I want to be dating anyone."

A long silence followed.

Elania whispered, "I guess I'll see you around then." As soon as the last word left her mouth, she promptly got up and walked over to her family, leaving Richard sitting by himself and feeling as utterly alone as he had experienced his entire life.

After another twenty minutes, he told his grandfather that he was going to head back to his place to call it a night. As he walked back to the mobile home, he felt incredibly tired—physically and emotionally. As soon as his head hit the pillow, he was out like a light.

Nightmares awoke him in a cold sweat on two different occasions, but both times, his fatigue pulled him back into slumber. When he finally opened his eyes in the morning, the sun was shining brightly through the kitchen window. Looking around, he could see that he was alone in the mobile home. Glancing at the clock, it was eight fifteen. His grandfather had gone on their traditional Sunday morning run without him. Myriad questions raced through Richard's mind. *Did someone tell him something after he left last night to go to bed?* His thoughts consumed him for another twenty minutes until Helaku finally walked through the door.

"Richard, what it that thing around your neck?"

Suddenly shocked back into the moment, Richard realized he had removed his shirt when he went to sleep, as he often did, and never put it back on. He was still wearing the necklace. Panic shot through him.

"I also ran into Chenowa on my way back to the house after my run, and he told me some very unusual things. He said that Ahote didn't hit the tree after all. He told me that you actually did this to him on purpose. He had no idea how you did it, but that's what he told me. What the heck is going on here, Richie? Does that necklace have anything to do with this?"

Richard's heart sank into his stomach, and a knot the size of a softball formed in his throat. He felt like he was going to be sick, but after a few moments, he composed himself. "Grandpa, you better sit down. I've got something I need to tell you."

Over the next hour, Richard methodically recapped the past two weeks, including his parents' conversation and the confrontation with Ahote. He kept expecting the old man to cut him off, telling him that it was the craziest made-up thing that he had ever heard, but he just sat there and listened.

Finally, after thirty seconds of silence, Helaku said, "Richard, my son, what you have just shared does concern me greatly. Parts of me are exceptionally upset and disappointed in you and your parents for making the decisions that you did. However, given the circumstances, I can understand how your intentions were largely good. I feel your regret with respect to the poor choices you've made, especially with respect to your confrontation with Ahote last night. I may have some information that might shed some light on this.

"There was a tale that I was told as a boy. As the story goes, many, many years ago, there was a great warrior who was the defender of our tribe. He was known simply as the Spirit Walker. Every twenty years or so, he was chosen by the previous defender as he grew too old to continue his role. Part of that transition was the passing down of the title and all the responsibilities that go with it. Perhaps this necklace is part of these duties they spoke of. Our people have always worshiped nature in all of its forms, but most of all, they worshiped the bear for its strength, the deer for its speed, the mountain lion for its ferocity, and the eagle for its ability to fly to the heavens. I suppose it's possible that this necklace in some way embodies the spirits of these four animals within it, and this is what gave the Spirit Walker his power. As unbelievable as it sounds, it would seem that you have somehow uncovered this lost treasure and taken it upon yourself to become the next Spirit Walker."

Richard stared at his grandfather with confusion and uncertainty. "So what do I do now?"

"Not sure," the old man said. "On the one hand, something this powerful should probably be destroyed for fear that it might fall into the possession of someone with nefarious intentions. On the other hand, this item is a priceless treasure for our people, and it should be put in a museum someplace where all of us can enjoy it. This, however, opens up the possibility that it could be stolen and used for evil purposes. As you know, my son, I am a very spiritual person, and I believe that we each have our own fate and destiny. Perhaps this is your fate, Richard. It was said that when the Spirit Walker chose his successor, he chose not the strongest or the bravest warrior but the one who was the truest of heart. I have known you your whole life, Richard, and I know in my soul that you are an honorable person with a good and just heart. You have made mistakes, as we all have. However, deep down, your spirit is kind and true. I firmly believe that you are regretful of your past errors, and if given the opportunity, you will do right with these abilities moving forward. Perhaps the last Spirit Walker indeed chose you to be the next in line? Only time will tell if you can live up to this great honor."

Richard was utterly stunned at this unexpected turn of events. Did he actually have what it would take to be the next Spirit Walker? And what exactly did it mean? He was uncertain of so many things, but there was one thing that he was perfectly clear about. From that moment forward, he would never use the powers of the necklace for purposes of greed, pride, revenge, or any other aspect of personal gain. It would only be used in the defense of his friends, family, and others in need of help from evil in any form he might encounter. From that day forward, he would be the Spirit Walker!

CHAPTER 8

One might be surprised by just how little there is for an animal spirit-powered superhero to actually do in today's modern society. Following the confrontation with his grandfather, weeks had gone by with literally nothing occurring that would provide even the slightest provocation to use his abilities for much of anything. After some time, Richard even stopped bringing the necklace to school altogether. The first time he left it home, he felt exceptionally exposed—almost naked. However, each day, it got a little easier, and at some point, he nearly forgot about it. He had heard almost nothing from Ahote and Chenowa, except an update from his mom that it would be six to eight weeks before everything would be healed, but that they expected his cousin to regain full use of his hand.

By October 12, with Halloween just around the corner, all thoughts turned to the Once Upon a Scary Night dance. Along with the traditional festivities, there was also a costume contest that awarded prizes for the scariest, most original, and funniest costumes, including individual and group categories. After building up his confidence to ask Jenny to the dance as his date, Richard's plan was quickly dashed when she ran up to all three of them at lunch that day, nearly bursting with excitement. "Oh, my god, guys. I've got the best idea for the Halloween dance. The four of us can dress up at the Village People! Wouldn't that be hilarious? We'd win the group competition for sure!"

Richard, Hector, and Tommy looked at each other with a mixture of confusion and trepidation.

"You know that the Village People were all gay guys, right?" Hector said.

"Of course, I know that, silly. That's why it would be so funny. Plus it would totally be a great pro-gay rights statement, and you know I'm all about equality and diversity. And since we are one of the most diverse groups in the whole school, it makes perfect sense for us to do this. Tommy, you'll be the police officer. Hector, you can be the cowboy."

"Oh, no," Richard said. "Let me guess. I'll be the Indian. You know I should be deeply offended by this."

Jenny said, "Oh, stop it, Richie. You're always telling us about how you take pride in embracing your heritage. Plus, we know that you already have the outfit for it."

She wasn't wrong. Having participated in many traditional ceremonies at the reservation, Richard did have access to a complete Native American ensemble. He even had a full chieftain's headdress that his grandfather gave him after he got a new one a few years ago. Yet despite all of this, the whole idea seemed ridiculous, and he still felt quite uneasy about it. He tried desperately to think of an alternate theme.

Hector said, "You know, she's got a point guys. This would be funny as heck—and great for making time with the ladies!"

"And exactly how is dressing up as a bunch of gay guys supposed to make you look appealing to girls?" Tommy said.

"It's reverse psychology, man," Hector said. "Just about every girl I know is all into gay rights and equality and stuff. They all know that we're not really gay, but by dressing up this way, it shows just how confident we are in our masculinity. Plus, we'll show them that were all for that equality junk too. I'm telling you, man, the girls will eat this up! So, Jenny, if we do this thing, who are you planning to dress up as?"

"Oh, I totally got this!" she said. "I'll do a reverse drag and go as the biker guy. I've already got the leather pants, and my sister has one of those old leather biker caps from a play she did a while back. I'll put my hair up under the cap, and I just need to get a fake moustache and a leather vest. It will be so awesome!"

"So that's four of us," Tommy said. "What about the other members? One was a construction worker, I think?"

Jenny giggled. "Oh, yeah. I already talked with my friend from art class. You guys know Bobbie. Anyway, he's totally down with being the construction worker, so we're all set."

"Isn't Bobbie actually gay?" Richard said.

"Of course he is," Jenny said. "That totally completes the group. We'll be the quintessential representation of diversity."

"It would be pretty damn funny now that I'm thinking about it," Tommy said.

Oh, you've got to be kidding me, Richard thought. *Now Tommy is on board with this thing too? Am I the only one who thinks this is a bad idea?* He could still play the insulting his people's heritage card if he really wanted to, and if he pressed hard enough, they would probably give in, but he really didn't want to be the only wet blanket of the group. Richard finally gave in and agreed to go along if everyone else was willing. Plus, the idea of seeing Jenny in tight leather pants intrigued him quite a bit.

As the details of this diversity extravaganza were being coordinated by Jenny, things kept trucking along as normal.

In science class, Richard was working on an experiment with Chris Consorte.

"So did you hear about Joe's Dinner on First Street?" Chris asked.

"No. What happened?" Richard said.

"So apparently this biker gang showed up the night before last. At first, they just pretended to be regular customers, but when the check came, they just laughed and swore at the waitress. When Joe came over and threatened to call the cops, they totally went off on him and tore up the whole place!"

"Are you serious?" Richard said with shock and anger.

"Yeah, it totally sucks. They beat the heck outta Joe as well. Broke his jaw and everything. By the time the cops showed up, the biker guys had taken off. The police are still looking for them. As far as I know, the place is still closed while they're fixing it up."

"That's horrible! I've eaten there probably thirty times. Where the hell does a renegade biker gang come from all of a sudden?"

"No clue? Crazy stuff though, eh?" Chris answered.

"Yeah. Pretty crazy."

For the rest of the class, Richard thought about the incident. A criminal biker gang causing havoc seemed like an appropriate use for his abilities. After cross-country practice, Richard nearly sprinted home. He tied the necklace around his neck for the first time in nearly a month, hopped on his mountain bike, and started pedaling the seven miles to Joe's Diner.

The place was trashed. Several of the windows were broken, and someone had nailed large sheets of plywood over the openings. Looking through one of the unbroken ones, he could see that the inside looked even worse. The jukebox was smashed in, and there were broken plates and glasses everywhere. Something else immediately caught his eye. On one of the walls of the restaurant, in red spray paint, "Lobo del Diablo" covered nearly the entire wall in foot-high cursive letters.

He heard something behind him and whirled around with his fists up and ready. His lightning-fast movements were met with a shrill scream from a terrified woman in her fifties. After a moment, he recognized Laverne, one of the waitresses who had probably served his family half a dozen times.

"Laverne, it's me, Richie. Don't freak out. I just heard something from behind me, and I guess it scared me a bit."

"Scared you! I just about peed myself—you scared me so bad just now. After what happened the other night, my nerves are as frazzled as can be. I know I should have made Earl come with me."

"Why are you here?" Richard asked.

"Joe asked me if I could come down and get some stuff out of the safe for him. He's afraid those thugs will come back and try to rob the place while it's closed. I just hope that there's still a place to open once he's better."

"He doesn't have insurance to cover the damages?"

"Oh, he's got insurance for that, but with his jaw and arm broken, it will be five or six weeks before he'll be able to cook again. Most of us just can't go that long without work. Suzie's already filled out an application at the Olive Garden on Beaker. It breaks my heart to abandon him like this, but I don't know if I'll have a choice."

"So you were here when it happened?" Richard asked.

"Oh yeah. I was here all right. About a dozen of those degenerates pulled up on their motorcycles. Most of them looked like they were in their early twenties, but some seemed like they could still be in high school. They were all strutting around, trying their best to look tough and intimidating. Unfortunately, Julia ended up waiting at their table. She's a pretty young thing, and they harassed her like you wouldn't believe. I offered to take over for her, but she insisted that she could handle them.

"After they ate, they all got up and started to leave before paying. It was not like a dine-and-dash sort of thing. They were not in a hurry at all. Once she saw what they were doing, she rushed over to give them their bill. After handing over the check, one of them dropped it on the floor. When she bent down to pick it up, he smacked her on the behind so hard that you could hear the spank across the entire restaurant.

"Joe saw what was going on and charged out from the kitchen to put those guys in their place! I don't know why he didn't just call the cops, but he was mad as hell. He wasn't going to let those creeps assault one of his girls without retaliation. That's when things really went bad! It's all just kind of a blur when I think back, but within five minutes, they beat poor old Joe to a pulp, smashed the heck outta the place, ran out, jumped on their bikes, and rode off. I'm still totally traumatized by the whole thing."

"Do you remember which way they went?" Richard asked.

"North on First. I saw them drive off as I was tending to Joe."

That would make sense, Richard thought.

The restaurant was at the north end of the city. By riding that direction, they were only about five minutes from the edge of town. Once they got into the unincorporated areas, they could have taken any number of side streets and trails. On motorcycles, they could have gone completely off-road. Richard stayed with Laverne until she got what she needed out of the safe and made it back to her car before getting back on his bike and riding home.

The following morning, Richard told Hector the whole story and asked if he had ever heard of Lobo del Diablo.

"What? Because I'm Mexican, I'm supposed to know all about some random Hispanic gang?"

"I didn't say that," Richard said. "I'm just asking if you've ever heard of those guys. There really bad news, and I'm thinking that we should do something about it."

As the realization hit him, Hector spun around as excited as a six-year-old on Christmas morning. "Dude, did you say that I think you just said? We're gonna do some real-life superhero stuff, aren't we?"

"Well, I'm pretty sure I'll be the one doing most of the superhero stuff, as you so eloquently put it, but I can't do squat unless I can find those guys. Supposedly, the police have been looking for them for the past few days, but they haven't found squat."

"Don't sweat it, bro. I know these homeys who are in the know about this sort of stuff. I'll ask around at lunch today."

For the remainder of the walk to school, Richard's head was consumed with all manner of questions and scenarios for what he would do if they actually figured out where to find those guys. The only sensible thing would be to tip off the police and let them deal with the criminals since that was their job, but what would be the fun in that? It hardly takes superpowers to call the cops, but the unfortunate reality of the situation was that he really had no idea what the heck he was doing. For all he knew, those guys had guns. Despite his super speed, strength, and agility, he was not bulletproof and could quite easily be shot and killed! Richard eventually put it out of his mind since he still had no clue where they were. *Once we know more, we'll figure out our next plan of action,* he thought.

At lunchtime, Richard, Jenny, and Tommy all sat down at one of the tables. After a few minutes, Jenny said, "Hey, where's Hector?"

Richard said, "Oh, yeah. He said something about needing to meet with some guys at lunch to discuss some... uh... school stuff."

This poorly constructed response apparently was sufficient to distract Jenny, and she quickly changed the subject to their upcoming Village People performance.

With only about eight minutes left of lunch, Hector ran up to the table. "Hey, Richie. We need to talk dude! I got some news about that... uh... Spanish assignment."

"Oh, yeah. I've got to head to class a few minutes early. We can talk about it on the way." Richard grabbed his backpack.

Once they were a few yards away, Richard said. "Nice going, smooth talker. You couldn't have made it any more obvious that something's up?"

"Sorry, dude. Just really excited to tell you the news! So I talked to those guys we spoke about, and one of them heard from his brother's friend that a Mexican biker gang has an old farmhouse they hang out at about ten miles outside of town. They used to call themselves the *Jinetes Libres*, or Free Riders, and they were pretty low-key. They grew and sold weed to pay for food and gas and were involved in some small-time theft, but nothing too serious. Then, about a month ago, something happened. Out of the blue, they changed their name to Lobo del Diablo or Devil Wolf and stepped up their illegal activities! There was the incident at Joe's Diner, and they also apparently took out this guy who was growing pot not too far from them when he refused to turn over all of his customers."

"What do you mean by took him out?" Richard asked.

Hector said, "What do you think I mean, dude? They killed his butt! Even worse, after they killed him, they apparently let their dogs have at him. The body was pretty torn up when the cops found it."

Richard thought, *If this information is true, we are dealing with something far worse than a bunch of rebellious kids with bad attitudes. These people are killers! Perhaps just calling the police on these guys is not such a bad idea after all. Of course, all of this news still leaves us without much in terms of how to find the killer bikers.* "So you got any idea where this old farmhouse might be?"

"One of the guys said something about a road off the main highway called Birch or maybe Maple... some kind of tree. That road takes you into the foothills, and it's apparently somewhere back there."

"Not exactly something I can plug into Google Maps, eh?"

"Hey, it is what it is, man. Criminals tend to keep their locations secret to most folks. Guess you take what you can get. So what now?" Hector asked.

"Not sure. But I think I'm in the mood for a bike ride tomorrow."

The following day was Saturday, and after breakfast, Richard told his mom that he was meeting up with his friends across town to catch the matinee of the new superhero movie and would probably have lunch afterward. His mom offered to drive, but he insisted on taking his bike. "Coach tells me it's great cross-training to help my running without the additional impact."

The story made perfect sense, and his mom bought it completely. After packing a couple of bottles of water and some snacks and putting on the necklace, Richard headed to the garage to get his bike.

Curious as to just how fast he could go on a mountain bike with the assistance of the necklace, he had downloaded a free speedometer app on his iPhone the night before. Once he got out about a mile past Joe's Diner, he looked around. With no cars in sight, he decided to let loose. His legs drove the pedals faster and faster, and the scenery was flying by him in a blur. He had no idea how fast he was going, but when the bike started shaking violently, he had to slow down for fear of it flying into pieces right underneath him. It was probably good that he reduced his speed when he did. A minute later, he noticed a small, poorly paved side street coming up on his right: Oak Road.

Well, it's a tree, so I guess we'll give it a shot.

As he turned onto the smaller path, curiosity got the best of him. He pulled out his iPhone and opened the app. Taking a second look to make sure that he was reading it correctly, it clearly showed eighty-seven miles per hour as his top speed. He glanced at his jeans, T-shirt, light jacket, and bike helmet. *If I'm going to do this again, I should invest in some better clothing.*

For the next two hours, Richard crisscrossed along more than a dozen side streets and dirt roads. Finally stopping in frustration, he hopped off his bike, took off his backpack, and removed a water bottle and snack bar. Enjoying a moment of relaxation, he closed his eyes and took a deep breath. Fall was fast approaching, and the cool breeze felt amazing. A sound caught his attention. Richard saw a large brown eagle flying high above him. *Now that's what I need to find these guys. If I could only get a five thousand-foot view over the area, I bet I could find them in no time.*

As soon as the words left his mouth, a bizarre feeling came over him unlike anything he had ever experienced. His eyes became blurry, and his head began to spin. It was like he was having an out-of-body experience. For a moment, he thought that he was having a heat stroke! His eyesight came back, and it was better than it had ever been, and he appeared to be hundreds of feet off the ground. Glancing around in utter panic, he realized that he had magically turned into a bird. Completely freaking out, Richard looked down. To his utter amazement, he was staring at himself next to his bike about three hundred feet below. *I get it! I didn't turn into a bird after all. I must have projected my consciousness into the eagle I saw flying overhead. That must be what the feather's supposed to do!*

After taking a few moments to regain his equilibrium, Richard scanned the earth for as far as his eyes could see. It was a truly amazing feeling, unlike anything he'd ever experienced. After soaring around for ten minutes, he spotted a small structure a couple of miles off a secluded road to the north.

As he flew closer, he could see a large barn with an old farmhouse next to it. Now flying directly overhead, he saw several motorcycles parked in front of the barn. The main barn doors appeared to be shut, but a small side door was open. He caught a glimpse of a tough-looking biker walking into the structure. *This has got to be it!*

There was only a single road leading into the property, and it was blocked off by a chain-link fence. The fence would probably look like it circled the entire property to someone on the ground, but from his vantage point, he could see that it only ran about fifty yards on either side of the gate before dead-ending in the thick foliage on either side.

Continuing to investigate the property, Richard noticed a side trail that broke off from the road leading up to the property that wound through some woods and then accessed the area from the south. It was pretty overgrown, and it was unlikely that they even knew it went anywhere. If he ever needed to get quick access to the property, the side road would be the way to do it.

Richard was still at a bit of a loss about how to turn off this rent-a-bird thing and return to his body. Deciding that it would probably be a good idea to retrace the path of getting to the farmhouse, he willed the eagle to turn around and fly back to where his physical body was. He took careful mental notes of all the connecting roads, and once his body came into view, Richard was fairly confident that he could find the place from the ground if needed. Moments after seeing himself again, the same uneasy vertigo feeling came over him, and he was back. After taking a few moments to fight off a feeling similar to seasickness, he slowly got to his feet and picked his bike up off the ground.

Wow. That was trippy! What the heck am I supposed to do now? He counted about a dozen motorcycles outside of the old barn, but he clearly didn't have sufficient information to go bursting in there. *They could have chains, knives, and guns! No. This was a recon mission and a damn successful one! Let's head home and regroup.*

The ride home was notably longer than the one to get there. Even after getting back to the main road, Richard feared going too fast since it might cause the bike to start falling apart. A crash at eighty-five miles per hour with no physical protection other than a plastic bike helmet didn't sound very appealing. It gave him a lot of time to think, and the longer he thought about it, the more the idea of just going to the cops made a lot of sense to him. That was their job after all. He could tell them that he just happened to be riding his bike in the hills and came across the old barn with motorcycles parked in front of it. He could take them right to the property, and they would take care of the rest. He'd still be the hero of sorts for finding their hidden lair, and most importantly, he wouldn't have to risk getting shot! It wasn't exactly being the courageous superhero from the movies, but as long as the bad guys were caught, everybody wins, right?

He texted Hector on his way back and was not the least bit surprised to find his friend waiting for him when he finally got home. As Richard recapped the day and detailed his out-of-body experience with the bird, the excitement in Hector's eyes was palpable. It nearly broke Richard's heart when he had to share his thoughts about turning everything over to the police.

"You're gonna do what?" Hector said. "You go through all the trouble of scoping the place and finding a secret way to get into their compound—and then you let the cops have all the fun arresting these guys? You ever see Batman call the police to take down the Joker? Hell no! And he didn't even have any superpowers!"

Richard said, "Batman is a fictional character who cannot die because he's not real! And even if he was real, he has all sorts of bulletproof armor and stuff. Most importantly, he's not a fourteen-year-old kid!"

Hector got very quiet. Then after a measured pause, he said, "Just think about it for a day. Give it until this time tomorrow, and if you still want to go to the cops with this thing, I'll support you 100 percent. Obviously, they have no idea that you know where their hideout is, so there's no reason for them to go anywhere in the next twenty-four hours, right?"

"Fine," Richard answered. "I'll give it a day and think about it."

"Attaboy!" Hector said. "Say, you should come over to dinner tonight. Mom's ordering pizza from Papa Giorgio's, and there is always tons of extra food. Oh, and we could also watch that vampire movie that we wanted to see last year, but our moms wouldn't take us because it was rated R. I somehow talked my dad into buying the DVD. You can just crash at my place afterward."

"Sounds like a plan."

Richard did his best to enjoy the evening. The pizza was delicious, and the movie was actually pretty awesome, but his mind was elsewhere. Was he taking the easy way out by simply showing the cops where those guys were and letting them risk their lives to do his dirty work? After all, this was Bentleyville. They didn't exactly have a military-grade SWAT team at their disposal. They'd be sending in deputies who were only a few years older than he was with little more than pistols and maybe bulletproof vests—and no superpowers. What if one of them was killed? Would that be Richard's fault? His mind raced throughout the evening, and he tossed and turned for most of the night.

The following morning, Hector's mom made the family chocolate chip waffles and bacon for breakfast. He was still groggy from the poor night's sleep, but after a couple of cups of coffee, he was starting to feel like his old self again.

"You're staying for the game, right?" Hector's mom asked.

"The game?" Richard asked.

"The 49ers are playing the Dolphins at ten."

"Oh, yeah… sure. I'll stay."

Hector's family had been big 49er fans for as long as Richard had known them. Hector's dad grew up watching them in the Montana years as he affectionately referred to them, and he had remained loyal to them through more than half a dozen coaching changes and many lackluster seasons. About two-thirds of the way through the first quarter, there was an unexpected knock at the front door. It would not have been so unusual on its own, but it was not a friendly knock. It was an open-up-in-the-name-of-the-law-level knock!

Hector's mom answered, and Richard was surprised to see his dad standing there with a look of utter shock in his face. Realizing that something was very wrong, she invited him in.

After walking into the family room, he whispered, "I just got back from the hardware store. I stopped by to pick up some supplies for a site. There were cops all over the place."

Richard knew the store well. It was the one Jenny's family owned. *Something bad must have happened there. Are her parents all right? Wait… today is Sunday. On Sundays, Jenny works in the store to help out her dad while her mom goes to church. Maybe it was just a break-in last night, but that would not justify his pale complexion and demeanor.*

Ernie said, "A group of men barged in about an hour ago. Pretty sure it was that biker gang that tore up Joe's Diner last week. They took all the cash on hand, knocked over a bunch of displays, and just as they were leaving, they grabbed Jenny—and took her with them! Her dad tried to stop them, but they beat him up and took off. They apparently had an old cargo van with them along with the motorcycles they were riding. One of them pulled Jenny into the back of the van, and they all took off. Philip called 911 as soon as they left, but by the time anyone got there, they were long gone. The police are looking all over for them, but they've had no luck so far. I know Jenny's a good friend, and I came straight over here to let you know."

Richard was shocked, stunned, and paralyzed with fear. *How could something like this happen? This is a quiet little town in the middle of nowhere. Things like this just don't happen here!* Snapping back to reality, he looked over at Hector. Something besides tears was welling up in his eyes. It was rage! *Damn right,* Richard thought. *Those bastards picked the wrong girl to mess with. If they were looking for a fight, they're damn sure gonna get one!*

Hector said, "Hey, Mom. Richie and I are going outside to take a walk to clear our heads. We'll be back in a while. Call me if you get any news."

"Of course, sweetie." She was openly weeping.

Once outside, Hector turned to Richard, eyes still red with fear and anger. "Dude, I'm so sorry, man! This is all my fault. You wanted to go to the cops yesterday, and I told you to wait and think about it. I'm such an idiot! Let's go down to the store now and tell them where to go to catch those a-holes!"

"No!" Richard shouted. His despair and confusion had been replaced with determination and focus. "You were right yesterday. I'm the one with abilities, and they just made it personal. I'm taking care of this!" His mountain bike was still on the side of the house.

"Dude, what are you doing, man?" Hector said. "You can't just go riding over there on a bicycle wearing a T-shirt and some jeans. You need some kind of protection and a disguise, man."

"A disguise?" Richard asked.

"Yeah, bro. Every superhero's gotta have something so people don't figure out who they are. If these guys—not to mention Jenny—see you going all super-dude on their butts, everyone will know what's up, and then who knows what the hell is going to happen! Don't worry, man. I got a plan."

Hector had a very valid point. Richard really had no plan whatsoever, and that's never a good strategy regardless of what abilities you have. Within moments, they were riding to Tommy's house. Hector was on his phone the whole time, and Tommy was largely up to speed by the time they arrived. The garage door was already open, and Tommy was waiting for them.

"Dude, I can't believe this is actually happening!" Tommy said as they dismounted their bikes. "I checked the gas tank, and it's full."

"Gas tank?" Richard asked. "I don't know how to drive a car."

"Not a car," Hector said. "A motorcycle!"

Behind Tommy, Richard could clearly see his brother's Kawasaki Ninja 300 parked inside the garage. He must have left it at home when he went off to college. It was a thing of beauty—jet-black with green accents and racing stripes.

"You've driven dirt bikes before, right?" Hector asked. "This thing works basically the same way—only faster! And his brother left his riding suit and helmet with a mirrored visor. That will give you a lot of added protection, and the helmet will cover your face and completely hide your identity."

Richard had to admit that it was a pretty great plan. The bike would give him the additional speed he'd likely require, and if he and Jenny needed to make a fast getaway, she could get on the back of the bike with him. He was starting to get pretty excited until he actually tried on the leather jacket. Since Tommy's brother was six foot three and weighed nearly 260 pounds, the jacket hung on Richard like a wet tent. There was no way he'd be able to fight effectively in that thing.

Tommy said, "Yeah. I was afraid of that. Don't sweat it, guys. I've got a backup plan." Going back to the cabinet in the garage, Tommy pulled out a much smaller jacket and pants. Like the first one, it was mostly black, but it had several sections where the black had been replaced by bright pink leather. "James bought this for his girlfriend for her birthday, along with a matching helmet, so the two of them could go riding together."

Richard groaned. "Really? It had to be pink. Let me guess, you have a matching tutu to go along with it?"

"Beggars can't be choosers. At least it should fit better."

Reluctantly, Richard tried on the outfit, and it fit nearly perfectly. Once everything was on, Richard tried moving around a bit, including throwing a few kicks. The leather pants were far too restrictive. "I think I'll stick with my jeans, but the jacket, boots, and helmet will work great!"

"Right on, bro! Wonder Woman to the rescue!" Hector yelled with just the slightest hint of sarcasm. It was a horrible time to be cracking jokes, but the unexpected levity helped break up the intensity of the moment. Even Richard had to chuckle to himself for a second. "Tommy, just so you know… something could happen to this motorcycle. If it comes between saving Jenny and protecting the bike, the motorcycle's gonna lose."

"Don't even worry about it, man," he said. "This is Jenny we're talking about. You do what you got to do. I can always just report the bike stolen or something. Pretty sure he's got insurance on it."

"Pretty sure?" Hector replied.

"And if not, it's been nice knowing you guys," he replied with a smirk.

Hopping on the bike, Richard turned to his two friends. His helmet was on, but his visor was still up. "Okay, guys. I guess this is it! Wish me luck."

"You got this, man!" Tommy answered. "Now go kick some butt and get Jenny back!"

Richard turned the key, and the beast of a machine throttled to life. Lowering the reflective visor of his pink-striped helmet, he shot out of the garage like a cannonball. It had been nearly a year since he had driven a motorized dirt bike, and it took a few minutes to get the familiarity back. It was a completely different machine. Its speed, power, and maneuverability were amazing. Unfamiliar with its capabilities, Richard nearly crashed twice in the first five minutes while getting a feel for it, but utilizing his enhanced dexterity, he quickly adjusted, and by the time he made it to the main road, he was pretty confident with his proficiency. Though he wanted to get there fast as humanly possible, he knew that every police car in the city was on the lookout for a bunch of guys on motorcycles. He opted to keep largely within the speed limit until he pulled off onto Oak Street. Once off the pavement, he tore down the smaller paths with a vengeance. Doing his best to retrace his steps from the day before, he found that it was much trickier navigating from the ground than viewing everything from three hundred feet up.

After ten minutes and a couple of wrong turns, he found the side trail that would allow him to access the compound without having to go through the front gate. Afraid of ruining the element of surprise, he decided to get off the bike. He pushed it up the steep trail and positioned himself silently. He could make out the farmhouse through the trees, but he felt confident that he was still completely hidden.

Though he could see a few motorcycles and a couple of guys walking around, there was still a lot about the situation that was completely unknown to him. If only he could get a better look at what the heck was going on. Wait. Perhaps he could. Looking up in the sky, he noticed a black crow flying overhead. Would his ability work with any bird—or only the eagle he had hijacked the day before? *Only one way to find out I suppose?* Closing his eyes, Richard concentrated on the image of the bird in his mind. At first, nothing happened, but he took a deep breath and refocused. The vertigo came over him, and he was airborne again. Taking a moment to orientate himself, once fully in control of the bird, he swooped down and landed on a fence post about twenty yards from the barn.

He could clearly see six motorcycles and the gray van that had been hidden from his view earlier. Two of the biker guys were smoking outside. They were both Latino, in their twenties, he guessed, and had at least twenty tattoos between them. They looked tough, but neither appeared to be carrying a gun. Something in one of their pockets looked like a switchblade, but Richard could not be sure. It was a truly bizarre feeling. It was almost like being invisible. He was staring right at them, and none of them had the foggiest idea what was going on. A thought involving the girls' locker room popped into his head momentarily, but he quickly dismissed it. *This is serious business. Jenny's life is at stake!*

Deciding to take a closer look, Richard willed the crow to take flight again. This time, it actually landed on the roof of the cargo van. It would allow him a much better view of the open barn door. The two thugs noticed the crow and said a couple of things to each other in Spanish, but they didn't see too concerned.

Richard could see three more men playing cards at a round, beat-up kitchen table. They each had a beer, and several empty bottles were scattered along the ground. One of the men had a pistol stuck in the back of his pants. The reality of at least the possibility of getting shot hit Richard hard, and an uncomfortable knot began to form in the pit of his stomach. *Where's Jenny?* His visibility of the inside the barn from this angle was still quite limited, and large sections of the structure remained out of sight. He had no choice. He had to get a better look. He took flight again and swooped right into the doorway. Once inside the structure, he angled his trajectory up and found a perch on one of the rafters. He was twenty feet off the ground, which was exactly what he wanted! Richard could see the entire inside of the barn, and the sudden realization of what he might see hit him like a ton of bricks.

What if Jenny was hurt, being attacked, or dead? The thought horrified him, and for several seconds, he could not focus on what he was seeing. Thankfully, a sound grabbed his attention. Jenny was in a loft above the main area of the barn. Her mouth was gagged, and her hands were tied with duct tape, but she appeared to be relatively unharmed. A large wooden ladder on the ground had apparently been used to get her up there in the first place, and she was trapped in the upper section of the barn. It was a good ten-foot drop, and it was unlikely that anyone would risk the jump. If they did, a sprained ankle or similar injury would most likely prevent a speedy getaway.

For Richard, it was actually a better scenario than he could have hoped for. Being so high above everybody else, the chances of Jenny getting accidentally injured in the conflict that was soon to follow were very small. Taking a final survey of the building, Richard saw one more man at a makeshift bar that they had set up underneath the loft. The two men from outside had come back in, and he realized that all six of them were looking at him. Panic shot through him for a moment. *Wait. I'm a crow. What are they going to do—shoot me?*

Having only spoken Spanish until that point, one of the men switched to English. "Dude, what the heck is with that crow, man? It's just up there staring at us. It's kinda giving me the creeps."

Another one said, "Crows are bad luck, man. You better shoot it."

Crap! Richard had no idea what would happen to him if they shot the bird when he was inside its consciousness, but he was quite sure he didn't want to find out. Leaping off his perch, he flew down through the door and back to his motorcycle. Once he was back in sight, it only took a quick mental shift before he was in his own self again. The same uneasy feeling hit him again, but it was not nearly as bad as the day before. Within a few moments, he was fine. *Okay. There's a total of six guys, and at least one of them has a gun. This is not just throwing around a bunch of sophomores. This is the real deal. Am I ready for this?*

Despite his enhanced abilities, he had only a leather jacket and a motorcycle helmet for protection. Neither would stop a bullet. He still had an opportunity to turn back. He could tell the police exactly what to expect, but how long would that take? It would be an hour at best. Any number of situations could change between now and then. *No!* He had the information he needed to act now, and with Jenny's life on the line, that's exactly what he was going to do.

Taking a deep breath, Richard focused his mind on the task at hand. Gunning the throttle on the Kawasaki, he shot down the steep path that would bring him out of the foliage and into the main area of the property. Once on flat ground, he turned slightly to the right and sped past the front of the barn toward the side door. Seeing all six Harleys lined up next to one another, he swerved his bike next to them and gave the first one a powerful kick, sending it smashing into the one next to it, ultimately knocking all six to the ground. *A quick getaway will likely be required once I get a hold of Jenny,* Richard thought. *And the few extra seconds it will take them to untangle their bikes from the ground could make all the difference.*

Flying around the side of the structure, Richard could see that several of the men at the table were looking toward the sound of the falling motorcycles. One of them had gotten up and was making his way to the door to investigate the noise.

Richard was speeding toward him at fifty miles per hour!

For a moment, the man froze—and Richard feared that he would have to drive straight over him. Fortunately, at the last second, the biker dove to his right and narrowly missed the vehicle as it drove right into the barn and directly toward the table where the others were sitting.

The five men at the table could only stare at the oncoming assault. Just before hitting the group head-on, Richard abruptly turned the bike to the left, causing it to skid until its side was parallel to the table. Moments before impact, Richard jumped up, pushed off from the foot pedals, and launched himself ten feet into the air. His momentum sent him flying twenty feet across the room, and a tuck-and-roll landing left him relatively unscathed. With tremendous force, the Kawasaki smashed into the table, sending the five men flying in all directions.

Richard took advantage of the momentary chaos to find the man with the pistol. The biker was still getting to his feet and was grasping for the gun in the back of his jeans. He managed to get the gun freed from his trousers, but before he had a chance to point the weapon, Richard struck out with a crushing front kick. The blow struck his opponent square in the chest and sent him flying into the side of the barn. The pistol landed thirty feet away. Following the impact, the man slumped to the ground and did not appear to be getting up anytime soon.

The others bikers were getting back to their feet.

Richard identified a second foe reaching for what appeared to be another pistol. Grabbing one of the legs of the now overturned table, Richard pulled with all of his might and hurtled it toward the second opponent as the gun was coming into view. The heavy wooden projectile knocked the biker unconscious. *Two down… four to go!* Richard fought to retain his focus.

A flash of silver caught Richard's attention. A steel chain was being swung at him by one of the other opponents. The man was aiming for Richard's head, but he managed to raise his right arm in time to block the blow. *Wow—that hurt!* He was grateful for the added protection of the leather jacket, which kept the painful blow from being much worse. As the chain wrapped twice around his forearm, Richard grasped the steel with his right hand and pulled toward him as hard as he could. Still grasping the other end of the chain tightly, the biker was yanked awkwardly straight toward him. Richard met him with a clothesline maneuver that would have made Stone-Cold Steve Austin proud. The impact sent both of his feet flying up, and his neck and upper back hit the cement floor with a sobering thud. *Three down!*

The biker who had narrowly missed getting run over darted toward the farmhouse. One of the two remaining antagonists was in his late teens or early twenties and was probably five foot eight and about 160 pounds. The second one was at least six foot two and weighed at least 250 pounds. The bigger opponent lunged at him and thrust a switchblade directly toward Richard's neck. Countering the attack with a side block from his left hand, he deflected the strike and knocked the blade to the ground. Richard shot out his fist, grasping the man by his leather vest, pulling him closer, and meeting him with a tremendous head butt. Richard was still wearing his helmet, and his opponent shrieked and winced in pain before going limp. Richard pushed the unconscious biker toward his last opponent, and the smaller man was helplessly pinned beneath the larger one.

Holy cow! Did I just really do that? Despite the seriousness of the situation and the still present danger, Richard could not help but take a moment to relish the sheer awesomeness of what had just happened.

With all his immediate opponents at least momentarily taken care of, Richard picked up the switchblade and leaped up to the loft area where Jenny was being held captive. She was absolutely terrified. Her hands and feet were wrapped with duct tape, and a handkerchief tied around her mouth muffled any attempt she made to scream. Richard decided to remove the mouth restraints before attempting to cut away the tape.

Jenny screamed.

Richard didn't know it was even possible for a human to achieve such a high octave.

"Who the hell are you? Are you one of them? I guess not since you just beat them all up. You're clearly not the police. Who are you?"

Aw crap! I gotta say something, and I can't use my real voice. She'll recognize me in a second. I need to use a fake voice. What the hell do I say? An idea shot into his head. Without thinking, he answered with a horrible Arnold Schwarzenegger impersonation. "Come with me if you want to live!"

"What?" Jenny replied, looking more confused than ever.

Cringing at how ridiculous he knew he sounded, he had no choice but to continue the charade. "Don't move while I cut the tape away. Then we'll get the hell out of here!" After freeing his friend, Richard helped Jenny to her feet and walked to the edge of the balcony.

She took one look down and shot a stare back at him with a "What? Do you want me to jump?"

Richard momentarily contemplated trying to explain, but knowing that he was pressed for time, he reached down behind the back of her legs, lifted her into his arms, and jumped off the edge. Focusing on his legs, Richard managed to cushion the impact as the two of them hit the ground. He could not help but take in the amazing feeling that welled up within him as she stared into his mirrored visor. There was still fear in her eyes, but at the same time, there was an understanding that everything was going to be all right. He had just rescued from six criminal bikers the girl who he clearly had very profound feelings for, and he was now holding her in his arms, ready to ride off into the sunset. He thought that were it not for the group of men slumped throughout the room who all wanted to kill them, it would be a really romantic moment.

One of the men started to move again, and Richard snapped back to reality. "We got to get out of here." Richard was still using his Arnold voice and knew he was completely killing any possibility of mutual romantic thoughts on Jenny's part. Reaching down to the handle of the motorcycle, he pulled up hard. The vehicle lifted off the ground, and by maneuvering the angle of his arm, he managed to turn the bike so that it hit the ground again with both wheels facing directly toward the open doorway.

"Whoa!" Jenny said.

Smiling to himself, Richard hopped on the bike and said, "Get on, and hang onto me as tight as you can!"

Jenny jumped on the back of the bike and grabbed around the middle of Richard's stomach, grasping her hands together tightly. Richard was thoroughly enjoying the experience, and between the adrenaline racing through his system and the hormones coursing throughout his body, he'd never felt so alive.

Just before Richard gunned the throttle on the motorcycle, the smaller of his last two opponents shouted, "This isn't over, man! The Wolf is going to come for you, and when he does, there ain't noting that you're going to be able to do to stop him!"

It took a moment for Richard to regain his composure. *Who the hell is the Wolf—and what can he possibly have in store for me?* Noticing that a couple of the others were stirring again, Richard revved the engine forcefully, sending the vehicle flying out of the barn. He turned toward the trail, and Richard's heart stopped as the man who had left the barn was holding an Uzi machine gun. *Not good!* Richard spun his bike to the left and sped around the back of the barn. Given the angle of his opponent, Richard knew it would take only a few moments to get the Kawasaki to a point where the structure would block the line of sight for his opponent. Fortunately for them, it apparently took that long for the Uzi-wielding man to point and shoot.

Rat-tat-tat-tat-tat-tat!

Jenny screamed at the terrifying sound. After the first few shots, Richard could hear the rounds hitting the barn. For a few moments, they were somewhat safe. Flying around the back of the structure, Richard stopped for a moment to catch his breath and decide what to do next. He could hear the others exiting the barn and pulling their Harleys apart. He had maybe thirty seconds to do something, and both paths out that he knew of were cut off.

Straight ahead, Richard noticed a small overgrown trail leading toward the hills directly behind them. When he was surveying the property in his original eagle form, he vaguely remembered another trail that ran in a different direction, and he hadn't given it any further consideration. Now it appeared that it was their only way out.

"Hold on!" He gunned the bike, and they shot across the last sixty yards of the property and onto the dirt trail. Glancing at the rearview mirror, he could see three Harleys flying around the barn and into view before they disappeared into the foliage.

The two quickly traversed their way up the narrow pathway. Small branches smacked Richard's visor every few seconds, and the trail continued to slope up. Having no idea where they were going, Richard could only hope it would wind down at some point and intersect with another road that would get them back to the highway. Uncertain if he was still being followed, Richard stopped and let it idle for a few seconds. As soon as he took a breath, he heard the roar of the approaching motorcycles and a loud gunshot.

"Crap! They're shooting at us again. Got to go!" They took off up the winding trail. Rounding a bend, Richard looked up and saw a straight, steep trail that led to what looked like a break in the tree line at the top of the hill. *Need to hit this fast!*

In a few seconds, the others would be where they were now, and they would have an unblocked shot. Even worse, with Jenny still clinging to him, she'd most likely be the one to take the bullet if they connected! It was a pretty steep path, and Richard was fairly confident that the Harleys would have a much harder time getting up the trail than he would on the Kawasaki. *If I can just get through those trees at the top, I can see blue sky. The path must slope back down, and with any luck, the others will not be able to get up. We can make our escape!*

Noticing how the path dipped down for about twenty yards before shooting up, Richard accelerated as fast as he could to gain as much momentum as possible. The two of them barely weighed two hundred pounds combined, and they gained speed rapidly. As they hit the incline, Richard could feel the tug of gravity in his gut as it pulled against their momentum. It reminded him of being on a roller coaster as it hit the bottom of a big hill and then shot up, leaving his stomach somewhere on the floor of the car.

A pistol shot rang out as they approached the top of the hill. Richard could hear the bullet hit the ground about ten yards away. *Got to keep pushing!*

A second shot hit only a few yards away. They're adjusting their aim. The next one will hit us for sure! *Just about there. Just need to gun it hard one last time!*

"We made it through the trees! Oh, hell!"

CHAPTER 9

Immediately after Richard and Jenny flew through the trees at the crest of the hill, they were met with the clear skies they were anticipating. What they were not expecting was the trail they were traveling on abruptly coming to an end and falling off into a steep ravine, some two hundred feet below.

Still focused on the bullet that flew past them moments earlier, it took a second for Richard to realize what was about to happen, and that second would turn out to be a critical one. He hit the brakes on the Kawasaki as hard as he could, but it was too little, too late. Without the benefit of pavement to generate friction, the vehicle's momentum caused it to slide across the loose dirt and right off the edge!

For the first moments after they officially become airborne, time seemed to slow to the point where it nearly stopped altogether. Richard could see the rocks far below as the front of the bike started pointing down. It would clearly not end well, and Richard was all too aware that it would all be his fault. *Who the hell am I to be playing superhero? I'm just a stupid kid with no more common sense than the average refrigerator. I could have easily called the police, and maybe things still would have gone south, but more than likely, the day would have ended with Jenny coming home safe to her family tonight.* Instead, his foolish antics would cost him his life—and the life of the person he cared so much about. She may not even be aware of what's happening yet, but that would all change in another second or two. *In all likelihood, her last thought before being dashed on the rocks below will be,* Why the hell did I get on the back of a motorcycle with this big dumb idiot! I'd have been better off staying with the bikers!

Just as Richard was ready to concede to his failure and ultimate demise, a bizarre awareness came over him. His body felt exceptionally light. He assumed it was just the weightlessness of falling to his certain death, but something was different. Richard felt the weight of the motorcycle pulling against his hands as they still gripped the handlebars. He simply let go, and the bike fell away, leaving Richard somehow floating in space.

Jenny screamed.

Glancing down to his waist, Richard could see Jenny's hands still gripping around his waist, but slipping down his hips, as her weight pulled down. In a panic, Richard reached back to grab her, but before he could get a good hold of anything, her grip gave way. For a millisecond, she was slipping away from him, but just before falling beyond his reach, Richard turned his body and shot out his right hand, grasping her wrist as she fell. Jenny in-turn grabbed his wrist with her hand and held on as tight as she possibly could. Moments later, Richard looked down past Jenny to see the motorcycle smash on the rocks below into at least a hundred pieces. Parts of the vehicle were still airborne when it became apparent that they were apparently not hurtling to their imminent deaths after all. So what the hell was actually happening to them? Looking around, Richard could see that they were descending toward he rocks below, but at an amazingly slow speed. Kind of like what a feather looks like as it's gliding through the air toward the ground.

"The feather!" Richard yelled. Apparently, it could do more than just kidnap the brains of random birds after all.

Jenny was still clearly traumatized and could only stare back at the mirrored visor of Richard's helmet with a combination of fear, confusion, and awe in her expression. About twenty seconds after riding off the ledge of the cliff, the two touched down on the earth below with no more impact than if they had jumped off a curb. Still clearly dazed, Jenny was unable to speak in complete sentences and could do little more than mumble "What... who... why... holy cow!" Seeing that despite the significant mental trauma of the past ten minutes, she would be all right, Richard smiled widely with gratitude, realizing how unbelievable everything had somehow turned out. Remembering to go back to his Arnold voice, he was about to say something, when he was interrupted by voices from above.

"What the hell? They're not dead? How is that possible, man?"

Glancing up, Richard and Jenny could see two of the bikers looking down from the top of the cliff in utter disbelief. One of them still had a pistol him his hand.

Crap! It would take some marksmanship on their part to hit us, but we are both still very much in range of bullet fire. We need to get out of there ASAP! Realizing that the random large rocks that surrounded them would significantly slow Jenny's progress, Richard bent down, hoisted her onto his shoulder like a sack of potatoes, and took off toward a wooded area about thirty yards away. Focusing all of his abilities on his agility, he nimbly hopped from boulder to boulder.

Jenny was screaming at the top of her lungs the entire way. Shots fired out from above, and one hit a rock about ten feet away. Richard's zigzag moments, and the increasing distance made them more difficult to hit. After a few seconds, they disappeared into the trees. Once out of sight from the bikers, Richard set Jenny back down on her feet and took a moment to catch his breath. Despite all the amazing things the necklace could do, Richard was still human, and as the adrenaline of the moment started to wear off, he felt utterly exhausted. Listening carefully, he could still hear the men talking up above.

"Man, do you suck! My grandmother can shoot better than you! Now how are we supposed to get 'em? How do we even get down there?"

"Hell if I know," the other man replied. "Let's head back and see if any of the other guys know a way."

"I guess... but the Wolf ain't gonna be happy!"

Since they had a few minutes to compose themselves and come up with their next course of action, Richard calmed himself. After getting back into character, he said, "Are you all right?"

For a good five seconds, Jenny did not move or speak. She stared off at a peaceful-looking oak tree in front of her. Finally, she said, "What the heck just happened? And who in the world are you? You're clearly not a cop. Are you some kind a Special Forces chick or something? I mean, the things I saw you do were incredible!"

"Chick?" Richard cried out in his normal voice before realizing what he was doing.

"Oh, sorry!" Jenny said. "Well, you were obviously using that fake voice, and I guess because of your small stature and the pink stripes on your jacket and helmet, I just kind of assumed." Her expression changed from embarrassment to surprise, but with a hint of familiarity.

Glancing over Richard's shoulder, Jenny said, "What's that over there?"

Fearing that one of the bikers had somehow managed to make his way down the cliff, Richard immediately spun around, ready for a fight. To his surprise, no one was there to face him. After a few moments, he turned to ask what Jenny thought that she saw. In the seconds when his back was to her, Jenny had closed the distance between them. When he turned back, she was right next to him. Momentarily stunned, Richard did not see her hand shoot up toward his helmet. Before he could figure out what was happening, she flipped up the mirrored visor, revealing his shocked and all-too-familiar face.

"Richie?" She slumped to the ground with her back against a tree. "What? Where? How the hell is this possible?"

"It's a long story," Richard answered. "I'll tell you everything, but for now, we need to find our way out of here and get home."

For the next thirty minutes, they wandered through the woods, totally and completely lost. Richard talked nearly nonstop, describing everything that had happened since discovering the necklace. When he noticed a beautiful brown hawk circling above them, he said, "Wanna see something hella cool?"

"Are you kidding me?" Jenny said. "What I've experienced in the past hour has been the most amazing and terrifying experience in my entire life! What the heck could you possibly surprise me with now?"

"Did mention that I can control birds?"

Stopping dead in her tracks, Jenny looked at Richard blankly. "Really? So, in addition to being Captain America, you're also Dr. Doolittle?"

"Not exactly," he said. "What I'm able to do is to sort of transfer my consciousness into a bird, so that I can temporarily control it and see what it sees and hear what it hears."

"I gotta see this!" she answered.

Sitting cross-legged on the ground, Richard placed his hands on his knees and closed his eyes. He took several deep breaths and got very calm.

Jenny stared at him until a screeching brown hawk swooped down at her. She screamed, and the bird swooped to the right and landed on a large branch about ten feet away.

The creature had rich chocolate-colored feathers, a bright yellow, razor-sharp beak, and eyes like jet-black pearls.

"Richie, is that really you in there?"

The bird nodded its majestic head.

"OMG! That is so cool! Oh wait! Do something neat. Do a little dance!"

The hawk turned its head sideways and stared back at her. After a few moments, the bird began moving its head and body up and down in a rhythmic pattern while opening and closing its wings in alternating turns. It wasn't exactly the tango, but the feathered creature was indeed dancing.

Jenny shrieked and clapped her hands with excitement.

Looking back at her, Richard had to smile. After the horribly traumatic events that Jenny had experienced over the past several hours, being able to see her so happy made him feel amazing. After another minute of the dancing nonsense, Richard willed the majestic bird to take to the air again. After all, he had a reason for borrowing the creature. He needed to find a way out of there, and getting a five hundred-foot view of the area seemed like the best way to accomplish that.

Soaring up, the landscape opened up, and as the trees and hills shrank beneath him, he could make out a dirt road about half a mile to the north. There were no signs of any cars on the road, but it should eventually get them to a main highway. Richard carefully studied the landscape so he could navigate his way from the ground. After a few minutes, he could see their bodies below. Richard opened his eyes and blinked several times as Jenny's face came into focus.

"Are you back?" she asked.

"Yeah. I'm okay. I know where we need to go. There's a dirt road up ahead. I saw the way."

"That is pretty friggin' amazing! I just gotta say." Jenny was smiling from ear to ear.

"Yeah, it's pretty cool. Trippy, but cool. But we really need to get moving."

Doing his best to identify the trees and rocks he had studied from the air, they made their way to the dirt road. Richard was much quieter. There was still much to tell her, but he wasn't in the mood anymore. He had seen something in Jenny's eyes after his latest bird trick. He could see genuine feelings for him, and as Richard had feared since finding the necklace, he had no idea if the feelings were for him as the friend who she had known for the past three years or for the wannabe super-kid who rescued her from a criminal biker gang? He'd never know for sure. The cat was out of the bag, and further detailing his accomplishments seemed trivial and juvenile.

They turned left on the dirt road. Richard was pretty sure heading west would get them back to the main highway. After a few minutes, they heard something coming up the road from behind. Fearing imminent danger, Richard spun around and positioned Jenny behind him.

An old Ford pickup was making its way down the gravel pathway directly toward them. At first, Richard feared that it might be one of the bikers, but eventually, he saw an old man in the driver's seat. Realizing that their potential ride might drive right past them, they waved their arms to get the driver's attention.

Coming to a stop in a cloud of dust beside them, the grizzled figure leaned his head out the window and squinted his heavily wrinkled eyes. His bifocals must have been a least a quarter-inch thick.

"What are you two young ladies doing out here in the middle of nowhere?" he asked.

Two young ladies? Richard thought. *Are you kidding me?*

As he was about to tell the old fart where to stick it, Jenny said, "Oh, my god! Thank goodness you came by. Me and my friend were riding her motorcycle, and we ended up accidentally going down this big hill and smashing up the bike. Then we got totally lost, but thankfully, you found us! Is there any chance that you could please drive us back to town?"

"Sure thing, darling," the man said. "Hop on in. Happy to be of assistance to a couple of damsels in distress."

Jenny led Richard around the front of the truck and opened the passenger door. Jenny scooted over to the middle spot as Richard climbed in after her.

He thought about saying something, but he stopped himself. This half-blind geezer thought he was a teenage girl, and speaking now could reveal his true identity. At best, the guy would likely be embarrassed; at worst, he might reconsider giving them a ride.

After several minutes of silence, the man said, "So if both of you were riding the motorcycle, how come she's the only one with a helmet and a proper jacket?"

Without a moment's hesitation, Jenny said, "Yeah, Suzie! Why didn't I get a jacket and a helmet? I told you that we shouldn't go riding until I had my own equipment, but you promised that you'd be careful! Now look at me. I'm a disaster!"

"She's right, Suzie!" the old man said. "You should have never talked your friend into going out riding with you without proper protection. She could have gotten badly hurt—or killed! You should be ashamed of yourself!"

What the hell is going on here?

Jenny was trying not to laugh hysterically, and Richard had to fight the urge to laugh as well. After tirelessly repressing their giggles for the next twenty minutes, they arrived in town. They had actually made it out in one piece!

Richard said, "You can let us off here, sir. That would be great! Thank you so much for your help." His horrible attempt at a female voice nearly sent Jenny into hysterics again.

The old man pulled the truck over to the side of the road, and Richard and Jenny climbed onto the sidewalk. They were still several miles from home.

"Thanks again!" Jenny called out as Richard closed the door to the truck. Turning back to Richard, she asked. "So why the heck did you have the guy let us out here? We're still like ten miles from my house. I'm sure he would have been happy to take us the rest of the way."

"That's right. We are ten miles from your house, but we're only two blocks from the police station."

"Do we have to do this now?" Jenny asked. "I'm so exhausted. Can't we just go home? I can fill in the police later. Oh, hell. What exactly do we tell them? I'm guessing that you're not ready to go public with that mystic-animal-thingamajig contraption yet, eh?"

"Correct! And *we're* not going tell them anything. *You're* going to tell them what happened, and I'm not even going to be mentioned in the entire conversation. Just tell them that you somehow escaped from the barn and ran off into the forest. After wandering around in the woods for an hour, you found the dirt road. That old guy picked you up, gave you a ride back to town, and dropped you off here. And then you tell them exactly where to go to arrest those scumbags!"

"I don't know where they took me. They had my head covered," Jenny said.

"Tell them to go out of town about twelve miles until they get to Oak Street. Take a right, keep going a mile and a half, take a left at a huge oak tree, go another three or four hundred yards, and take a right on an old dirt road that goes up into the hills. Three miles down that road, they'll find the compound."

"And where will you go?" she asked.

"I'm gonna run home and wait for you to be the hero who escaped from a ruthless biker gang and saw them brought to justice." He took off the leather jacket for the run home.

"Wait!" Jenny was starting to tear up. Taking several steps toward him, Jenny embraced Richard with all of her might and buried her face in the crook of his neck. "I never really got a chance to thank you for saving me. I have no idea what's going happen to all of us after this, but I'll always remember that you came for me. You're the best friend anyone could ever ask for!"

After a few more seconds, she released him and gave him one last smile before turning toward the police department. She almost had a skip in her step as she walked away from him.

Smiling widely, Richard said, "Don't look so happy. You just escaped from being kidnapped. You're supposed to look traumatized!"

Smiling from ear to ear, she said, "I don't know. I'm feeling pretty happy right now. You think I'll be able to fake it?"

Richard didn't have to answer. Jenny's flair for the dramatics was legendary, and he had every confidence that she'd easily be able to play the innocent young girl who miraculously escaped the clutches of certain death at the hands of her captors. Richard began the ten-mile run. In case he needed them in the future, he carried the helmet in one hand and the jacket in the other. Normally, it would have made the run awkward and difficult, but he was still wearing the necklace and barely noticed them.

After crossing the main highway through the middle of town, he took off down a street that ran through a residential neighborhood where he wouldn't draw too much attention. Sure, some people would see a kid running pretty darn fast, but it would not likely cause anyone to take more than a second look.

Once he felt that it was safe to do so, Richard's strides grew longer and faster. He was still pacing himself, but the houses flew past him as he sprinted down the road. The feeling was incredible as the wind blew through his hair. He was breathing hard, but he did not feel winded. The oxygen flowed easily in and out of his lungs. His grandfather had described a special type of runner's high that he was only able to achieve on three occasions during his many races. He described it as a spiritual experience in which all physical pain and discomfort disappeared, making him feel completely at one with nature and the universe. He was certain that this feeling it was what his grandfather was describing.

When he was back in his neighborhood, he glanced down at his watch. It was four thirty-five, approximately thirty-two minutes after he began his run. *Wow! Ten miles at roughly a three-minute, thirty-seconds per mile pace! Not too shabby, if I do say so myself.* He slowed to a jog for the last half a mile. As soon as he turned onto his street, he saw his family and Hector's family walking home from the opposite direction.

Hector ran toward Richard. If Richard had not been wearing the amulet, Hector's leaping bear-hug would have knocked him over. "You did it, bro! You saved her! I knew you could do it, you super-powered freakazoid!"

"What's happening?" Richard asked. "When did you guys hear about Jenny?"

Barely able to catch his breath, Hector said, "So after you took off on the bike, I went home. By then, everybody was getting ready to go over to Jenny's house to sit with her parents. They were really upset and seemed to appreciate having us there for moral support. The sheriff was there with two of his deputies. They had all their men out looking for Jenny—along with state troopers and some officers from Redding, Chico, and Santa Rosa. The local ABC News team was there as well. It was all pretty crazy. Your mom asked about you a couple of times, but I just kept telling her that you were really upset and that you'd be back soon. About ten minutes ago, the police radioed the sheriff to let him know that Jenny just walked into the police station, basically unharmed. After that, her folks and sister raced back to the station to see her. The rest of us celebrated and hugged and stuff, and then we all headed home—and that's where we saw you just now."

"And where the hell have you been all day?" Richard's mom asked. "I don't know what to say to you, Richard. One of your best friends gets kidnapped, and you just go riding off on your bike to who knows where? Listen, I understand that you were upset and people deal with this sort of thing in different ways, but when Jenny's parents needed support the most, we were all there to be with them. All of us except you! It was really rather embarrassing for your father and me. Even your sister was there, and she barely knows Jenny. I just wish you would spend a little more time thinking about others."

Richard's head was churning in a sea of emotions. His family's current opinion of him as some sort of a selfish a-hole infuriated him. He took a second to compose himself. If he was in her shoes, Richard would be pretty upset. Glancing over at Hector, Richard could see that her words angered him as well. Hector's blood was starting to boil, and he was just about to lash out when Richard grabbed his shoulder and gave him a stern look.

Hector managed to keep his mouth under control, but Richard was afraid that he was going to have a stroke!

When Richard's mom headed toward their house, Hector said, "Dude what the hell, man? How can your mom go off on you like that? You're the one who saved her, bro! How can she walk away, thinking that you're some kind of self-centered jerk! You gotta tell her what really happened!"

"No, I don't!" Richard said. "And neither will you—or Tommy or anybody! That was tough for me to hear as well, but it's okay. We know what really happened, and that's got to be enough. Superheroes all need to have secret identities, right? If the bad guys knew who they really were, they could target their friends and families to get back at them. That's just the price we pay. Remember what Uncle Ben told Spidey. With great power comes great responsibility."

Hector took a deep breath and said, "All right, bro. I'll keep it to myself. But you gotta tell me all about it! Was it totally awesome?"

Grinning from ear to ear, Richard said, "I ain't gonna lie, man. It was friggin' incredible!"

They headed to Richard's house and went up to his room. In private, he replayed the entire encounter in explicit detail—every punch, kick, jump, and fall off the cliff.

Hector's eyes filled with wonder and amazement.

Richard thoroughly enjoyed retelling the story. After the verbal thrashing at the hands of his mom, it felt really good to receive some positive feedback for his heroics.

After Hector went home, it was dinnertime. To Richard's delight, it was Chinese food from the Golden Wok. Normally, a Sunday night would include a home-cooked meal, but with all the chaos of the day, he was not surprised that his mom had gone with the easier option.

Once everyone was seated at the kitchen table, his mom turned to him and said, "Hey, sweetie. I want to apologize for being so upset with you earlier. We know Jenny is very important to you, and apparently being on your own was the way you believed you could best deal with your feelings. I should not have been so hard on you. The only thing that matters is that Jenny is okay, and we should all try to get back to normal."

Richard appreciated the sentiment and glanced at the TV in the family room. A news break caught his eye. A reporter was standing in front of the police station with print clearly shown below him in white block letters: "Local Kidnapped Girl Found Unharmed."

"Oh, look!" Richard jumped out of his seat. "It's the news. They're doing a story about Jenny."

The family rushed to the other room and turned up the volume on the television. A suited man in his forties said, "Good evening, everyone. Michael Cosyn reporting for you tonight from the Bentleyville police station where a truly amazing story played out today that could have come right out of a Hollywood movie! This morning, at approximately ten o'clock, local businessman Peter Lee was working in his hardware store with his daughter Jennifer when a group of five men barged into the establishment and proceeded to rob him and cause significant damage to the store. Just before departing, they grabbed fourteen-year-old Jennifer and left, taking her with them!

"Bentleyville police were immediately called to the scene, and shortly thereafter, an all-out manhunt began, involving law enforcement personnel from six cities and three counties. It was believed that the men who kidnapped Jenny were the same ones who vandalized a local restaurant several days earlier and sent its owner in the hospital. The search continued throughout the day, and at approximately 4:10 this afternoon, young Jenny miraculously walked into the police station—unharmed! She had somehow managed to free herself from her captors, who were keeping her in an abandoned farmhouse in the foothills north of town. She made her way through a densely wooded area until she came upon dirt road and flagged down a passing car. Thankfully, the Good Samaritan stopped and gave her a ride to the police station.

"Jennifer was not permanently traumatized by the incident, and she actually had the wherewithal to lead the authorities back to the location where she was being held! In fact, we have someone on the scene there now! Angela, are you there?"

The screen split in two, and the second window showed an attractive woman in her twenties with a burly police officer in SWAT gear. After a moment's pause to verify that she was now live, she said, "Good evening, everyone. Angela Ratzburry reporting from just outside an abandoned farmhouse in the foothills north of Bentleyville. I'm here with Sergeant Christopher Garner from the

Humboldt County SWAT Division. Sergeant Garner, can you tell us what happened?"

"Based on the guidance provided by Miss Lee, my division was able to locate the property, and through the coordinated efforts of city and county forces, we entered the two structures and promptly apprehended four assailants. Miss Lee quickly identified all four of them as the men who had abducted her earlier. They are on their way back to the station to be questioned about the whereabouts of the rest of their organization."

"Was there much resistance from the assailants when your men entered the property?"

"No. In fact, it was one of the easier operations we've had in a while. The group must have been attacked by a rival gang—or possibly were fighting among themselves—since all four men had sustained fairly significant injuries prior to our arrival. There were several broken bones, at least two concussions, and numerous cuts and bruises."

The camera panned back to Angela and moved in for a close-up.

"Thank you, Sergeant Garner. Quite an amazing story! There are still a lot of questions to answer here, but what's important is that Jennifer Lee is now home safe with her family. Michael, back to you."

He continued on for another minute or two before switching over to a different story, but Richard was no longer paying attention.

Looking over, his dad finally said, "Richie, is there something funny that you want to share with us?"

"No, Dad. I'm just really glad that Jenny's back and is okay."

CHAPTER 10

The following day, the ABC News affiliate was at the high school in hopes of getting a one-on-one interview with the amazing girl who singlehandedly thwarted a criminal biker gang. Despite Principal Bell's efforts to hold off the mass disruption of a news team on campus until at least lunchtime, at ten thirty, an announcement came over the loudspeaker that would unofficially end all hopes of any actual education taking place for the remainder of the school day.

"Attention, Jennifer Lee. Please report to the gymnasium at your earliest convenience. There is a group of people here who would like to speak with you regarding the events of yesterday. Any of your fellow students who wish to join you for moral support are invited as well—provided they can conduct themselves in a professional, civilized manner."

As the collective student body quickly made its way to the gymnasium, there was a buzz of gossip and rumors in the air like nothing Richard had ever seen.

Richard, Hector, and Tommy managed to get seats four rows down from the top of the bleachers. A camera crew was set up in the middle of the gym, and two chairs were positioned directly in front of the camera. An attractive blonde woman was being primped by a makeup person. It was the same woman from the TV interview with the SWAT guy.

Jenny was being assisted by a studio beautician. In her usual hot pink lipstick and turquoise eye shadow, Richard could only imagine the conversation she was having with the professional cosmetician.

After a few minutes of getting everything situated, Principal Bell made his way to the center of the room, just to the right of the camera crew. He tapped the microphone twice, and once the feedback died down, he said, "Good morning, everyone. Today is a very special day for one of our students who had a truly life-changing experience. I spoke with Jenny this morning to make sure that she was okay with sharing her story in such a public forum. As a credit to her bravery and selflessness, she also felt it was important that all of you share in this experience with her."

"Selflessness?" Hector whispered. "What the heck is this dude talking about? I guarantee you that Jenny is absolutely loving every second of this. I just know it!"

Principal Bell said, "ABC News is here to interview Miss Lee, and I expect all of you to behave with the upmost courtesy and represent your school with the dignity and respect it deserves. Anyone who does not show such respect will be promptly removed from the auditorium. Is everyone clear?"

"Yes, Principal Bell," the crowd mumbled.

Principal Bell returned to his seat, leaving only Jenny, the reporter, the cameraman, and a couple of lighting people on the main floor of the gymnasium. After a few minutes, the reporter sat down next to Jenny, and one of the people behind the camera began a countdown with his right hand: five, four, three, two... action!

"Good evening. Angela Ratzburry reporting from the gymnasium of James Garfield High School. I'm joined here today with freshman Jennifer Lee. Those of you who tuned in yesterday may have seen my report from the abandoned farmhouse outside of town where the criminal biker gang that had been causing havoc throughout this quiet town for the past several weeks had been thwarted through the heroic efforts of this young lady sitting with me today. Fourteen-year-old Jennifer Lee was brutally kidnapped from her father's hardware store scarcely more than twenty-four hours ago. In most cases like this, the story ends in tragedy—but not today. Jenny escaped her captors and led police to their headquarters where most of them were apprehended!"

"Jenny, I can only imagine how terrifying this must have been for you. Can you try to explain to the audience what exactly took place yesterday to the best of your recollection?"

A hollow feeling began to form in the pit of Richard's stomach. *This could go really badly,* he thought. *It's one thing to come up with a frazzled story for the police as someone who had just escaped captivity, but this is different. She is being interviewed by a reporter on national TV. She is going to be looking for details she would have to generate quickly and effectively, and they will need to match up with whatever she told the police. She could easily flub up and get caught in a lie. Could my involvement come out? What are the consequences of that?* Sweat was beading on Richard's forehead.

Jenny said, "Well, Angela, the whole event was totally surreal, and I'm still kind of in disbelief that this thing actually happened to me. It's all sort of a blur, but here's what I can remember. I was working down at Lee's Hardware on Blain Street when five biker dudes barged in, ran up to the counter, and demanded all the money in the cash register from my dad. Now that I'm thinking about it, they were actually really dumb to rob us when they did because we had only opened half an hour earlier. Aside from some petty cash we had on hand, we hadn't taken cash from a single customer. Weird, huh? After they took what little cash we gave them, they started knocking over a bunch of displays and stuff. All of a sudden, one of them grabbed me and put a knife to my throat! My dad did what he could to help, but they just beat him up. Before I knew it, I was in the back of a van—and they were driving away. Two of the men stayed in the back of the van with me, and one of them drove. The other two took off on motorcycles. The two men in the back duct-taped my hands and tied a scarf across my mouth in case I tried to scream."

"Did you scream?" the reporter asked.

"No. I kept quiet because I wanted to focus on everything I could hear and see because I knew the information could be critically valuable to me. I was sitting in the back of the van, and even though it had no side windows, I still could see out the windshield. I was able to make out a few landmarks and realize they were taking me toward the north end of town. Once we were out of town, I figured I was screwed big-time, but after about fifteen minutes, we turned off the main road. I caught a glimpse of a sign for Oak Street. After another few minutes, we turned again. I noticed a big gnarly tree on the side of the road. Before I knew it, I was being dragged toward an old barn."

"What happened next? You must have been absolutely terrified!"

"Oh, yeah," Jenny said. "I was so scared, but I knew I needed to keep my wits about me. This was life and death after all, and if an opportunity came up to escape, I had to be ready for it. Once I was inside the barn, they instructed me to climb up this ladder to a loft. Once I was there, they removed the ladder, trapping me about fifteen feet off the ground. They just left me there.

"Once I was alone, I started looking for something to free my hands. Luckily, I found an old rusty nail in one of the support beams. I used the nail to cut through the tape. Once my hands were free, I looked around for something I could use as a weapon. I eventually found an old two-by-four and hid it under some straw. In the rear of the loft, a small window looked out toward the back of the property. I saw an overgrown trail that seemed to lead into the wooded hills behind the building. *That's where I'll run if I can get out of here,* I told myself!"

"Simply amazing composure you displayed!" The reporter was making every effort to convey as much drama as possible into each syllable. "Did they ever return for you?"

"Yes, they did come back for me. At least one of them did. He came alone and was carrying a backpack with him. Since he was by himself, I knew it was my one shot of getting outta there! He set the ladder up and climbed into the loft. When I saw him coming, I sat down and did my best to wrap the tape around my hands to make it look like they were still tied. He said that he had some water and a snack in the bag for me. I still had the handkerchief tied in my mouth, so I grunted and motioned for him help me with it. Once he removed the gag, I asked him to take out the water since my hands were numb from being tied up all morning. He reluctantly agreed. Once he set the bottle of water down, I reached out with both hands, still looking like they were tied up, but I hit it in such a way that it fell on its side and started rolling toward the edge of the loft.

"The man turned his back to me and reached over to grab the bottle before it fell. He was only turned away for a couple of seconds, but that's all that it took. I quickly grabbed the two-by-four from its hiding place, and just as he started to look back, I swung the board and knocked him out cold! Once I saw he was unconscious, I scampered down the ladder and made a bee line for the trail. It was pretty overgrown, and within a few seconds, I was completely out of sight. I kept climbing up the trail. I heard some commotion when they discovered my escape, but by that time, I was long gone!"

"Then what happened?" The reporter was sitting at the edge of her seat.

Taking a deep breath and a dramatic pause to compose herself, Jenny said, "Well, I just knew that I had to find my way back to civilization. I guess I just kept wandering around in the woods until I came across a dirt highway. Thankfully, a lady drove by in a jeep and gave me a ride back to town. Once I got to the police station, I was able to lead them to the farm by using the handful of street signs and landmarks I remembered. I guess the rest is history."

There was an unusually long silence as Angela turned toward the camera. "What a truly amazing story! In all of my years of reporting, I can't recall ever meeting a young woman like Jennifer. You demonstrated such courage and resiliency in the face of such terrifying danger. I think I can speak for everyone at the station when I convey our admiration, and our thanks, that you're okay after this truly harrowing adventure. Michael, back to you."

"And cut!"

All the students' eyes were as wide as saucers as they whispered to each other. The girls were especially impressed with the tale, and he overheard a couple of them talking about putting pink and green streaks in their hair.

Richard watched his friend as the sound crew removed her microphone. *Jenny is without question the world champion, undisputed, heavyweight queen of bullshit!* He was more impressed with her tale than many of the students who believed it was real. Her attention to detail was incredible! And she showed such raw, unfiltered emotion. If he had tried to recap his story of what happened on national television, there was no way it would have come across half as impressive or believable, and it actually happened to him!

An unexpected emotion came over Richard as he looked down at his friend: jealousy. After this, Jenny would most likely attain celebrity status in their town. She would be heralded for her bravery, determination, and levelheadedness, and she could bask in all the perks that come with such fame. Richard would remain the same dopey freshman he had always been, and he was actually the hero of this whole thing! Sure Tommy, Hector and Jenny would know the truth, but was that really enough for him? He was starting to get a bit annoyed until Jenny caught his eye and mouthed, "Thank you!"

His entire disposition changed, and any negative feelings were replaced with pure happiness. *What kind of a big jerk could feel bad because his friend did exactly what he told her to do—and did a damn great job of it? This actually went just about as well as it possibly could have gone. With all the attention on Jenny, there is basically no chance that anyone will even give me a second thought. And even though a little fame and admiration would have been nice, it is all for the best.*

CHAPTER 11

For the next couple of days, the high school and much of the entire town of Bentleyville was in a frenzy with all things Jenny Lee. By the end of the week, things had finally calmed down to something at least approaching normal. It was also officially just one week until the Halloween dance and consume contest. Though Richard had fleeting hopes that—between her kidnapping and subsequent rescue and fame—she might decide the timing may not be quite right for her Village People extravaganza, it became abundantly clear that she fully intended on proceeding as planned.

Jenny even pulled some strings to get them access to the gymnasium on Saturday so they could practice their routine and get their timing down to a military level of precision. This met with some initial objection from Hector and Tommy, but ultimately, resistance was futile. At eleven o'clock, all four of them, as well as Jenny's friend Bobbie, were present and accounted for. And to add insult to injury, she insisted that they make Saturday a full dress rehearsal.

Richard felt absurd in his Native American garb and chieftain's headdress, and the rest of the gang looked equally dorky, but they did seem to fit the part. The one person who most certainly did not look bad on stage was Jenny. The skin-tight leather pants, crop-top white T-shirt, and leather vest showed off her figure quite nicely.

Throughout the week, Richard racked his brain for what to do next with respect to the recent change in their relationship. Clearly, Jenny had feelings for Richard, and he was pretty certain that she knew that the feelings were mutual, but neither of them dared to make the first move. Richard was still completely unsure if these new feelings Jenny appeared to have were genuine, or simply a by-product of saving her life. He was terrified of making the first move since it might come off as creepy to Jenny, Hector, or Tommy.

Hector said, "It's really tricky, bro. I mean, it's Jenny. If the two of you dated, and then it didn't work out for some reason, it would be kinda weird. I mean, Tommy and I would need to pick sides and stuff."

"You think it could go that badly?" Richard asked. "Of course, if it came down to it, you'd pick me, right?"

Hector smirked. "I dunno, dude. She's a lot better at *Overwatch* than you."

After several performances of "YMCA," the rehearsal ended.

That night, Tommy stayed over at Richard's house. They had become much closer in the past few weeks, but Richard never did get the full story of what happened when his brother's motorcycle disappeared into thin air. As luck would have it, no one noticed that it was missing for the rest of the day. That night, Tommy snuck down and kicked in the side door to make it look like someone had stolen it. Fortunately for Tommy and his brother, the motorcycle was insured. James was actually somewhat relieved when his mom gave him the news. He was still making payments on the vehicle, and it was getting more difficult with his other school expenses.

Richard appreciated the time he was able to spend with Tommy when it was just the two of them. He appreciated Richard's suggestion to refrain from using his abilities unless it was absolutely necessary. He still found everything about the necklace fascinating, and he suggested additional testing in a controlled environment to gain a better understanding of his specific abilities. He also brought a perspective to the situation that Hector did not possess.

The rest of the evening was filled with more run-of-the-mill chitchat about school, sports, gaming, girls, and general stuff that fourteen-year-old boys talk about. Richard's mom baked a frozen lasagna and served it with garlic bread and Caesar salad. They also polished off a two-liter bottle of Coke. Following dinner, they watched *Monty Python and the Holy Grail* for about the thirtieth time. They spent the next two hours laughing, belching, and farting until they drove the rest of the family out of the lower half of the house. Richard's sister was particularly vocal about how disgusting she thought they were, which made the whole thing all the more hilarious.

For Richard, the following week flew by in the blink of an eye. With a ton of school assignments and a cross-country meet on Wednesday, Friday arrived before he knew it. The big Halloween dance was that evening. Even though he was pretty sure the dance would end up being a lot of fun, he still had mixed feelings. On a strictly egotistical level, he feared looking foolish performing a song and dance number in front of the entire school dressed as a gay Indian chief. On a more personal level, if news of it ever got back to his grandfather—or others on the reservation—he'd have hell to pay. Mocking his people's tradition, even if done in good spirits, was looked down upon sternly, but he was too far into it to turn back now.

Throughout the week, Jenny's excitement level had been at about a twelve, and she took it to a whole new level. She shrieked, "OMG! OMG! Tonight's the night, Richie! *So* excited!"

Mrs. Wexler said, "Miss Lee, can we please take a seat and try to control ourselves so the rest of us can actually learn something today. We've heard all week about your upcoming performance this evening, and I'm quite certain that everyone who is planning on attending will make a point to appreciate this spectacle that you've been chatting about nonstop for the past several days."

"Sorry, sorry. I'll be good. I promise!" Jenny sat down and remained nearly silent. After thirty minutes, she leaned over to Richard and whispered, "So, after school, go home, get all your stuff, and bring it over to my place. We can all get dressed there, and my mom will drive us all over in the minivan. Given that we're a group, we certainly can't show up individually!"

Richard nodded, but in his head, he thought, *What the heck have you gotten yourself into?* The rest of the morning went by without incident.

By lunch, Jenny was back to her hyper-psycho energy level and went over the plans for the twelfth time that week. Several other students came up to the group as they ate and mentioned how excited they were to see the performance.

Jenny's popularity skyrocketed, and groups of people were vying for her attention. If not for their upcoming performance, Richard feared that she might have abandoned their group of jolly misfits altogether. *What will happen next week after all of this is over? Will she dump us for a group of older, cooler, more popular kids? Granted, none of them have superpowers, but that's hardly common knowledge to the rest of the student body. Will it be enough to hold her loyalty?*

At four thirty, everyone made their way over to Jenny's house. Her parents were very kind and gracious, and her mom prepared at least two dozen egg rolls and pot stickers for everyone to snack on while they got ready. Her dad still showed several bruises and a black eye from his encounter with the bikers, which upset Richard greatly, but when he asked how he was doing, Richard was met with a warm smile and stoic assurance that it was only a few bumps and bruises—and that he'd be fine in no time. On at least three different occasions, they thanked everyone again for their support while she was missing. Neither of them said a word about Richard not being there that day, but he felt tremendously guilty all the same. It was a ridiculous thing to feel, given the fact that he was actually the one who saved her, but Richard still couldn't shake the feeling.

After stuffing themselves with snacks and soda, everybody went to different rooms in the house to get dressed in their costumes.

For several weeks, Richard hadn't brought the necklace to school, and he certainly had no plans for thwarting any crimes at the dance, but in the end, he decided to go for it. He even took the fashion statement one step further by wearing it outside of his shirt for everyone to see! It would be their own private joke for the rest of the gang. After everyone was ready, they all piled into the van for the quick trip to school.

As they got out of the van, several of Jenny's friends rushed over to compliment everyone on their look. Jenny's glow of stardom had not quite dissipated. Twenty or thirty people surrounded them as they entered the gymnasium. Richard noticed a couple of parents who appeared to be checking ID cards at the door, and for a moment, he froze in fear. He had left his at home. Fortunately, given the bulky costumes many students were wearing, making it difficult to easily access a wallet, the parents appeared to be pretty lenient toward those who couldn't quickly produce one. As it turned out, the parents didn't even ask as they walked past.

Once inside, they could take in the full experience of the Halloween dance. Richard had heard a lot about it from Hector's sister, but her descriptions did not do it justice. Black and orange metallic streamers cascaded along the tops of the walls and flowed from a large disco ball mounted to the ceiling out toward the walls, forming something that resembled the inside of a circus tent. Fake cobwebs were everywhere, and there were six skeletons, a dozen candelabras, and at least a hundred imitation spiders and bats. Four lights were pointed at the disco ball, and orange and purple bulbs caused a kaleidoscope of colors to engulf the room. At the far end of the gymnasium, the raised stage was forty feet across and thirty feet deep.

Plenty of room for us to make complete fools of ourselves, Richard thought.

"Oh my God. This is so awesome!" Jenny said. "This is even better than I imagined it would be. We are so going to win this thing!"

"Nothing like being on stage and strutting your stuff to look good for the ladies, eh?" Hector bumped his elbow into Tommy's stomach. "And best of all, Halloween is the one time that girls can get away with dressing hella provocative without coming off as too slutty."

A number of students were dressed in some pretty interesting attire. It was a high school dance, so there was nothing too over to top, but several young women dressed as nurses or French maids with fairly short skirts and fishnet stockings. *I just hope Horn-Dog Hector can keep his mind on the routine.*

The DJ had an impressive collection of speakers and turntables. Contemporary music was playing, and the dance floor was about 60 percent full. Richard thought about asking Jenny if she wanted to dance for a bit to help pass the time, but she seemed way too excited about their performance to think about dancing. There would be plenty of time after their routine to get her out on the dance floor. Once the pressure was off, she could enjoy herself. He had thought extensively about whether he would try to initiate something if they ended up in a slow dance together. She would likely be in a great mood, especially if they won the contest, and the memory of his daring rescue would still be fresh in her mind. After going back and forth in his head about a million times, he decided to proceed with a wait-and-see strategy. If he ended up in a dance with her—and if he felt that the mood and timing were right—he'd definitely try to go in for a kiss. It could still go badly, and even if it went well, it might still screw up their dynamic with Hector and Tommy, but he had repressed his feelings for Jenny long enough. If he could get up on stage and make a total jackass out of himself in front of the entire school, then he had the courage to try to move their relationship past the friendship level.

After forty minutes, the DJ abruptly stopped the music.

Vice Principal Dillard got up on stage with a microphone. After a minute of quieting down the crowd, she said, "Good evening, everybody! So great to see so many of you here tonight for the first official dance of the school year! I'd normally comment on how lovely everyone looks, but given several of the costumes I see out there, a number of you actually look downright dreadful!"

A painfully awkward silence ensued.

"Okay. I guess we'll get started with the individual costume contests. As with past years, we'll have different categories. When I call each category, everyone who wants to participate can come up onto the stage. Each student will step forward and be judged by your applause level. Once everyone has been evaluated, myself, Principal Bell, and Mrs. Lima will declare the winner of each category. After we've handed out all the individual awards, we'll move on to the group categories. So, without further ado, let's bring on the first category of individual contestants: scariest costume!"

Six or seven students made their way up on stage. Most were fairly uninspiring, but one of the kids looked like he had just stepped off the set of *The Walking Dead*. He easily won the category, and the prize was four movie tickets and a gift certificate for a large pizza at Papa Giorgio's. The funniest costume category had the largest number of entries. Most were pretty lame, but a few were over the top—ranging from downright offensive to bordering on obscene. The person who ended up winning was the current student body president. Kirk Wexler wore an old lady outfit with a curly white wig, thick glasses, an ill-fitting muumuu that covered an enormous bodysuit, breasts that hung down past his waist, and a rear end that was at least three feet across. When he was called to the front of the stage, he asked the crowd in his best old lady voice if they had seen her lost puppy. After this went on for a few seconds, he turned around so that his back was to the crowd, revealing a small— obviously fake—dog squashed between her gigantic butt cheeks. As tasteless as it was, even Richard had to laugh when he saw it. Following this spectacle was the third and final category of the individual participants: most original costume. That group brought out the nerdiest of the nerds, and they could almost count how many times each of them had been to Comic-Con by looking at them. Several of them were pretty interesting, but the one who eventually took the prize was a steampunk version of Iron Man. Nerdy or not, it looked really cool, and Richard could only imagine the cost and hours that must have gone into making it.

During the individual rounds, Jenny managed to hold it together pretty well, but as soon they finished, she pretty much lost it. She had checked ahead and knew that their group was the second of the eight groups. She was not happy about this placement since it left six other groups to go after them. In those types of competitions, the later ones tended to fare better. She was thoroughly convinced of it, but they would have to make the best of it.

The first group consisted of four students portraying characters from *Game of Thrones*. One slender girl had a long white wig and two small, cheap-looking plastic dragons on her shoulders. She was supposed to be Khaleesi. A freshman from Richard's science class wore a short blond wig and a crown and appeared to be King Joffrey. The third was dressed in leather and furs, sported a shaggy black wig, and carried a plastic long sword. Though he could not be certain, Richard was pretty sure it was John Snow. John Sandal came on stage last—to build suspense and because he was walking on his knees. His shoes came out from under his knees to give the appearance of having stumpy legs. With a curly brown wig, it was clear that he was supposed to be Tyrion Lannister. Whatever favor he hoped to gain from the crowd with his creative interpretation of a little person went horribly wrong, and the students began groaning and booing him almost as soon as he made his appearance. Just about everyone Richard knew, considered Peter Dinklage one of the most talented and coolest actors around, and this feeble attempt to mock him brought nothing but disdain and hatred from the audience. Richard almost felt bad for the four of them as they attempted to go through some dialogue they had previously planned, but the negative reactions from the crowd drowned out any hope of gaining approval from anybody.

"I guess we're up next!" Hector whispered.

They walked up a small set of stairs and made their way onto the stage.

After the *Train wreck of Thrones* was finally over, Mrs. Dillard came out and said, "Okay, everybody, quiet down. Our next group category participants are four young students, one of whom I'm sure you all remember quite well from our assembly on Monday. Please give a big round of applause to Bobbie Spicer, Tommy Parker, Hector Ramirez, Richard Locklear, and—of course—Jenny Lee!"

"Is it just me or do you guys feel like a bunch of Beyoncé's backup singers?" Hector whispered as they made their way to the front of the stage. The costumes were instantly recognizable, and even though no one in the auditorium, outside of some of the faculty, was even alive the last time the band had a hit, their impact on pop culture seemed to hold up.

Several people shouted, "Yeah, Village People!"

Richard was still nervous about looking foolish in from of the entire student body, but before he could allow his concerns to expand into an all-out panic attack, the music began. He had no choice but to get back into character and complete the performance.

Apparently, practice does make perfect because everyone absolutely crushed it. The performance went off without a hitch. Everyone's movements were synchronous, their lip-synching was on point, and they had nearly the entire auditorium clapping along with them as they hit the chorus: "YMCA… you'll find it at the YMCA." By the end of the song, even Richard had to admit that the experience was an absolute blast. The reaction from the crown was unbelievable. Cheers, whoops, and hollers could be heard for a good thirty seconds after they finished.

Once everyone was offstage, Jenny gave them all a huge bear-hug accompanied by a shrill squeaking sound that was simultaneously painful and endearing. Whether through design or pure chance, Jenny hugged Richard last. From his perspective, she appeared to hold on a few seconds longer than with the others.

Richard was still wearing the necklace, and he could easily hold her off the ground. As she jumped into his arms, her body pressed firmly against his. Finally setting her down and taking a step backward, he looked into her eyes and smiled widely. She stared back at him with a look of pure joy and excitement. Richard could not remember feeling happier. Even with her fake moustache, she looked absolutely adorable. That said, he certainly could not go in for what would be their first kiss while she was wearing that awful thing. He would need to hold off until the end of the contest. If they won, they would call all of them back up to the stage. He knew Jenny would want to receive their award in full costume. After the contest, Richard was fairly confident he could convince her to take that thing off, and that's when he'd attempt to make his move.

As the next act took the stage, dressed as some tacky superhero ensemble, Jenny leaned over to Richard and asked him if he could get her some punch. She was absolutely parched, but she did not want to miss evaluating any of their competition.

Happy to oblige, Richard began making his way through the crowd. When he was almost across the crowded dance floor, a dark hooded figure stepped in front of him. He stood about five foot ten and was wearing a black cloak that extended all the way to his feet. The hood completely covered his head, revealing only a skeletal face. It was obviously makeup, but it caught Richard off guard. Two rubber prosthetics on his forehead sloped down to his cheekbones, and a separate piece covered his jawline.

Richard did not recognize the student in the Grim Reaper costume, but it was a big school.

"You should be ashamed making a fool of yourself like that. That's your heritage you're making fun of, man."

The words and tone of voice stunned Richard.

The dark figure continued, "I'm gonna do you a big favor and not mention any of this crap to the Wolf when you go see him tonight."

Richard's blood turned to ice, and a cold sweat formed on his brow and the back of his neck. *What the hell? I thought they already arrested most of that gang? Even if they didn't, how the heck could they know who I am? I was wearing that motorcycle helmet the whole time. And if they know who I am, why in God's name would they encounter me in such a public forum? None of this makes any sense!*

The hooded man said, "So this is what's gonna happen. You're going to casually follow me outside and get into a car that's waiting for us. We're gonna go see the Wolf. He's been wanting to speak with you for a while now. And if you try to do anything stupid, a bunch of people are going to get hurt!" He pulled back one side of the cloak, revealing an Uzi submachine gun. A shoulder strap held the weapon at his side, hanging just beneath his armpit.

Terror and panic shot through Richard like a lightning bolt. A weapon like that could easily wound or kill dozens of his classmates—and even his best friends if they were unlucky enough to be in the crossfire. Suddenly remembering who he was and what he was wearing, he stopped himself before flying into a full-blown panic attack. *There's just one guy here, and I should be able to take him out before he gets off a single shot!*

The dark figure said, "Don't get cocky, hero-man. I'm not alone." He motioned with his head toward his left.

Two other figures in similar attire opened their cloaks to reveal their guns. *Crap! There's two more of them, and they're at least twenty feet away! Even with my speed, there is no way I can get to all three of them before one or more open fire on the crowd! This is really bad!*

"Hey, bro. I thought you were getting some punch?" Hector said. "Dude, what's up with Skeletor? He looks like somebody just peed in his Cheerios."

The dark figure took a step toward Hector.

Richard said, "Hector, I'm going to leave with these guys for a while. You need to go let Jenny and the others know that I had to leave. Don't worry. I'll be fine."

Richard could tell that his friend understood that he was most certainly not going to be okay if he left. With one last look at Hector, Richard began walking toward to the exit with the skeletal presence.

The two other hooded figures also made their way toward the exit, and the full gravity of the situation sank in for Richard. He had taken on armed thugs before, but he had the element of surprise on his side. This time, they appeared to have all of the advantage.

CHAPTER 12

Once Richard and his three kidnappers were in the parking lot, he saw a fourth man beside an old gray Ford. The two others stayed thirty feet behind them.

This must be by design, Richard thought. If they got too close, there was a chance he could take out all three before they started shooting. If he tried to do anything, by the time he clobbered the guy next to him, the other two could make Swiss cheese out of him. All-consuming fear coursed through Richard as he approached the vehicle. Taking on the biker gang to rescue Jenny was scary as heck, but it was nothing compared to what he felt now. He could only hope and pray that they did not try to take the necklace from him. Even if they knew who he was and were aware of what he could do, it did not necessarily mean they knew *how* he was able to do what he could do, and he was wearing the only outfit he could possibly have on where his necklace did not look out of place. It could easily be mistaken as a prop for his costume. As long as he had the necklace, he had a chance!

Richard slowly climbed into the back of the sedan, and two of the gunman got in on either side of him, sandwiching Richard with the barrels of their guns resting against his ribcage. The third gunman got into the passenger seat and pointed his gun at Richard.

This is it! There's no way I can possibly get out of this. No matter how strong or fast I am, I can't do anything at this point. I've just gotta stay here like a sitting duck and see what happens.

The twenty-minute drive that followed was the longest car ride Richard could ever remember taking. Every second felt like an eternity, and he replayed so many of the events in his life over and over again. For many of the episodes, he was generally proud of his actions, but there were also many not-so-proud moments when he showed significant character flaws, ranging from cowardliness to jealousy to wrath. His errors in judgment and bad decisions screamed out at him. What concerned him the most was that he truly believed that he would be meeting his Maker that night. He had no idea what sort of a life grade he would receive from the Big Man.

The vehicle made its way into the hills, and to his amazement, it headed directly toward the Tolowa Reservation. Less than a mile from the entrance, the sedan turned off on a side road. It drove several miles down a windy dirt road and pulled into a large clearing surrounded by enormous redwoods and other foliage.

Through the windshield, Richard could make out other figures. Torches lit up the clearing. The person who Richard had been speaking with earlier opened his door and exited. "Get out!"

In the clearing, Richard was repeatedly prodded in the back with the end of the Uzi as he walked toward the lighted area. A forceful push sent him stumbling into a patch of earth directly in front of a small wooden stage that appeared to have been built recently.

A solitary figure in a black hooded robe stood on the stage with his back to Richard. Even in the poor lighting, Richard could clearly see Lobo del Diablo embroidered on his back.

After a few silent moments that felt much longer, the figure slowly turned around and faced Richard. His face was hidden in shadows, but the figure Richard assumed to be the Wolf was actually much smaller than he had expected. Richard could have sworn the legendary leader of the biker gang was only a few inches bigger than he was. Still utterly terrified at the entire situation, Richard remained silent.

The figure said, "You really think you're some hot stuff, don't you! Showing off your abilities and taking down a bunch of helpless kids not much older than yourself—but without any enhanced abilities to protect themselves."

Richard's hurricane of emotions shifted from sheer terror to partial confusion. He sensed a familiarity in the voice and struggled get his head around it. He fought to regain his composure.

The mysterious figure said, "Using your powers to dominate those weaker than you is a pretty regular thing for you, isn't it!" Following a dramatic pause, the hooded figure reached up, grabbed the sides of the hood, and slowly pulled it back until it fell behind his neck.

As the shadows concealing the face of his adversary disappeared, Richard's eyes nearly popped out of his head. "Ahote?"

"You surprised to see me?" he replied.

Struggling to put more than two words together, Richard said, "How? What? Why the hell would a bunch of biker dudes be following you? You're just a stupid kid like me?"

"But that's the big difference, my petulant cousin. You're not just some average kid. You have special abilities, don't you?"

"How did you find out?" Richard asked.

"The day you crushed my hand, I was in the emergency room until two o'clock in the morning. They managed to splint up my hand and sent me home until they could perform surgery the following afternoon. Even though I only had a few hours of sleep, the pain in my hand woke me up by six thirty. I happened to be walking through the kitchen when I saw Grandpa running past our place. To my amazement, you were not running with him. I knew that you had stayed over the night before. I went into our closet, pulled out my dad's pistol, and walked over to his place with all intentions of shooting you!"

"So what happened?" Richard asked. "I was still asleep, but I don't recall getting shot."

Ahote said, "To be totally honest, I got there and froze. I stood there for probably twenty minutes or longer, unable to do anything but look at Grandpa's place and fume in an absolute rage. For some reason, I just couldn't get myself to kick in the door and start shooting. Grandpa must have cut his run short. I dashed behind his mobile home and crouched beneath a slightly open window. When he walked in, you were wearing the necklace."

"And that's how you learned about it?" Richard said. "You decided that kidnapping my girlfriend was some kind of twisted way of getting even with me for screwing up your hand? That doesn't explain why a renegade biker gang would all of a sudden want to start taking orders from a big dweeb like you!"

"It's funny you say that," Ahote said. "There was one particular detail of your story that I paid special attention to. You made one casual mention of a second set of remains in that tomb with you. If the skeleton you investigated had some sort of magical artifact on it, perhaps the other body had something of value on it as well. And I was right!" An ancient necklace was tied around Ahote's neck.

Richard said, "But even if you thought there might be something with the other remains, how the hell did you ever find them? My dad moved and reburied them over a month ago. I don't even know where they are."

"And that's where the one other key detail that you were kind enough to mention came into play. There was a momentary comment about your dad's coworker. As luck would have it, my father knew Fred fairly well when they were both working for Uncle Ernie. He had a bit of a gambling problem, and one time, he got in over his head a bit and did something rather desperate. He stole a bunch of equipment from a job site, and he told your dad that someone had broken into one of the storage containers. Your dad filed an insurance claim, and that was pretty much the end of it. I decided to pay old Fred a visit, and in exchange for not making your dad aware of what really happened, he helped me excavate and rebury the remains—but only after I retrieved this!"

Ahote's necklace had many teeth with small, jet-black stones between them. All of the teeth came from the same species. It was difficult to tell for sure, but they appeared to be canine in nature. Most likely, they were wolves' teeth.

"So if you knew about the necklace, why didn't you have your goon squad take it from me while they were bringing me over here?"

"Oh, and what would be the fun of that? Certainly, someone like you—with no morals—might think of such a strategy, but unlike some people who try to deny their heritage, I actually honor mine. Ours has been a tribe of warriors for more than a thousand years, and I will not disgrace my lineage by simply slaughtering you like a helpless sheep. I will defeat you in combat like a true warrior. And maybe, for the sake of our grandfather, by dying in combat, you will regain some of your honor."

Richard's feelings began shifting toward hope. "So let me get this straight. You and me will fight—just the two of us—and the best man wins? Your guys aren't going to start shooting at me if I start winning, are they?"

"My god... you're pathetic. You've fallen so far from your roots that you don't even know what honor is anymore. Of course, my men will not interfere. Someone with any integrity would know it without saying, but since I'm dealing with you, I'll make it crystal clear." Shifting his eyes from Richard to the others, he said, "My fellow wolf pack, you honor me with your presence here tonight, but let me be clear in saying that none of you will interfere in any way with the battle between me and my cousin. If any of you becomes involved in this fight, you will most certainly face the full fury of my displeasure!" He glanced at Richard. "Satisfied?"

"Fair enough. So let's stop screwing around and do this!" Ahote slowly walked toward the edge of the wooden stage.

Richard carefully removed his headdress and tunic, leaving him shirtless. The shirt was a bit small and would significantly impede his movement. Preparing himself mentally for the fight, he started feeling pretty good about how things should turn out. *Okay. Let's assume he's got wolf speed and strength now. Bears are way stronger than wolves, and deer are way faster. Throw in the agility of a mountain lion, and I should be able to mop up the floor with this jerk! I bet the second guy in the cave was my guy's sidekick or something. Ahote must not really know what I'm capable of.*

Hopping off the stage, Ahote untied the small rope securing his cloak and let it fall to the ground. He was also shirtless and shoeless. The only thing he was wearing was a pair of basketball shorts that went down to just above his knees. He began hopping around and rotating his neck and shoulders to warm up as he raised his fists in preparation for combat.

Still unsure if the other criminals would do as they were told, Richard decided to make it a fair fight, but he'd strike fast and hard, trying to end it quickly. *If all goes well, I'll beat him senseless until he calls off the fight. If he really has this honor he keeps talking about, he'll let me go—and everything will be okay.* "So you ready?" Richard asked

"Let the fun begin!" Ahote sneered.

With lightning speed, Richard sprinted the twenty feet separating them and threw a side kick at his cousin's head.

Ahote managed to dodge the blow and retaliated with multiple hand strikes.

Richard managed to maneuver out of the way of the first strike and blocked the next two. Seeing a window of opportunity, he attacked with a jumping front kick that landed squarely in Ahote's chest, sending him back into the wooden stage. The force of the impact broke several of the boards.

For a moment, Richard was afraid that he might have accidentally killed him. To his relief, his cousin began to move in the rubble. *He's got to have broken ribs. No chance he's getting up from this.*

Ahote slowly got to his feet, stared at his opponent with sadistic contempt, and started chuckling.

The other bikers took several steps backward.

What the hell is going on here? Something is very wrong!

"I have to say, cousin, that was a pretty good shot. This is going to be more fun than I anticipated. It's my turn now!"

Ahote stood up straight, and Richard immediately noticed the small black spheres on his necklace beginning to glow. To his shock and horror, the stones and teeth sunk into his skin, like they were just sucked up by his body until the artifact was completely gone.

"What the hell?" Richard said. This necklace obviously worked very differently than his, and he became exceptionally uneasy.

Ahote jerked his head back and puffed out his chest. As he did, sickening sounds that appeared to be snapping bones and cracking joints emanated from his body. Brown fur began appearing on his chest. His hands contorted, his fingers began to lengthen, and horrible claws began to grow from them. A ferocious roar brought Richard's eyes back up to Ahote's face, which was now twisting and deforming before him. His jaw was stretching away from his skull, and large fangs were replacing his teeth. Hair appeared all over his face, and his ears grew and shifted toward the top of his head. Wrenching back and forth as the metamorphosis was occurring, Ahote's feet stretched up, his back hunched over, and thick fur covered him.

Terrified beyond all rational thought, Richard looked on in unreal astonishment as his cousin turned into a werewolf. *Oh, crap!*

After the transformation was complete, the creature looked directly at Richard and appeared to almost smile through its fang-filled maw. Crouching down to regain its balance, the beast leaped at Richard.

Realizing he had milliseconds to react before it tore him to pieces, Richard dove to his left, somersaulted, and ducked under the swing of the powerful claws.

The monster spun around and leaped toward him again.

Richard saw several boards from the stage and managed to avoid the two-inch claws that came inches from tearing his face off. He grabbed a two-by-four and turned back toward his foe.

Huge, open jaws were flying straight toward his head. Falling to the ground, he pulled the board in front of him, grabbed it with both hands, and shoved it into the middle of the fanged mouth. The incisors clamped down on the board, and the fangs sank into the wood. Looking beyond the snarling mouth, Richard saw purely inhuman eyes staring back at him, totally devoid of any trace of human emotion. Only primal animal instinct remained.

Realizing that certain anatomical features on his foe should have remained generally in tack, Richard kicked the creature's groin as hard as he could. The beast let out a sharp shriek and jumped back several yards, allowing Richard to scramble back to his feet. Sensing that the pain the beast was in would be his only opportunity to make an offensive strike, he lunged forward and swung the board at the creature's head with all his might.

The beast barely got its arm up in time to stop the blow with its forearm. Richard heard a definite crack and hoped it was the sound of the beast's bone and not the two-by-four.

Richard swung again, this time lower and to the opposite side, aiming for the body. With the monster expecting another high shot, its arm was raised. Richard managed to get the swing under the elbow and landed a powerful blow to the side of its chest. The strike knocked the wind out of his opponent, but the board snapped in half, leaving Richard with a largely useless twenty-inch piece. Realizing he was defenseless, Richard looked for another weapon.

When he looked back a second later, four razor-sharp claws headed straight toward him at lightning speed!

Richard did his best to jump backward and avoid the strike, but the reach of the creature was longer than he anticipated. Three of the four claws tore across the front of his chest, producing lacerations that were six inches long and a half-inch deep. Shrieking in pain and terror, Richard scampered backward, his hand grasping at the burning tears in his skin. The wounds were bleeding significantly, and he used every ounce of willpower to keep his wits about him. *This fight is over if I go after him again. Focus. I've only got two choices here: stay and get eaten alive or run!*

Noticing the fear that the bikers had for the horrific beast, Richard got an idea. He began moving backward toward several of them, while still facing Ahote. Sensing victory, the beast lunged, jaws wide open, and went in for the kill. Fear and adrenaline momentarily eased the searing agony radiating from his chest. Richard ducked, drove his legs forward, and aimed his shoulder at the knees of the beast. The creature managed to get one of them turned to the side, but Richard could clearly hear the left one pop as he hit it squarely at the joint. After another high-pitched shriek, the beast leaped over Richard and scrambled onto the one uninjured hind leg and its front legs. The aggressive movements of monster caused several of the armed men to run as far away from the beast as possible, which left an opening into the forest, which was only about a hundred feet away.

Richard sprinted toward the trees as fast as he could. He heard one of the bikers calling out and the sound of a gun firing just before he reached the tree line. Flying through the foliage, he navigated his way under branches, over logs, and through bushes in hopes of gaining some distance from the creature before it began its pursuit. Richard heard the angry roar of the beast echoing through the forest and the sounds of something large and powerful tearing its way through branches and vegetation.

Richard soon found himself alone in the forest. After a few minutes, he decided it would be okay to stop for a second to catch his breath and figure out where he was. The blood from his chest wound had run all down his stomach, and long streaks of red cascaded along his trousers. He'd lost quite a bit of blood. As soon as the adrenaline started to wear off, Richard felt terrible. The searing pain in his chest returned, worse than ever, and his head started to spin. Slumping down next to a tree, he wrapped his arms around himself to conserve his warmth. He was still shirtless and wet with blood and sweat in the middle of the night in late October. *You just need to rest here for a minute—and then you can start running again.*

Several minutes later, he felt no better. In fact, he felt worse. Then it occurred to him that he still had his iPhone with him. He opened it up, but there was only a flicker of one bar of coverage. *It's unlikely that a call will get through, but I gotta try.* After four failed attempts, he gave up. *Perhaps a text might work.* As he moved the phone around, he'd intermittently see a second bar for a second. Maybe *it's enough to send a text.* Unsure if a group text would be more, or less likely to get through to someone, he decided that his best chance would be to try to message Hector and hope for the best.

With his hands shaking from the cold, it took a full minute to compose a text: "Bro, please help! I'm in the middle of the forest somewhere not too far from the reservation where I used to live. No idea how you're going to find me, but please try. Hurt and need help! Thanks!" After hitting Send, Richard used what little strength he had left to get to his feet. Holding the phone overhead, he walked around, hoping to somehow find enough coverage to complete the transmission.

Finally, after thirty grueling seconds, "Message Sent" popped up on his screen.

He let out a huge sigh of relief and sat back down against the tree. He pulled his legs up to his chest and wrapped his arms around them to conserve what little body heat he had left. *Still got no idea how the hell he's gonna find me in the middle of a forest, but at least there's a chance.* The odds certainly weren't in his favor, but he had no other options besides praying for a miracle.

As he sat shivering, a million little details of the forest caught his attention. A three-quarter moon provided a good amount of light to illuminate the trees and bushes. A squirrel darted up a tree about twenty feet away, climbing up and disappearing into the branches. A blue jay was eating seeds off the ground. Despite his terrible physical discomfort, the forest was actually quite pleasant. Richard's mind began to drift to various scenarios, including what would happen if no one found him. By morning, either the blood loss or the hypothermia would most likely be the death of him. That would pretty much be it! *I suppose there's worse ways to go. I really enjoy nature, and kicking the bucket in this beautiful forest surrounded by magnificent redwoods, moss-covered boulders, squirrels, and birds would not be all that horrible, I guess… wait—birds! I can control birds! How did I not think about that before?*

Glancing back to where he had seen the blue jay ago, he initially could not find it! He panicked for a few seconds, but he found it again within a minute. In his battered, half-frozen, and delirious state, Richard had no idea if he could make it work, but he had to try. Closing his eyes, he tried his hardest to focus on the bird. *Be the bird. Be the bird!* The shaking of his body made it terribly difficult to concentrate. His mind calmed for a few moments, and he became the blue jay.

Taking to the sky, he soared to the tops of the trees, and the sheer grandeur of how huge these redwoods were really sunk in. Reaching the open sky, he looked around in hopes of making out a landmark that might give him an idea of what direction to start flying. Seeing a tiny glint of what might be a headlight, Richard took off toward it. Glancing through the trees toward the earth, only blackness stared back at him. He asked himself on several occasions what exactly he expected to see down there, but he found himself looking nonetheless.

A slight speck of light caught his eye, and he quickly landed in a treetop to take another look. At first, he could not find it, and he was just about to take flight when he saw it again—way down through the trees. There were no roads out here, so it must be someone on foot with a flashlight. Maybe a forest ranger? Perhaps one of the bikers? In either case, he needed to take a closer look. Flying down through the branches, the shimmer of light grew more and more noticeable. After dipping beneath the canopy, he could clearly see a person walking through the woods. Only fifty feet away from the figure, Richard could see that the person had a smartphone in one hand, a flashlight in the other, and was dressed like a cowboy. *It can't be. There's no way Hector could have possibly gotten to me so quickly. I only sent the text twenty minutes ago.* To his utter disbelief, his bird eyes were looking at his friend right in front of him—and only a mile or so from his physical body. *I just need to let him know that this bird is actually me.*

Swooping down, the bird flew right in front of Hector and began squawking loudly. It had little effect because Hector was strangely engrossed with his cell phone. Taking the situation up a notch, Richard willed the bird to fly down and land on the cowboy hat. Once he made contact, he started pecking the top of the hat.

"What the hell? Stupid bird!" Hector waved his hands up over his head, batting the bird aside.

Now that Richard had gotten Hector's attention, he began flying right in front of his face.

"Dude, I'm gonna smash you with this flashlight if you don't leave me alone, ya friggin' bird. I've got to find my friend out here. Oh wait! You're a bird! Dude, is that you, Richie?"

Landing on a log, the bird nodded until the message became clear.

"Oh, bro! Thank God it's you, man. Where are you at? Can you lead me to you?"

For twenty minutes, Hector followed the blue jay as it flew back and forth, trying to navigate its way back to Richard's body through the forest. Finally, after flying ahead about two hundred yards, Richard made out his body curled up in a ball at the base of a tree. Landing just a few feet from him, his consciousness snapped back into his head. The pain and discomfort came rushing back and woke him up with a jolt. Using what little strength he had left, Richard said, "Hector, over here!"

After a few moments, Richard could hear the rustling of bushes and the glow of the flashlight growing closer. Once his friend was in sight, Hector rushed over and helped prop him up into a sitting position against a tree. Tears welled up in their eyes as they looked at each other.

"Oh, man, am I glad to see you, bro! I didn't think I'd ever find you."

"How did you get here so fast? I only texted you twenty minutes before I found you in the forest. It would have taken longer than that just to drive here from town."

"I was already in the area. As soon as you left with those Grim Reaper dudes, I found one of my boys, Luis, and we made it to his car in time to see you guys leave. We followed you, and I guess the thugs you were with didn't notice. As soon as they turned down that dirt path, my boy chickened out on following them any farther. We stayed there until I pulled you up on the app."

"What app?" Richard asked.

"A couple weeks ago, Tommy found this GPS tracker app that we downloaded onto our phones. He put it on your phone as well."

"When the heck did he do that?"

"About a week ago. I guess you asked him for help downloading a game or something, and he loaded it on your phone at that time. We were gonna tell you, but I guess we forgot. If we were supposed to be your support team, Tommy figured there might be a need to track you down at some point. Great thinking on his part, eh? At any rate, I pulled you up on the tracker app and saw that you stopped moving about a mile after turning down the dirt road. We were just about to call the cops when we saw you take off into the forest. We turned the car around and did our best to follow, but you kept getting deeper into the woods. When you stopped moving, I jumped out and took off into the forest. Fortunately, Luis had a flashlight in his car."

"So I guess I didn't need to use the bird stunt after all, eh?"

"No, man. That bird saved your butt big-time! The signal kept getting weaker and weaker as you got deeper into the woods. We'd pretty much lost you when you sent that text. That message was just enough to give me a general direction to go in, but if it wasn't for your help, it could have been hours before I stumbled across you." Hector gasped when he saw the blood that covered most of Richard's upper body and the front of his pants. "Crap! You're hella messed up, dude! That's a lotta blood. And why the hell did you take your shirt off? You're going to freeze to death out here! Can you follow me back to the car? I think it's about two miles from here. I'm pretty sure I can find my way back."

"I don't think so," Richard whispered. "I can barely move, and my head is spinning. You're gonna need to go back for help."

"Don't worry. I got this, brother! Before I go, take my shirt so you don't freeze to death waiting for the cavalry." Hector unbuttoned the long-sleeved cowboy shirt and pulled off his T-shirt. Carefully working with Richard to avoid further aggravating his injuries, he pulled the T-shirt over his head and helped him with the long-sleeved shirt to give him a second layer of clothing for added warmth.

What could I have possibly done to deserve friends like this? How does the saying go—a good friend is someone who's willing to give you the shirt off their back? Hector is the literal embodiment of that standard.

"Okay, man. I better get going. Gonna freeze my cojones off, but I guess the cold will make me run faster, right?"

Richard said, "Hector, I can't thank you enough. You're absolutely a lifesaver!" With what little strength he had left, he reached out his right hand.

Hector walked back and grabbed it firmly. As they shook hands, an odd sensation came over Richard. It felt like something was draining out of him. It was not painful or especially unpleasant, but it was very unusual. Looking up at his friend, he could see Hector's eyes widening and his body shaking slightly.

Releasing their handshake, Hector said, "Man, I'll be back as fast as I can." He disappeared into the bushes.

After Hector jogged fifty or sixty feet, he felt an amazing lightness in his body. His feet starting to move faster and faster. Expecting to be out of breath any minute, he instead felt better than he could ever remember. As the trees and bushes flew past him, a realization hit him. *Holy cow! Richie must have somehow transferred his super speed into me? Oh, hell yeah! Let's do this!*

For the next ten minutes, Hector flew through the trees, hurdling logs, ducking under branches with ease, and loving every second of it. The exhilaration was amazing, and he felt as if he could run forever. At the road, he could just make out the taillight of his friend's car about a mile ahead. With a clear path in front of him, he started sprinting. Everything around him became little more than a blur as he raced to the car.

After twenty seconds, his lungs finally started to burn, but he continued to push on. Once he was a hundred yards from the car, he began putting on the brakes. He slowed to a jog as he reached the vehicle.

Luis had since fallen asleep. Startled into consciousness, he floundered to find the button to roll down the window. "Dude! You scared the crap outta me! Don't do that again! So did you find him? And what happened to your shirt?"

"I did," Hector answered. "He's about two miles from here. You gotta call 911. The battery on my phone just died. That GPS app eats up juice like crazy."

Luis glanced at the clock in the dashboard. "Two miles? Wow, you made great time! So is he hurt? Is that why he's not with you?"

"Great guess, Einstein. You think I told you to call 911 so they could bring him some cookies? Yes, he's hurt! Now get out your stupid phone and make the call!"

Richard stayed in the fetal position, and he actually felt a bit better as time passed. The two shirts helped tremendously with the cold. His violent shivering generated some body heat, which was caught between the layers of cloth and eventually warmed him to a point where he could start to think rationally again. He was still not comfortable by any stretch, but he was pretty confident that he would not freeze to death while waiting for help. He was fairly sure that the bleeding had finally stopped. Once he quit exerting himself, his body was finally able to start clotting the wounds on his chest, and though he was still very weak, he was optimistic that he would not bleed to death.

After what he guessed to be about an hour, he heard voices in the forest. Hearing his name made his heart soar, and he nearly started to giggle with joy until he realized that he'd most likely need to yell back so they could find him. He was still unbelievably tired, and taking the deep breath to call out would likely disrupt his wounds. *I suppose I could just stay here and let them find me. Pretty sure they'd come across me eventually. No. I can't do that. They might take a wrong turn and end up out of earshot before I realize it. On top of that, Hector did so much for me tonight. I can do this one thing for him.* Rolling onto his back to allow for full expansion of his diaphragm, Richard sucked in deeply and yelled, "Over here!"

The pain was excruciating, and he prayed that he would only have to do it once. After two minutes without a reply, Richard started gathering his strength to shout a second time.

A beam of light shot out from behind a tree and hit him squarely in the eye.

"I see him over here!"

It was not Hector's voice—it was most likely an EMT or a park ranger—but it was the most beautiful sound Richard had ever heard.

CHAPTER 13

A piercing bright light slowly pulled Richard out of unconsciousness and back into reality. He was startled at first by the unfamiliar figure standing over him, but as his head cleared, the events of the past day started to come back to him. He was in a hospital bed, and the person standing over him appeared to be a doctor. He looked competent enough. He was in his forties and had thinning hair and what looked like three days' growth of a beard. His glasses were halfway down his nose, and after looking into Richard's eyes with a small flashlight, he stood up and pushed them back in place like Coach Jed would often do. "He's coming around now," the man said.

"Oh, sweetie!" Richard's mother said. "Oh, Richie, my poor baby! What the heck happened? Hector said that a couple of guys grabbed you as you were leaving the dance and took you up into the hills where you were attacked by a mountain lion."

Still pretty groggy, Richard opted to use his current mental state as an excuse to not fill her in on all the details. "Hey, Mom. Glad to see you. I can't quite remember what happened. It's all kind of a blur."

Richard's mom hugged him firmly, aggravating the wounds on his chest and sending streaks of pain straight into his mind. That instantly cleared up any lingering grogginess. She quickly pulled back. "Oh, Richie. Did that hurt? I'm so sorry. I'm just so glad to see that you're okay! He's going to be okay, right, Doctor?"

"He lost a good amount of blood, but we replaced that, cleaned out and stitched up his chest wounds, and have him on an antibiotic to fight off any sort of infection. I'd like to keep him here overnight just to be safe, but he should be fine to go home tomorrow morning."

"Let me go get your father and sister. They just left a few minutes ago to grab some lunch in the cafeteria." Richard's mother exited along with the doctor, leaving him alone in the hospital room. As crazy as Hector's story was about getting kidnapped and being attacked by a mountain lion, it wasn't really that far off.

Fighting off a splitting headache, Richard struggled to remember what exactly had happened. He clearly remembered the part where he was nearly torn to pieces by the big monster who just happened to be his cousin, but after that, it all got kinda hazy. He remembered running through the forest, stopping to rest, and the cold. Boy, did he remember the cold! He knew that Hector found him, gave him his shirt, and left to go get help. At one point, he was being carried through the forest on a gurney, and then he was in the ambulance.

Glancing down and lifting the covers, he could see the bandages on his chest. He let his head fall back on the pillow and looked up at the ceiling. *The necklace! Where is it?* In a panic, Richard glanced around the room. There were no signs of his clothes. *Don't panic. When you go to the hospital, they remove all of your clothes and store everything for you. Unless the clothes were already thrashed—and they just throw them away! What if they thought the necklace was some stupid prop from my costume and tossed it? What if it's gone forever! I can't just leave this world with a crazed Ahote wolf running around and causing havoc. Crap! I'm not dead yet, and I'm quite certain that he'd very much like to rectify that fact. What if he goes after my family this time?*

Richard was nearly hyperventilating when his mom returned with his dad and sister.

Ayiana said, "What's wrong, Richie? You're white as a ghost. Are you in a lot of pain? Do you need me to call the doctor?"

He fought to calm himself. "No, Mom. I'm okay. I'm just trying to figure out what happened. Do you know where they put all my stuff?"

"I'm not sure, sweetie. I think that they cut most of the clothes off to avoid aggravating your wounds. Do you want me to look around?"

"Yes please." Richard tried his best to hide the panic in his voice.

Richard's dad said, "So how are you feeling, son?"

Realizing that he'd need to calm the hell down to keep them from figuring out that something was up, Richard took a deep breath. "Hey, Pop. I'm okay. My chest hurts like hell, but I'll live."

"You gave the three of us quite a scare when we got that call from Hector last night, telling us that you were on your way to the hospital."

Richard thought, *I gotta see Hector. He'd know what happened.*

"I think I found your things," Richard's mom called out from the other side of the room. Reaching into the bottom of a closet, she pulled out a large plastic bag with clothes in it. Streaks of blood covered the plastic.

"Thanks, Mom. Can you set it over here next to me? I just want to see if my phone and wallet are mixed in with the clothes. Say, is Hector here?"

"No, dear. His parents came to pick him at the hospital last night. He called me a few hours ago, but you were still out like a light. Did you want me to call him?"

"Yes… uh, I mean no. Can I just borrow your phone for a minute? I want to call him myself."

"It's no problem for me to call. I know you're still not feeling well."

"No, I'm good." He fought to keep his voice down at a somewhat normal volume. "I just really want to give him a call to thank him for saving my life. Do you guys mind leaving the room for a few minutes? I'm just feeling really emotional right now."

Now who's the Academy Award-winning actor? Richard thought. *That little performance even impressed me!*

"Oh, sweetie." She handed him her cell phone. "We understand. Come on, everyone. Let's give Richard some privacy."

As they walked out of the room, Richard overheard his dad saying, "If the kid wanted privacy, he should have said something earlier. I could have finished my lunch."

Richard's mom punched her husband's shoulder.

Milene turned back toward him and said, "Hey, bro. Glad you're not dead… I guess? I would have liked your room though."

Richard could not help but chuckle at the comment—until the pain of his chest wound quickly brought him back to the moment. He grabbed the plastic bag and pulled it onto the bed. He fumbled with the plastic tie and began tearing at the plastic until it gave way, sending clothes flying all over his bed. In a full-blown panic, he rummaged through the clothing until his iPhone, keys, and wallet fell out unto the covers. He tore through everything a second time, but there was still no necklace! *It can't be gone. It can't be gone! I've only got one hope left!* He pulled out his mom's phone, scrolled through his mom's contacts, and called Hector. It was three of the longest rings of his life. His heart was racing a mile a minute, and he had completely broken out in a cold sweat.

After what seemed like an eternity, Hector said, "Oh, Mrs. Locklear? How's Richie doing? Is he okay?"

"It's me. I borrowed my mom's phone. They're down the hall. Tell me that you have it!"

"Have what? Your wallet? Your phone? No, man. I didn't think to grab either one. Sorry, man. Is one of them missing?"

"No! My wallet and phone are right here. I mean the necklace! It's gone!" Rich felt nauseous and light-headed.

"Oh, that? I grabbed it last night. Figured it was in safer keeping it with me. Ha! Dude, you should have heard your voice, bro. You were freaking hard!" Hector was barely holding back his laughter.

"You decide to screw with me now?" Richard felt a mixture of relief and fury. "You're aware that I'm in a hospital and that I nearly died yesterday? Are you trying to give me a heart attack after going through all the effort of saving me?"

"Sorry, Richie. I wasn't thinking. I knew that you'd realize it was gone and lose it, and I thought it might be a hoot to have a little fun with you. I didn't think you'd get so upset about it. Don't worry, man. I've got the necklace safe and sound. I've got you covered. You gotta tell me what happened!"

Richard sighed and sank down onto his bed. It felt like the weight of the world had been lifted off his chest, and the fatigue of his outburst overwhelmed him. He was unbelievably tired. Richard finally said, "Don't worry about it. You taking the necklace was one of the smartest thinks you've ever done! I owe you another one, brother. I've got to get some sleep, but I'll fill you in on everything once I'm back home tomorrow. You ain't gonna believe it!"

Richard ended the call just as his mom poked her head in to check on him. "Richie, did you speak with Hector? Were you able to thank him the way you wanted to?"

"Yeah, Mom. It was good. Thanks for letting me borrow your phone. I think I'm going to rest for a bit. I'm super tired."

The following day, Monday, Richard returned home. That afternoon, he started feeling better. As soon as school was out, Hector, Tommy, and Jenny came over to visit. His mom must have cautioned them with respect about his fragile state because Jenny whispered, "Richie, are how you feeling?"

Once Hector could see that Richard's mom was on her way back down the stairs, he quickly closed the door, pulled over the computer chair, and rested his forearms on the back support. "Okay, man. You gotta tell us what happened out there!"

Tommy sat in a bean-bag chair, and Jenny sat at the foot of Richard's bed. After sitting up and positioning another pillow behind his back, Richard told them everything in detail. When he told them that Ahote was the leader of the band of outlaws that had been terrorizing the town, his three friends looked on in silence, but their expressions spoke volumes. Richard described in detail how his cousin had transformed him into a werewolf, but he didn't go into a lot of specific details about his battle with the beast.

The three of them were in shock and Tommy had a particularly puzzled look.

After a long silence, Hector said, "Dude, you just fought a freaking werewolf! You're totally a superhero now, brother! Tommy, we've got to come up with a cool name for him and design a costume or something."

"Let's not get too excited about this, Hector," Tommy said. "Remember that this thing is still out there. If it is a werewolf, we might have much bigger problems. Everything I've read about werewolves says they're pretty much invincible unless you've got a silver bullet. I don't know about you, but I don't have access to a gun, any significant amount of silver, or any equipment. I wouldn't know how to make silver into a bullet if my life depended upon it."

"I don't think it's a werewolf like the way they portray them in the movies," Richard said. "I mean it was definitely part man and part wolf, but I'm pretty sure it's still flesh and bone. I got in a few good shots, and it can be hurt. The only reason I was able to escape is because I somehow managed to take out one of his knees with a shoulder block."

"Well, that's some good news at least," Tommy said. "As long as it's not supernatural, we should be able to find some way to kill it! Aw, snap. I forgot for a second that this thing is actually your flesh and blood. This must be really hard on you, dude."

Richard paused and then said, "It is… obviously I have no great feelings of fondness for Ahote, but he is my aunt's oldest son. I love my auntie a lot, and it would destroy her if something happened to him, but it would be even worse if she ever discovered what a horrible thing he has become. Perhaps there's a way to take the necklace from him before he transforms into the beast."

"That would be the best-case scenario," Hector said. "We just need to come up with some sort of plan to try to make that happen."

With his mind racing through different scenarios and strategies, Richard realized that Jenny had not said a word since she came in. She just looked blankly at the wall on the other side of the room. Richard said, "Guys, why don't you go downstairs and get a snack or something? Give us a minute here."

When it was just the two of them, Richard closed his bedroom door.

Jenny was sitting on his bed, and she looked up at him with tear-filled eyes.

"Are you okay?"

She leaped up and wrapped her arms around him.

Still injured and not currently wearing the necklace, he nearly fell to the floor with the enthusiasm of her grasp. He fought off the pain of the newly aggravated chest wounds and hugged her back with what little strength he had.

"You nearly died out there yesterday!" Her head was buried in the crook of his neck. "When Hector took off after you at the dance, he only had time to tell me that these three skeleton dudes grabbed you and that he was going after them. That's all that I knew for the rest of the night—until he called me Sunday morning after he got you to the hospital. I totally lost it once he left. I couldn't even go onto the stage after we won the costume contest. Did you know we won?"

"No. Somehow, it never came up in conversation—until now," Richard said.

"I'm serious, Richie!" she said. "If you'd have gotten seriously hurt or killed, I don't know what I'd do. You're like my best friend in the whole world, and I just couldn't bear to lose you. And now that I know what's really out there—and that it wants to kill you—I'm absolutely terrified!"

"Yeah. I'm pretty scared too. I'm still trying to process this whole thing. At this point, I can't just sit back and do nothing. That monster is still out there, and if he hasn't heard already, he will soon figure out that I'm still alive. Who knows what his plan of attack could be? Next time, he could go after one of you or my family. I wouldn't put anything past that bastard."

Jenny took a step back and looked him in the eyes. "Just know that, whatever happens, we'll be there with you."

"Thanks. That means a lot to me, but I can't ask any of you to put your lives in danger because of my mistakes. When it comes down to it, it's going to have to be me and Ahote."

"How could any of this be *your* fault?" Jenny asked.

"It's a long story, but I can promise you that my actions inadvertently led to where we are now. At least I still have the necklace! Without that, I'd be a goner for sure. Speaking of the necklace, are the guys still downstairs? I need to get it back from Hector. He took it off me in the forest for safekeeping. I'm pretty sure I heal faster when I'm wearing it."

"Oh, you mean this?" Hector and Tommy walked in with the necklace, four sodas, and a container of Chips Ahoy cookies. "Your mom thought we must be hungry and thirsty, and she loaded us up."

After taking the necklace from his friend, Richard fastened it around his neck. Within seconds, he felt better. As his strength returned, he said, "Hector, thanks again, buddy. That was some fast thinking taking this off, before taking me to the hospital. That decision will likely save my life the next time I run into Ahote."

"No problem, bro," Hector answered. "Like I said, I got your back. Besides, it ain't like the thing is going do me any good, right?"

"Guess not." Richard leaned back against his headboard.

"But you already knew that, right?" Tommy said. "You already tried to use the necklace last month, and it doesn't work on you because you're not a member of Richie's tribe."

"Yeah, I know," Hector answered.

"So why bring it up again?" Tommy said. "And at the end of your comment, you posed it as a question—as if to ask Richard if he might know something that you don't. What are you getting at?"

The three friends looked curiously at Hector, and he finally said, "Okay. Something happened in the forest that I wasn't able to explain. At first, I didn't tell anybody. I'm not sure exactly what's up, but Rich was able to let me borrow his deer speed for a while."

"He did what?" Tommy shouted.

"It was just after I lent him my shirt and needed to find my way back to my buddy's car to call for help. Right before I left, he shook my hand to thank me, and I got this weird, tingly feeling all over me."

"I remember that!" Richard said. "I felt like I was a goner if he didn't come back with help pretty quickly. As I shook his hand, I actually thought to myself—please go as fast as you can!"

"So you didn't give him the necklace, right? He took that off of you later?" Tommy said.

"No. I still had the necklace on, and I didn't have a clue that this happened until just now. But now that I thinking about it, I kind of remember getting a weird feeling when we shook hands. It was like something was being drained out of me."

Jenny said, "So let me get this straight. You let Hector try on your magic necklace—and not me? And then you gave him your super-animal running? So do you still have it?"

Hector said, "No. It only lasted for about thirty minutes."

"Interesting." Tommy rubbed his chin between his thumb and index finger and looked at Richard. "So, taking into account this information, you should be able to transfer any of these abilities— at least temporarily—to one or more other people. This gives us a number of other options that we didn't have before."

"Listen, guys," Richard said. "Like I was just telling Jenny, this is my problem. I'm the one who needs to deal with it. This thing is dangerous, and even if I could somehow transfer some of my abilities into one or more of you, I would never be able to live with myself if someone got hurt or killed! Plus, we don't have any idea how this thing works. The other night could have been a fluke, and even if I could somehow do it again, the abilities could disappear without a moment's notice—and you'd be a goner for sure. There are just too many unknowns for us to take the risk."

"You're right," Tommy answered. "That's why more testing is required."

CHAPTER 14

The rest of the school week was painfully slow for Richard. His head was a monsoon of thoughts, fears, and emotions about what his next plan of action should be for dealing with Ahote. Fearing for his family's life, he contemplated long and hard about telling them everything, so they would at least be aware of their possible peril, but he ultimately decided against it. Sharing his secret would only further involve them in this catastrophe, and he was pretty confident that Ahote wouldn't go full werewolf in the middle of town. It would create way too much attention that he absolutely didn't need or want. The last time, his actions were meticulously planned out, and it made sense that he would most likely use a similar tactic the next time. Detailed plans would take time. Though Richard had no actual proof pertaining to his theory, he was fairly confident that he had at least had a week or two before Ahote would try anything again.

Richard stayed home for a second day on Tuesday, but by Wednesday, he was feeling much better and went back to school. Having worn the necklace for nearly thirty hours straight, the wounds on his chest were healing at a faster-than-normal rate. He'd have three gnarly scars to show for it, but he believed that, in another week, he would pretty much be back to normal. His friends at lunch confirmed their plans to return to school on Saturday morning to conduct further testing on the power-transfer thing. Richard resisted involving his friends in the situation, but he had to agree that there was no harm in additional experiments in a controlled environment.

After school on Thursday, Richard could tell that something was off with his mom. She was sitting at the kitchen table with a glass of wine and staring blankly at the backyard. She never drank in the middle of the day, and there was tremendous concern in her eyes.

"What's wrong, Mom?"

"Oh, geez. You scared me, sweetie. It's really nothing, Richie."

"It's not nothing, Mom. I can tell. You're drinking wine at three in the afternoon."

"Okay. I guess you're old enough to handle it, and you should know what's going on with your family. In fact, I think it might have something to do with the guys who grabbed you on Saturday night and that mountain lion you were attacked by. Just promise that you won't tell your sister until we know more about what's going on."

Richard was very nervous. What could possibly upset her so much? Could Ahote have already done something else? "Okay, Mom. I promise. So what's up?"

"I got a call from Aunt Lisana a few minutes ago. The police just left her place. You remember when Ahote took off several weeks ago to stay with some friends? That's what he told your aunt the one time he called home. A few hours ago, three cop cars drove up and started asking her questions about several bodies they found in the woods not too far from the reservation on Sunday. Apparently, three people in their twenties were killed by some crazy animal, and when they asked a fourth person who was only injured in the attack, Ahote's name was brought up as being the person responsible. To make the story even crazier, the people killed and the person they asked were all part of the biker gang that kidnapped Jenny last week! The whole thing just doesn't make any sense! How could Ahote possibly get caught up with such people—and why would he be involved in the deaths of people who were attacked by a wild animal?"

What the hell? Ahote must have killed these three men, but why? They were supposed to be members of his gang. What would possess him to turn on his own people? Perhaps in his beast form, he doesn't have full control of his actions. After losing his primary target, he must have turned on his fellow gang members.

That turn of events likely brought an end to whatever leadership role he had with Lobo Del Taco, or whatever the name was of that gang he was supposedly commanding. He could not imagine that any of them would still follow him after he killed several other members. If he was largely on his own—and likely on the run—it would significantly diminish his ability to create another elaborate plan. The smartest move would be to leave the area, perhaps the state, and find a different group of delinquents to worship him for his mystical shape-shifting abilities. *Perhaps my best course of action would be to lay low and see if he shows up again. If he does, we'll deal with him at that time. No. I cannot in good conscience allow this creature I had a part in creating roam free, potentially putting dozens of lives at risk. I must find a way to take back the necklace or stop Ahote once and for all!*

"I know this is all a lot to process, honey," Ayiana said. "You've probably got a million things running through your head right now. This will all end up being a big misunderstanding, and everything will be okay."

"Sure, Mom," Richard answered. In his head, he was having a completely different conversation. *If only I could tell you what's really going on here. There are a lot of ways this could turn out, but in all likelihood, the result will be far from okay.*

On Friday, Richard shared the news about Ahote with Hector and Tommy. He thought about telling Jenny too, but he decided against it. The three debated the positives and negatives of this new information, and after some discussion, they unanimously agreed that Ahote could not just be left to whatever his devious mind could devise. They had to come up with a way to eliminate this threat!

The following morning, the four met up at the high school at eight thirty for a number of "ability-transfer experiments," as Tommy described them. On the track, Richard tried to reenact whatever he did to transfer his deer speed to Hector. It took several tries to get into the correct mental state to successfully hand off his abilities, but the fourth time worked—and Hector proceeded to run the hundred-meter dash in only 9.27 seconds. It was about half a second behind Richard's time, likely due to his shorter legs, but he seemed more than pleased by the time based on his celebratory yells and high fives, which everyone feared would draw the attention of the entire neighborhood.

In the weight room, Tommy insisted that he should be the person to try out the bear-strength ability. It only took two tries before the handoff occurred, and Tommy instantly felt the rush of superhuman power flowing into him. He started out with three hundred pounds on the bench press and put it up with minimal effort. He made four more lifts before finally stopping at 650 pounds.

Throughout these tests, Jenny kept pressing Richard to see what enhanced ability he would let her try. Bursting with excitement following Tommy's last lift, she said, "Okay, Richie. It's my turn! What are you going to give me? You've also got crazy dexterity, right? I'll take that once since we haven't tested it yet."

"I actually wanted to have you try out the bird-control ability. I know how much you liked it the other week. It's a really cool thing to be able to do."

"You want me to try the bird-control thing? What the hell is that supposed to mean? Tommy gets to be the Hulk, Hector gets to be the Flash, and I get to be Crazy-Bird Lady?"

"It's not like that," Richard said. "This is super important! As a bird, you can be our eyes and ears and let us know when Ahote's coming. This thing is fast, and every second will count. Plus, you can probably even distract him by flying by his head or something. Oh, and you have not lived until you've flown! Once inside the bird, you experience every possible sensation of flying. Trust me—it's awesome! It's way better than being able to do backflips and stuff."

"I don't know," she replied. "It still seems like I'm getting the short end of the stick, but I guess I can give it a try."

Richard sighed deeply with relief when she agreed to try out the bird-control abilities. Even thought everything Richard had told her was completely true, his motive was based entirely on her safety.

She could do her bird thing from dozens or even hundreds of yards away from any conflict. If it ever came to pass that the four of them actually went up against this monster, Richard wanted her as far away from the action as possible.

In the end, Jenny took to the ability like a duck to water, and within a few minutes, she took over the consciousness of a pigeon that was flying around the school. A few minutes later, she found she could control a second pigeon at the same time. Richard was stunned at this revelation; it had never occurred to him that he could possibly control more than one bird at a time. She was actually better at it that he was! Once she came out of her bird trance, Jenny nearly exploded with excitement on how amazing it felt flying!

"Mission accomplished," Richard whispered to himself. Thankfully, neither Jenny nor anyone else mentioned the feather's other ability of being able to fall great distances like a feather. It was something Richard did not want to test that day, and to Richard's relief, they didn't have to.

Throughout the morning, several more experiments were conducted to explore factors like whether more than one ability could be transferred at a time, how and when abilities could or would be transferred back to Richard, and various other aspects of the necklace that would provide critical information—when and if they needed to use them.

Tommy was fastidiously taking notes of every finding. After the morning was complete, he came up with several theories with respect to Richard's ability to transfer his abilities. Richard could only transfer his abilities to another person through physical touch. If an ability was handed off to another person, Richard no longer had access to it until it was returned to him.

He could transfer multiple abilities at a time, but no one—other than Richard—could have more than one enhanced ability at a time. He could transfer speed to Hector and strength to Tommy at the same time—but not speed *and* strength to only Hector. If any skin-to-skin contact was made following the transfer of abilities, the ability would switch back to Richard immediately.

If no physical contact was made after the transfer, the ability would automatically return to Richard based on a variable time frame. For Hector, the switch happened after ten minutes, but he also reported that it stayed with him for longer the first time. For Tommy, the ability did not transfer back for close to thirty minutes. For Jenny, it was about twenty minutes. He believed that the variance was due to something he called the "Hulk factor." Once the immediate danger passed, and the Hulk felt like he was basically safe, he would switch back to David Banner. Likewise, as long as someone was actively using the ability, it would not switch back to Richard unless physical contact was made. Tommy recommended further experimentation to add evidence to his hypothesis.

Richard was glad they conducted the tests since it provided them with a lot of great information on the mechanics of how the crazy thing worked.

Tommy made a point to clarify that his theories were based on minimal experimentation and were far from proven facts. Richard still had a lot of concerns with the last part.

"We did some good work here today." Tommy put his notebook and supplies into his backpack. "We know a lot more than we did before, which will help us tremendously if we ever find ourselves going up against that thing. Unfortunately, that's the one variable that we're still largely in the dark about. We still know almost nothing about this creature, which is very concerning."

"I may actually be able to help with that," Richard answered. "If there's one guy in the world who might know something about this thing, I think I know who it is."

The following morning, Richard's dad drove him up to the reservation. He had made plans earlier in the week to visit, and his grandfather was eager to see him after his harrowing experience. He thought about going up the night before, so they could go on their traditional Sunday morning run, but his chest was still healing.

His stomach churned like a wriggling octopus during the twenty-minute trip. He remembered the angst in his grandfather's face as he detailed his earlier experiences with the necklace. Richard was torn about the right course of action, and he would have to further burden his grandfather with even more devastating news.

Worst of all, he would need to explain how the entire thing was essentially his fault! If he had never attacked Ahote, his cousin wouldn't have overheard the details needed to find the second necklace. Richard did not know whether to share the information with his grandfather. It was a long shot that he would have any useful guidance to provide. Ultimately, he decided that it was the right thing to do. Richard had withheld important information from his grandfather in the past, and he decided that he would never do so again.

The two met with a hug as they always did, but Helaku was more gentle than usual. After a few minutes of chitchat between his father and grandfather, his dad left.

As Richard and his grandfather sat down in the family room, Richard was more nervous than ever.

"How are you, Richard? You had me worried to death when I got the call from your mother at the hospital. Thankfully, by then, she already knew you would be okay, but the fact that this happened to you upset me greatly. How are your injuries?"

"Not too bad. It's actually healing quickly. I should be pretty much back to normal in another week or so."

The slightest hint of the necklace peeked out from under his collar.

"It helps you heal faster, doesn't it?"

"It does. How did you know that?" Richard said.

"Just a hunch I suppose. It's really quite a miraculous thing you have there. Tremendous potential for good I imagine… if used correctly."

Richard could see where this conversation was headed. "And tremendous potential for evil if used improperly, right?"

Helaku said, "That's not what I meant at all. Did you mean the event with Ahote? I suppose that was a dark moment for you. It's actually a good thing that this event remains in your conscience. It will keep you on the straight and narrow if a similar situation comes up in the future. You must put that behind you and look ahead to the future. Tell me what happened last week."

He took a deep breath. "It's a good thing you're sitting down for this."

For the next twenty minutes, Richard detailed the encounter with the skeletal henchman, the drive out to the forest, and the encounter with Ahote. His cousin's appearance was initially met with confusion from his grandfather, but as the story continued, Helaku turned white as a ghost. Richard almost stopped several times, but he knew it would be less painful to get it all at once instead of bits and pieces at a time. The recap finished with his rescue in the forest and the discovery that he could temporarily transfer his abilities to other people.

Following his completion of the tale, they were totally silent. Richard was looking at his grandfather, and Helaku was staring out the window toward a majestic redwood about a hundred feet away. Richard guessed that his grandfather was likely desperate for the strength to process this tidal wave of horrible information he'd just received, and he looked to the strongest, most powerful thing he could think of for inspiration.

After several long minutes, his grandfather said, "I'm grateful that I removed all the alcohol from my home years ago because I could really use a drink right now."

"Can you ever forgive me for the mistakes I've made?" Richard asked with tears welling up in his eyes.

"Of course, my son. This is not your fault! Yes, your actions did unfortunately create the series of events that led us to where we are now, but that's different than this all being your responsibility. You did not convince Ahote to blackmail your father's coworker to help him find the second necklace, and more importantly, you did not use its powers for evil—as he has apparently done. If anyone here is to blame for this, it is me."

"You?" Richard said. "How could any of this possibly be your fault?"

"Ahote is also my grandson. I've known him his entire life, and I must not have shown him the love and support I should have for his character to turn out the way it has, especially after his father left. I tried connecting with him several times as I have with you, but he was difficult. Unlike with us, Ahote and I have no common interests, and conversations with him were challenging. Even as a young boy, there was anger and frustration in him. At some point, I guess I just stopped trying to get closer. He knows how close we are, and I'm sure that it angered him greatly. I should have done more to try to get through to him and make him a better person who would not have attacked you and Chenowa in the recreation hall, which is ultimately what started this whole disaster in the first place."

"Don't say that, Grandpa," Richard said. "If there's anything I learned through this whole crazy experience, it's that you're responsible for your own destiny. Chenowa had the exact same set of circumstances as his brother, and he turned out fine. Actually, he had it worse than Ahote because he didn't have an older sibling who was always beating up on him."

"Perhaps you are right, Richard. I believe that there may just be some owl spirit in that necklace as well, given the wisdom you have shown me today, and for that, I thank you."

Richard said, "Do you happen to remember anything in the stories you've heard over the years about a wolf creature and how someone might be able to defeat it?"

Helaku sat back in his chair and sighed deeply. He looked older, weaker, and more burdened by the world. The lines in his forehead intertwined like tangled vines as he furrowed his brow. "Now that I think about it, I vaguely remember a tale my grandfather told me. It was one of the tales he shared regarding the Spirit Walker."

"What can you remember about it?" Richard asked.

"To the best of my recollection, the tale involved a Spirit Walker who was on a quest to destroy a horrible beast that was terrorizing the tribe. There was no mention of this creature having a magical necklace, but as one might expect, details get lost through generations of sharing the tale. I can't recall many specifics except that their battle ended with both of them falling off a cliff to their death. It must have been by the sea since I distinctly remember mention of the sounds of crashing waves."

"So this thing can be killed like other animals?" Richard asked.

"Some compassion, Richard," Helaku said. "This thing is part of your family! Despite the horrific transformations that may have occurred in him, we should still refer to him as Ahote. We owe him that much. From what I recall, the creature from the story did die from the fall. Richard, you're not thinking about trying to fight Ahote by yourself, are you? It's far too dangerous!"

"If not me, then who?" Richard said. "He's already killed several people, and it's not like I can just go to the police and tell them that my cousin's a werewolf. Intentional or not, this abomination is my doing. I have to at least try to stop him."

Helaku slouched down in his chair and let out a defeated groan of acceptance. He gazed blankly at the wall of the mobile home. After several seconds of silence, he said, "Just promise me that you will do everything you can to take the necklace from him so we can end this whole thing without any further violence."

"Of course, Grandpa. I don't want this anymore than you do. Trust me! If there's any way that I can avoid going toe-to-toe with that… uh… with Ahote again, I'm all for that! But if it comes to that, I'm prepared to do what I have to. I need to have a backup plan in place. I don't suppose you have any idea where that cliff is that the creature and the other Spirit Walker fell from?"

After several minutes, Helaku said, "I think I may know of a spot. It's about a ninety-minute hike from here. I used to take girls up there when I was your age. The view was incredible, and when we'd walk close to the edge, they'd get all nervous and grabby. It kinda helped set the mood."

"Ew, Grandpa. I really didn't need a visual of you picking up on girls."

"How do you think I first kissed your grandmother?"

"Okay. I get it. So can you take me there?"

"I can try. It's been decades since I've been there, but I'm pretty sure I still can find it. We should leave soon. It's supposed to rain this afternoon."

After taking a few minutes to pack some water, the two headed out. The first thirty minutes or so were spent on trails that Richard had run many times. He fondly recalled his memories of those hikes and the time spent with his grandfather, and a great sadness washed over him when he realized that this could be the last time they spent time in nature together. Neither of them spoke a word, which was very uncharacteristic for them. There was a lot to think about.

About three miles into their journey, Helaku turned off onto an overgrown trail that Richard had never been on before. The path slithered to the north between redwoods and birch trees, and then it began to slope up sharply.

Glancing back at his grandfather, Richard saw something that he had never seen before. Helaku looked genuinely tired. Given the events of the past hour, it made sense that it would have had an effect on him. Richard had never seen Helaku look quite so old and frail. "Hey, Grandpa. You look pretty tired. Do you want to try wearing the necklace for a while? My friend Tommy believes that it works for me because I'm part of the same tribe as the last Spirit Walker. It should work on you as well."

Helaku stopped and looked at Richard with a mixture of hesitation and curiosity. After several moments, he said, "No. It would not be right. The Spirit Walker chose you to be the next in line. This privilege is for young warriors—not broken old men. Thank you for the offer, but it would not feel right."

"Well, at least let me make the rest of the hike easier for you." Richard grabbed his grandfather's arm.

As Richard felt his running ability pass through his grasp, Helaku's eyes widened, and he stood up straight as an arrow. He looked at Richard with wonder and amazement. "Richard, what did you do?"

"I told you that I can temporarily transfer one of my abilities to another person. You looked really tired, so I wanted to give you a boost. Feels pretty trippy, doesn't it?"

"It feels amazing! It's like I'm a young man again. I feel like I could run forever!"

"You should go run ahead," Richard said. "Really... try it out. I'll catch up with you eventually."

"Well, I suppose I could just run until we get to the top of the ridge. Just stay on the trail, and I'll wait for you."

As the old man began jogging up the path, he was overwhelmed by how light and energized he felt. His strides quickly increased, and he bounded up the trail like a deer. Faster and faster he ran, and he could feel his white hair flowing behind him in the wind. His senses and reflexes were heightened as well. It was unlike anything he had ever felt, and he had never been more at one with nature.

At the top of the ridge, the trail leveled off and was largely straight for the next mile or so. Feeling too good to stop, he accelerated into a full sprint. The thought occurred to him that he might very well give himself a heart attack and die right there in the forest if he kept up the pace. The concern was fleeting, and the experience was too incredible to end. If that was to be his last day on earth, he could not possibly think of a better way to go out.

Completely losing track of time, Helaku realized that he was almost at the cliff. Slowing to a jog, he stopped and walked up to the edge. The ocean cascaded endlessly in front of him. The cool ocean breeze felt refreshing against his face, and he closed his eyes and breathed in deeply through his nose, taking in all the smells and sounds of the seaside. Seagulls cried out above him, and the harmony of waves crashing on rocks echoed up from below. Salt and eucalyptus were in the air, and the scent took him back to the times he spent there with his wife as teenagers. Their whole lives were ahead of them—and what a life it was. Though their time together was much shorter than he would have wanted, the love they shared was too great to measure in years. It was a bizarre combination of feelings that he was experiencing. He could not remember feeling more alive, but he longed to be with Saswanna again in the spirit world.

He thought for a second about turning back for Richard, but then decided against it. The moment was too precious to disrupt. Helaku had no idea how long it would last, and he was not going to take any of it for granted. After a few minutes, the feeling was gone. Like smoke from a campfire, it vanished in the wind. Helaku felt his weight returning, and the pain and fatigue slowly crept back into his legs. He walked over a fallen tree trunk, sat down, and looked toward the sea and the darkening clouds.

After another five minutes, he heard footsteps approaching.

Richard bounded effortlessly along the path and smiled as he approached his grandfather.

"Thank you, Grandson!" Helaku said. "You have given me a gift unlike any I have ever received—or will ever receive again. I now know what it is like to be one with the spirits of the forest. For a few minutes, I was a young man—here with my love for the first time. It is a memory I will treasure for the rest of my days."

"We can do it again if you want," Richard said. "I can do it whenever I like."

His grandfather paused for a moment and said, "No. I think the one time is better. Whatever might happen the second time could not possibly compare to this experience, and it would only detract from it by trying."

"Suit yourself—but it will be a lot longer walk back. At least, it will be mostly downhill."

Richard surveyed the area. The clearing was exactly the size he was looking for. It was about sixty yards across and about forty yards deep. A sheer rock face lined the north end of the clearing and sloped down to the east, forming an L-shaped barricade. If he could somehow get Ahote there, there wouldn't be anywhere for them to go.

He had promised his grandfather he'd make every possible effort to take the necklace from Ahote without resorting to violence, but if he was left with no other option, he was prepared to do what was needed to end it. Inching toward the edge and carefully looking down, he saw jagged, black bounders staring back up at him. There was no beach—only stony shards rising and falling through blue-green water and white foam from the churning sea.

I really hope it doesn't come to this.

CHAPTER 15

Once Richard and his grandfather returned to the reservation, he had one more stop to make before heading home. He needed to speak with Chenowa. If there was one person who might be able to communicate with Ahote, it would most likely be his brother. Now that he had ended his association with the biker gang, he was really on his own—and likely looking for some sort of connection with just about anybody. After checking the rec center, he went over to his aunt's place.

Richard had really hoped that Chenowa would be at the center so he would not have to see her. She would likely be in anguish regarding the whereabouts of her eldest son and his possible connection to three homicides. Seeing her would just make the inevitable confrontation with Ahote all the more real—and the stakes all the higher.

Walking up the steps to the door, he could hear an old *Family Ties* episode on TV. Chenowa was there for sure; it was one of his favorite shows. Since they could only afford basic cable, his options were fairly limited. Richard hypothesized that—on some conscious or subconscious level—the show provided him with a brief escape to a reality with a family dynamic including a loving mother and father and siblings who all deeply cared for each other and generally got along well.

Opening the door, Lisana's eyes widened. "Richard? What a nice surprise! Come in, sweetie. Chenowa will be happy to see you." Following a hug that seemed to last a few seconds longer than usual, she released him and gave Richard a quick glance before turning back to the dishes. Richard felt her sadness in his chest like a weight pulling his heart toward his stomach.

Chenowa met Richard halfway to the couch. They greeted each other with their usual hand grasp, bro hug, and slaps on the back.

Chenowa said, "Great to see ya, cuz. It's pretty unbelievable what went down with you last week. You gotta show me those killer scars you'll have after you're all healed up. You doing okay, man?"

"Yeah, I'm good," Richard said. "But I was hoping that we could take a walk. Some stuff I wanted to talk with you about."

"Sure thing. Just let me grab a sweatshirt."

They walked along the northern edge of the reservation, and a lump that felt as big as a softball formed in Richard's throat. "So that's some crazy stuff that's going on with Ahote, eh?"

After a pause, Chenowa said, "Yeah, *crazy* is the word for it. Did you hear all the details? The police were here, and they think he was involved in the deaths of those three guys who were mauled to death by a bear or something. The whole thing doesn't make any sense."

"Have you had any contact with him since he took off?" Richard asked.

Chenowa looked surprised or panicked. "Why do you ask?"

Richard said, "I just got a feeling he's feeling pretty alone out there right now. Since he doesn't have many friends, I thought he might have tried calling or something."

"He sent me a text two days ago. It was from a number I never saw before. One of those burner phones? He told me that there was some stuff going on, but it was not what other people—specifically *you*—will tell me it is. He didn't go into much detail, but he basically said that situations had changed and I'd need to make a choice again between the two of you. He told me I needed to make sure I made the right choice this time! You have any idea what the hell he's talking about?"

Richard signed deeply and looked down at his shoes. "I do—and he's not lying to you. Situations have definitely changed, and you will need to choose a side again. That's actually why I'm here now...

to tell you what really happened, and how all of this will affect you and your mom. Let's go over to that bench. You'll want to be sitting down for this."

Over the next several minutes, Richard delivered a greatly abridged version of his tale regarding the discovery of the necklace and the events leading up to the confrontation with Ahote in the forest. After a moment to let everything sink in, Richard continued on with the remainder of the story, climaxing with the unimaginable reality that Ahote was now some sort of inhuman monstrosity who had nearly killed him in the forest. Richard kept waiting for his cousin to jump in or cut him off, but he just let Richard keep talking. There was at least a full minute of silence. Each second was torture, and Richard didn't know if he should say anything else.

After what seemed like an eternity, Chenowa said, "What kind of an idiot to you think I am? That old strip of leather around your neck with some animal parts hanging from it gives you superpowers? And my brother is a werewolf now! Am I missing anything here?"

"No, that's pretty much the gist of it. I know this all sounds totally unbelievable, but I swear to you that it's all true."

"Prove it!" Chenowa said.

Realizing that he'd have to do something if he was going to have any chance of getting his cousin to believe his story, he walked over to an old pickup truck that was parked about twenty yards away. Once he was directly behind the tailgate, he said, "Now don't freak out and start yelling or anything."

Richard took a deep breath, squatted, and grasp the bumper of the truck. Taking a moment to focus, he pulled up with a deadlift movement. Within a few seconds, he returned to a fully standing position with the back wheels at least two inches off the ground. Holding it for a few moments just to make sure his cousin got a good look, he carefully lowered the vehicle again.

Chenowa's pale face was overwhelmed with shock and disbelief, and he started swaying a bit. He sat down in the dirt, rested his elbows on his knees, and stared at the ground. "Holy crap! That thing is real? I mean really real? I guess I have to consider that what you said about Ahote could possibly have some truth to it as well. I mean you've never lied to me before. I just thought that you went Koo-Koo-Co-Co Puffs on me. After seeing this, I don't know what the hell to think."

"I know it's a lot to take in," Richard said. "I would not have burdened you with this, but I need your help. I believe you're the only person who can help me speak with Ahote and try to talk some sense into him. I'm hoping we can convince him to give back the necklace, so everything will just go back to normal."

"What if he decides not to return it and tries to kill you again?" Chenowa said.

"I won't lie to you. If it comes to that, and he transforms again, I'll do whatever is necessary to stop him! I guess the big question is if you are willing to help me."

After a few moments, Chenowa said, "I don't know yet. I'll need some time to think about everything. It's just a lot to take in all at once."

"Of course!" Richard said. "This is an unfair, unbelievably difficult thing I'm asking of you. You take as long as you need to decide—and just let me know. Of course, in the meantime, be sure not to tell your mom about any of this. God knows that she's been through enough this week—and it really is best if no more people know about this than are absolutely necessary."

CHAPTER 16

On Thursday morning, Richard heard back from Chenowa. It was an agonizingly slow three days, waiting to see if the calculated risk of telling his cousin everything would pay off or completely blow up in his face. He shared the details of his discussions with Hector, Tommy, and Jenny, and they all had ideas and opinions about what their next course of action should be. Richard was not prepared to do anything until he heard back from Chenowa. He was getting ready for school when he heard the familiar ping from his iPhone. Grabbing the device, he opened the text from Chenowa: "Richie, I gave it a lot of thought, and I'm pretty sure I can get him to meet with me. I won't tell him you'll be there, but the three of us can have a talk so I can get both sides of the story. I need to know when and where you want to coordinate the meeting."

Richard thought for a minute and then replied: "Thanks, cousin! I know that this was a hard decision for you. Give me a couple days to think about the best way to do this. I'll let you know."

After hitting Send, he sat down on his bed and started to feel nauseous. *This is really happening! I am intentionally going to confront this monster who nearly killed me less than two weeks ago. How am I going to do it? Will I simply meet with Ahote and Chenowa by myself or have the gang for backup? It would certainly be nice to have someone there with me, but having strangers there might spook Ahote, making it more difficult to negotiate.* His head was throbbing with the possibilities. He would need additional perspective, and he could really use input from Hector, Jenny, and Tommy.

The four of them talked about it at lunch and agreed to meet at Tommy's place after school to discuss several ideas. Tommy had a large chalkboard in his bedroom that he used to work on mathematical equations, and his parents would be working until after five o'clock. They would have the house to themselves for nearly two hours.

Tommy had set up a small ice chest with sodas, a large bowl filled with tortilla chips, and a smaller bowl with salsa.

Richard thought, *How thoughtful of Tommy to provide refreshments to assist in coming up with a plan that could very well get one or more of them killed.*

When Hector and Jenny arrived, and the four of them began throwing out ideas.

Tommy stood at the board with a piece of chalk in his hand. "So let's start by establishing our primary, secondary, and tertiary objectives. If I understand correctly, our main objective is to talk with Ahote and try to convince him to just hand over the necklace and end this whole thing without any incident. From what you've told us about this guy, our chances of success with this strategy are pretty small, but we still have to give it a try."

Tommy scribbled: "1. Negotiate."

Everyone nodded.

"If this scenario does not work, then our secondary strategy will be to try to forcefully remove the necklace from him before he has a chance to turn into the big, scary monster of death." He wrote: "2. Grab the goods."

Everyone nodded again.

"And if that plan does not work out, we need to come up with a way to get him—in his werewolf form—to a secluded spot on the side of a cliff. One or more of us will have it out with this thing, while somehow managing not to get killed, and push Fido off the edge to the jagged rocks below." Finally, he wrote: "3. Operation Splat." Two vertical lines separated the chalkboard into three distinct sections—one for each objective. "So did I miss anything?"

Richard said, "No. I think you have our three main goals down pretty well. We just need to work out the details."

"Okay. Let's start brainstorming then." Tommy answered.

For the next two hours, the four of them threw out ideas and discussed the specifics involved and the advantages and disadvantages of each tactic. One after another, most were scratched out for being too dangerous or for relying on Ahote reacting in ways that he most likely would not.

What eventually become apparent was that there was virtually no way Richard could do it all alone with any chance of success. The realization pained him greatly. The last thing he wanted was to put his friends in danger, but they were more than willing—and it did not appear that there were any other options at that point. Eventually, they established what seemed to be a pretty comprehensive plan of attack. It accounted for backup tactics and last-second adjustments if needed. It also provided a somewhat reasonable possibility of success—without any bloodshed by either party.

"I think we've got a plan here," Richard said. "Now if any of you are having second thoughts about this, just say so. We all know what we're dealing with here, and if anyone is getting cold feet, don't hesitate. There's no obligation for any of you to help me with this."

"Don't even sweat it, bro," Hector replied. "This is an adventure of a lifetime, and just like when you had my back against John Sandal and his goons, I've got your back here."

"That was a few sophomore bullies. This is a werewolf. Not exactly an apples-to-apples comparison," Richard answered.

"Apples, bananas, werewolves… whatever, dude. When I say I got ya, I got ya!"

"Same for me, Rich," Tommy said. "You think I'm gonna go through all the trouble to come up with this masterpiece and not be there to see it through?"

"Of course you can count on me," Jenny said. "You saved my life. The least I can do is return the favor."

There was a long pause as the reality of everything began to sink in. They glanced at each other and waited for Richard to put the plan officially into action.

Pulling out his iPhone, Richard opened up the last text from Chenowa. "We're all in agreement? Saturday evening at five in the woods near the reservation, right?" After the other three nodded, Richard typed the message to Chenowa. When the text was ready to go, he triple-checked it for errors. Exchanging last glances with everyone to look for any hint of hesitation and seeing none, he hit Send. "Okay. It's done."

After a few awkward seconds, Hector said, "We should all hang out tomorrow night. Go catch that new Jack Black comedy that came out last week. I mean… in case it's our last… er… well, you know."

"Yeah, we should definitely do that," Jenny said. "We all need a fun night together."

Richard and Tommy nodded, and the plan was confirmed. They would meet at the mall at six forty-five and plan on catching the seven thirty show.

Richard, Hector, and Jenny headed homes, and Hector and Richard walked together—but neither of them said a word the entire time.

A ping rang out from Richard's phone. It was a sound he'd heard a thousand times, but it somehow sounded more menacing and foreboding. They stopped, and Hector looked to Richard as he pulled the device out of his pocket. It was a text from Chenowa. Richard stared at it for several seconds before opening the chat window, wishing it would somehow disappear. Finally, tapping on the phone, the text popped up in front of him: "Chenowa heard back from Ahote. He'll meet me at the clearing we discussed on Saturday at five. It's on. He'll be there."

"Cool deal, man," Hector said, trying to hide the fear and anxiety in his voice. "It'll be fine, bro. I told you. We got this."

The cool breeze made it seem even colder than it should have, and ominous clouds were drifting in from the west.

Hector said, "Looks like a storm is coming in."

"I know," Richard said. "Looks like it could be a bad one."

CHAPTER 17

Richard awoke in dark silence. Realizing that his alarm had not gone off yet, he closed his eyes and tried to get back to sleep. However, within a few minutes, he knew that it wasn't in the cards. Glancing toward his alarm clock on his nightstand, he saw it was 6:05.

Alarm goes off in twenty-five minutes, he thought. *Might as well get up now and have an early start to the day.*

After getting out of bed and taking off the necklace, he made his way to the bathroom. With time to spare, he took an extra-long shower. It was unusually cold, and the hot water felt especially comforting. The details of the plan began to creep back into his head, but he quickly stopped himself before the racing thoughts took hold. *Not today!*

Stepping out of the shower, he strained to see a hint of his reflection on the mirror due to the steam that had accumulated during his twenty-minute cleansing. After drying, he used the towel to wipe a strip across the middle of the glass, revealing his jumbled wet mass of black hair and the three scars on his chest. They were almost completely healed, and only minor scabbing and redness remained.

He put on his boxer briefs, socks, and jeans. Every morning since his last encounter with Ahote, he would put on the necklace and cover it with a T-shirt. As he was bringing it up to his neck, he paused. After thinking about it for a few moments, he carefully rolled it up and stashed it in the back section of his underwear drawer. *Today is not about this thing,* he thought. *Today is about just being a fourteen-year-old kid again. It might be the last day I'll ever be able to do it, but for the next twenty-four hours, I'm going to pretend I never found that damn thing!*

Once he put away the necklace and finished getting dressed, he went downstairs, poured himself a cup of coffee, and talked with his mom about school while she finished making breakfast.

He met up with Hector twenty minutes later, and they exchanged their usual fist bump and smiled at each other. The necklace and whatever lay in store for them tomorrow were not to be discussed that day.

The school day that followed was perhaps the most enjoyable Richard had experienced all year. An amazing feeling of innocence seemed to permeate the air, and he felt a freedom from burden and all things grim, serious, and life-threatening. He was just a kid a few months into his freshman year, enjoying a Friday with his friends and schoolmates. Mrs. Briar even commented that he seemed especially chipper.

At lunch, the four of them sat together at an outside table in the quad and joked and gossiped like none of them had a care in the world. It was sunny, and a brisk November breeze made for a nearly perfect temperature.

Cross-country had finished for the season, and Richard could walk home with all three of his friends, which he had not been able to do more than a couple of times. As they chatted and goofed around, Richard exchanged a few crossing glances with Jenny that were somehow different than the ones they usually shared. His feelings for her, which had been temporarily put on hold due to the events of the past several weeks, came rushing back stronger than ever. Jenny turned off to the street that led to her house, and a block after that, Tommy did the same, leaving Richard and Hector to cover the last quarter of a mile alone.

"I'm gonna tell her how I feel tonight," Richard said.

"So you really going do it, eh?" Hector said. "Well, I guess tonight's as good a time as any—given that we might all get eaten by a werewolf tomorrow."

"Way to kill a moment, Mr. Sunshine. Got any more enlightening words of encouragement?"

"You know I'm only kidding with you. Seriously, you really should tell her. It's the right thing to do. It will make things kinda awkward with the four of us afterward, but you should still go for it."

"There's something else I've been thinking about—and you aren't gonna like it."

"Uh-oh. Does it have anything to do with the plan tomorrow? I don't think we'll have time to make any significant changes at this point."

"No, it's about the necklace. I'm pretty sure that, after we deal with this whole Ahote thing, I'm going get rid of it."

"Say what? Are you screwing with me? You find the greatest thing in the history of everything, and you want to get rid of it!"

"It just seems like every horrible thing that has happened to us the past few weeks has all been tied back to it. I think I want to just be an ordinary teenager again."

"Aw, come on, homey. We got a great thing going on here. You can't give up on it now! Just promise me that you'll think about it. Don't go making any rash decisions."

In front of Hector's house, Richard turned to his friend and said, "Okay. I'll think about it. See you in a couple hours. Gotta go make a dent on next week's term paper."

Hector came over at six o'clock to grab a quick dinner of KFC that Richard's mom had brought home before getting a ride over to the mall. The four had arranged to meet at the entrance to the mall closest to the movie theater, and by the time Richard and Hector arrived, Tommy was already waiting for them. The three of them chitchatted until Jenny finally walked in at 7:02, fashionably late as always. She wore a white Lady GaGa concert T-shirt, a short leather jacket, and blue jeans with several intentionally placed holes along both legs and embroidery on the front pockets. She also wore a black choker with a peace sign and had at least twenty thin bracelets around her wrists, which caused her to jingle like a bag of quarters as she walked. Though it was not an especially fancy or unusual outfit for her, Richard thought she looked really cute.

As the four of them made their way over to the ticket counter, Richard ran through multiple scenarios for how he was going to express his feelings for her. He definitely wanted to do it when it was just the two of them, but he wasn't sure if he should try before or after the movie. It would be easier to tell her before since it would relieve all of the anxious anticipation, and he could relax during the movie, but depending on how the conversation went, it could make it awkward for him—and everyone else. Ultimately, he decided to hold off until the movie was over. Whether the end result of his declaration was what he hoped for—or something very different—he'd end the evening with a bang!

After buying their tickets, they walked around the mall to kill some time before taking their seats. Their typical shenanigans ensued as they popped in and out of stores. Everyone was having so much fun that they lost track of time and nearly missed the start of the movie. By the time the four of them made it into the theater, the lights were already out and the previews had started. They were giggling as they fumbled around in the dark, trying to find seats.

Richard feared they'd get thrown out before the movie even started, but they found seats and enjoyed the show. The jokes and one-liners in the movie, which would have made a mortician chuckle, were downright hysterical. They laughed until their sides hurt and their cheeks ached.

The movie ended at nine o'clock, and Tommy, Hector, and Jenny all texted their parents for ride. Richard's mom had driven them, and Hector's mom agreed to pick them up. They made their way through the lobby and were just about to exit the theater when Hector stopped and started grabbing at his pockets. "Aw, hell. I think my keys fell in the theater when I pulled out my phone. Tommy, come with me to help look for them."

"You did what?" Tommy replied. "You clumsy super-dweeb. You think they'll let us back in to look?"

"Sure they will. Come on and help me look."

"Do you need us to help look too?" Jenny asked.

"No. We've got it covered. You too can stay here and look out for my mom when she shows up."

As they headed back into the theater, Hector gave one last look to Richard and threw him a quick wink of acknowledgement, which revealed his true intentions. Knowing that he didn't have much time to work with, Richard suggested that they wait outside to spot their parents when they drove up.

A knot welled up in Richard's throat, and he felt sweat on his hairline. In a panic, he froze. For a moment, he forgot how to speak. Fighting for the right words, and only coming up with nonsense, he decided to throw caution to the wind and just go with his heart—and hope that his head could catch up. "Jenny, I need to talk with you about something."

"What's wrong, Richie? Is it about tomorrow? Don't worry about that. It's a great plan, and I know it will all work out."

"No. It's not that. It's about us… I mean you-and-me us. Man, I'm screwing this up."

"What are you talking about? And why are you sweating? It's like fifty degrees out here."

"I really like you, okay? I have for a long time, and with everything that has happened the past few weeks, the feelings are stronger than ever. I guess what I'm saying is that I want to be more than just friends."

For several moments, Jenny stared back at him with an expression that he couldn't quite figure out. She was clearly trying to suppress some strong feelings that were bubbling up inside, but he could not tell if she was just trying not to smile too enthusiastically or if she was fighting the urge to laugh at how ridiculous his previous statement was. Panic was starting to sink in.

She said, "So what you're saying is that you want to be my boyfriend, right?"

"Yes. That's what I'm saying."

Jenny grinned widely and started to giggle. "I think I'll start off by saying it's about damn time! I was dropping every possible hint I could, and I was wondering if you were ever going to ask me. Of course, I'll be your girlfriend!"

She hugged Richard firmly, squeezing him with a surprising amount of strength given her small stature.

After a few moments, the two pulled away slightly and faced each other. Their noses were only a few inches apart. Staring deep into her eyes and seeing what he thought was the look he was hoping for, Richard slowly leaned in and turned slightly to the side. Jenny did the same, and after what seemed like an eternity, their lips met—and the two kissed for several seconds. There was none of that weird tongue stuff—only soft lips, the smell of her perfume, and the taste of her strawberry lip balm. It was a thousand times better than when he kissed Elania at the reservation. Richard wanted to truly savor this moment, but something stopped him. When he eventually pulled away, he was still smiling widely. There was a hint of hesitation in his eyes.

"What's up, sweetie? I can call you sweetie now, right?"

"There's one more thing I need to tell you." He gathered his courage for a second time. "After tomorrow, if we're able to resolve everything with Ahote once and for all, I've decided I'm going to get rid of the necklace and just go back to being a regular kid again."

"Okay. But why are you telling me this now?"

"I just want to make sure that when you said yes to being my girlfriend, you were saying yes to me and not my superpowers."

Richard was not really sure what sort of response he'd receive after delivering his last comment, but whatever he imagined, it was not the reply he received.

Jenny's smile immediately disappeared, and before Richard could say a word, she punched him in the shoulder.

"Ow!"

"You're a big jerk! What kind of a person do you think I am that I would only like you because you can do crazy things with a stupid necklace? I like you for you—for the person you are and the friend you've been to me these past years. You're totally awesome, you big clueless knucklehead." Her scowl quickly gave way to an adorable pout, which gradually morphed into a sly grin.

Richard struggled to think of something to say.

She said, "Now come over here and kiss me before you open your mouth and say something stupid again."

Confused by the sudden change of disposition, he decided it was best not to overthink the situation and go for it. He leaned in and kissed her a second time, which was even better than the first. The emotional roller coaster she had just taken him on seemed to add to the excitement. *If only this could go on for just a bit longer.*

Mrs. Lee's horn jolted the two out of their embrace as she parked right in front of the theater—only about thirty feet from them. Her expression was unlike anything Richard had ever seen. It was filled with a conflicting emotions, but at the same time, she was trying to hide any trace of them.

Jenny's pink face was beautiful, and her expression was absolutely adorable.

"I guess you gotta go, eh?" Richard said, breaking the awkward tension.

"Yeah. I guess I better. I'm really not looking forward to the inquisition waiting for me on the ride home, but I don't think she'll actually be too upset. She likes you. She wishes you'd cut your hair, but she still likes you. So everything is a go for tomorrow at eleven, right?"

The words hit him like a punch to the nose that was even harder than the one he just took to his shoulder. The words made perfect sense for her to say, given the situation, but they still hurt. In one second, she took him from one of the best moments of his life to the reality of the imminent peril they all would face tomorrow. He tried to hide his feelings of dread, and quickly said, "Yep… eleven o'clock in front of the school."

Jenny gave him one last quick hug and a kiss on the cheek before pulling back and making her way to her mom's car. The window rolled down a couple inches, and her mom's eyes locked squarely on his.

Richard figured he should say or do something. Raising his hand no higher than his shoulder, he waved slightly. "Good night, Mrs. Lee."

No words were returned, and her expression did not change as she pulled away. Awkward!

"S'up, Romeo?" Tommy was walking with Hector and grinning from ear to ear. Clearly, they were enjoying every second of this. "That's pretty impressive. I usually need to date a girl for about a month before I piss her off to the point where she wants to punch me. It only took you ten seconds!"

Richard blushed and turned to Tommy. "So how long did it take you to figure out that Hector really didn't lose his keys?"

"About five seconds. Hector's about as subtle as a rhinoceros in a china shop. Since his heart was in the right place, I went along with it for a few minutes. After that, we hung out just inside the entrance to enjoy the show."

"I guess it's gonna be kinda weird between the four of us now, eh?" Richard said.

"Yeah, it will," Tommy said. "But seeing that we've got a friend with superpowers and are getting ready to fight a werewolf tomorrow, I'd say that *weird* is sort of our thing."

CHAPTER 18

At eleven o'clock, they met up in front of the school. Richard was wearing the same leather jacket as the day he rescued Jenny, but he'd used a red Sharpie to change the pink accents.

They were all nervous but steadfast in their commitment to the plan. Little was said between them for several minutes until Luis pulled up in an old Plymouth Reliant. Hector had provided his friend with some details regarding what they were up to and trusted that he could keep his mouth shut. Luis was the only person that any of them knew—other than family members—with a driver's license, so there wasn't really another option.

The story that all four provided their respective parents for continuity was that they would be helping set up the gymnasium for the victory party celebrating the school's varsity football team when they hopefully won the league championship at a game that started at four o'clock. As luck would have it, the game was actually taking place at four o'clock, and the prep squad was planning to do some sort of event following the last game of the season. The event could go until eight or nine o'clock and provided them with the perfect alibi for the next eight or nine hours.

When the trunk opened, Richard and Tommy tossed in a backpack and a large duffel bag. Hector sat in front, and Tommy, Jenny, and Richard squeezed into the back. Tommy was nearly twice Hector's size, and it would have made a lot more sense for him to sit in front, but since Luis was Hector's friend, no one said anything when he called shotgun before climbing in. Once everyone was seated, Luis drove to the parking lot of the Lee family's hardware store.

As she often did on Saturdays, Jenny agreed to hold down the checkout counter while her father walked a few doors down to get a Reuben and a beer at his favorite sandwich shop. He normally brought his lunch to work during the week, but he liked being able to get out of the store for a bit on the weekends.

Jenny walked across the parking lot went into the hardware store. It was an agonizingly long five or six minutes before Mr. Lee exited the store and turned toward the sandwich shop. As soon as he was twenty yards away, Luis parked right in front of the entrance, and the other three ran inside. No customers were in the store, so there would be no one to blow their cover when her dad returned.

Jenny had already started pulling a length of industrial, synthetic rope from a large spool in the back of the shop. In the plumbing section, Tommy and Hector started looking through the selection of lead pipes. After a minute, they found a suitable choice that was three feet long and fifteen or twenty pounds. They also threaded two large nuts on one end of the pipe.

Hector grabbed a roll of duct tape.

Richard sprinted to the equipment-rental section of the shop and retrieved the biggest chainsaw they had. They met up at the entrance, raced out to the car, and place all of their items in the trunk.

Once the trunk was shut, Jenny ran back inside the store.

Richard, Tommy, and Hector climbed into the car, and Luis parked next door.

When Richard saw Jenny's dad walking back with his brown paper bag, he slumped down to ensure that her dad did not recognize him. There was no reason that he would be looking in their direction, but it was better to be safe than sorry. Her dad was smiling and whistling as he walked into the store, blissfully unaware of the tremendous danger his daughter could possibly be facing.

When Jenny finally exited the store and started walking back to the car, they all sighed.

She turned to Richard and said, "Okay. We're good. He doesn't suspect a thing. As long as he doesn't figure out that we borrowed the chainsaw, we should be fine."

"Okay then. Let's go," Richard said.

For the next twenty minutes, Luis drove out of town, into the hills, and northwest toward the reservation. There was barely a word spoken, and to make matters worse, the old car had a broken radio. There wasn't even any music to distract them. They only had the eerie silence of their thoughts to pass the time.

Richard's thoughts were screaming in his head. Had he done the right thing allowing his friends to get involved in this debacle? Without question, their plan required all of them to work, and it certainly had a much higher likelihood of success than anything involving only himself, but was that enough of a reason to endanger all of them? If it was only his life at risk, it would be a different matter. If he and Ahote had to fight again, regardless of the outcome, the threat his cousin posed to this world would be gone when it was over, and he was pretty confident that he'd be willing to go after him alone, even if it meant his demise. Richard knew it was not the situation they were in. If he fought Ahote alone and failed, his cousin's reign of terror would continue, and without the necklace to combat him, there was no telling the pain and suffering he could inflict upon those who Richard knew and loved. Even worse, he could take Richard's necklace and use it himself—or find another tribe member to corrupt with its power. There could be two monsters out there wreaking havoc on the world! That scenario was unacceptable. Richard had to do everything humanly possible to stop Ahote, and if his friends were willing and brave enough to offer their help, how could he turn them down? He would just have to do everything he could to keep them safe and hope for the best. It might not even come to that. It was possible they'd be able to get him to hand over the necklace or take it from him without a fight. *Perhaps luck will be on our side today?*

At twelve thirty, Luis dropped them off at the beginning of a dirt trail that was about a mile past the entrance to the reservation. Hector spoke with him, as Richard and Tommy unpacked everything from the trunk.

As Luis completed a three-way turn to drive back to town, the friends grabbed their equipment and headed into the woods. The dark clouds added to the foreboding feeling that was hanging over them. A cold wind was blowing through the trees from the west. They were near the ocean, and Richard could almost taste the salt in the air. It instantly took him back to the cliff and the waves brutally smashing on the boulders below. Hearing them in his head, the sound was louder and more forceful, and he could almost feel the icy waters washing over him and sucking him into the abyss. Catching himself, he forced the thoughts out of his head, refocusing on the tasks at hand. There was no time to allow worst-case scenarios to fly through his head. They had a strategy in place—a good one—and he needed to allocate all of his resources to its perfect execution.

After hiking for about thirty minutes, they arrived at the clearing where Ahote had agreed to meet with Chenowa in about four hours. From there, it would be another mile to get to the cliff. It was more than enough time to get everything ready, but they all agreed that allocating additional time was a good idea.

The path sloped up, and they all slowed down except Richard. With the necklace, he carried as much of the equipment as he could to take the burden off the others, but he still seemed to find himself fifty or sixty yards ahead of the others and would have to stop and wait for them to catch up. It made the hike seem much longer, and Richard became more anxious and impatient with every step.

At the clearing, Richard saw the horizon directly ahead of him. The clouds were even darker than before, and just as he looked out to the point where the sky met the sea, a lightning bolt illuminated the curves and contours of the billowing objects. For an instant, the clouds seemed to take on the appearance of a demonic face that was sneering at him ominously. Thunder cracked a moment later, and shivers cascaded through Richard's body like electric shocks.

A couple minutes later, the others joined him near the cliff. They slowly walked toward the edge and cautiously peered down. The jagged rocks glared back at them. Pools of seaweed-filled water surrounded the boulders, but the water levels were a bit lower than they were when Richard was there with his grandfather. He could see the concern in his friends' eyes as they looked down. Perhaps it was only a fear of heights, but it seemed like there was more to it.

Standing up straight again, Richard cautiously backed away from the edge and started walking toward the pile of supplies. Richard picked up the chainsaw, turned to his friends with a gaze of solemn determination, and struggled to think of something appropriate to say.

In the end, he abandoned hope of anything inspirational and decided to be satisfied with something practical. "Okay, gang. Let's get to work."

CHAPTER 19

Chenowa nervously zipped up his denim jacket to protect himself from the winds that whipped through the redwoods. His nerves were on high alert, and every snap of a twig or chirp of a bird caught his attention. It was twenty minutes before he was supposed to meet Ahote, and when he was suppose to meet up with Richard.

It was critical that everyone involved, including Chenowa, was informed of every aspect of their plan. It would likely only take a few minutes to get his cousin up to speed, but it was always better to allow more time than needed.

A rustling of trees came from the west. This initially startled Chenowa, but this quickly changed when he saw Richard smiling as he walked toward him. The two exchanged their usual shake and bro hug before Richard carefully walked Chenowa through the different aspects of the plan, starting with the best-case scenario of somehow convincing Ahote to hand over the necklace. If that didn't work, and if all else failed, Richard was prepared to fight the monster. Richard could see in Chenowa's expression that he still did not fully believe everything he was telling him, but he trusted Richard enough to follow through with the plan to the best of his ability—and judge for himself what was really going on once he could see if firsthand.

"Now this is the most important part!" Richard said. "If he starts to change, turn and run back toward the main road as fast as you can. It takes about a minute for the transformation to take place, and that should give you ample time to get the hell outta here! I don't think he'd want to hurt you, but I'm pretty sure that while he's in his beast form, he loses a lot of control over his actions. I can't risk you getting hurt or killed by accident. Do you understand?"

"Yeah. I got it. And you're going to do everything you can to keep from hurting him, right?"

"Absolutely! If I never have to go up against that thing again, it will be just fine by me!"

After a shake and a bro hug for a second time, Richard headed back into the forest.

Chenowa stood in the middle of the clearing, alone and trembling with fear and anxiousness. A tornado of thoughts flew through his mind as he awaited his brother's arrival. Did he actually have a clear side he was taking in the fight? Though there was still much he did not believe or understand, it was apparent that Richard and Ahote had kept important things from him. Perhaps this was for his safety, but it might have been for more self-serving or nefarious reasons. He loved Richard like a brother, but Ahote actually was his one and only sibling. Despite their differences, he comprised a third of their core family. Was he really ready to betray that bond? Ultimately, he told himself that he'd hear out both sides and make his own decision about how to proceed.

Fifteen minutes later, a second disturbance in the forest—to the east this time—caught Chenowa's attention, and he turned quickly to face the sound. A dark figure walked through the trees, and it took several moments to realize that Ahote was walking toward him. He was barefoot, and his baggy sweats were cut off just below the knees. The only other thing that he appeared to be wearing was a large black hoodie with the top pulled down to eye level. The shadows cast by the setting sun filtering through the trees that surrounded them, highlighted his jaw, cheekbones, and the tip of his nose, but it left the rest of his face darker, giving him an almost skeletal appearance. Perhaps Ahote could see, or sense his brother's uncertainty as he proceeded to lower his hood, revealing his full image. Chenowa recognized his brother, but Ahote looked thinner, harder, and colder. It was almost as if he'd been carved from marble. Whatever had happened in the weeks since Chenowa had last seen him, he was a changed person. Whether this change was for the worse was still to be determined. Chenowa's stomach was churning with nervous anticipation. Looking at his brother, he was uncertain about what to say.

Finally, Ahote said, "Hey, bro. Long time, no see. You look good. How's Mom?"

"Mom's not so good," Chenowa said. "She's a little upset after her oldest son took off two months ago and apparently joined up with a criminal biker gang. Oh, and then to top it all off, earlier this week, the cops showed up and grilled her for two hours about you possibly being involved in the deaths of three people! So NO… She's not doing so hot these days!"

For several seconds, Ahote looked down at his brother's feet. Glancing back up to his eyes, he said, "You don't understand, bro. It wasn't supposed to be like that. The biker gang was just a means to an end. I only needed them to help me get back at Richard for screwing up my hand and publicly humiliating me in front of everyone! Once that was done, I was going to come home and help you and Mom get off the reservation and move to a nice place like Richie's family."

"And what's so bad about living on the reservation?" Chenowa asked. "I love it there. I've got a ton of friends, and we've got the trees and the ocean. We don't have a lot of money, but who cares? And how exactly did you think you'd be able to provide all those great things for us by leaving school? There are not exactly a lot of high-paying career opportunities for high school dropouts."

"It's the necklace!" Ahote unzipped the hoodie slightly to reveal the item lined with wolves' teeth and shiny black orbs. "It has abilities that you wouldn't believe. It's incredible! Within a few days, I had an entire group of guys practically worshiping me. They would steal for me—and do whatever else I told them to do."

"And where are they now?" Richard said.

Chenowa and Ahote looked toward the sound, and Ahote blinked twice in disbelief, trying to figure out what was going on. A Latino teenager was standing in front of him with a smartphone in one hand and a small speaker in the other. A wire connected the two.

Richard's voice said, "Your biker gang abandoned you after you killed several of them in an uncontrollable rage, isn't that right?"

"Richard, is that you?" Ahote shouted at speaker. "Are you so cowardly and dishonorable that you could not face me in person? And why are you even here? Chenowa wanted to meet with me to discuss family matters that have nothing to do with you!"

"Chenowa suggested you meet him here because I asked him to. He knows everything, and I needed to speak with you. I asked him to set this up so that we could talk through this and come up with the solution that's the best for all of us. I had my friend Hector go in my place because I feared the sight of me might upset you to the point of doing something rash."

"And what exactly would you propose to be a solution that would be good for all of us?" Ahote asked. "If your idea is for the two us go at it again—and see once and for all who is the superior warrior—then bring it on! That's all I ever wanted."

"These necklaces are too powerful for either of us to have. We're just kids, and we don't have the maturity to be responsible with them. We should do the right thing and destroy them—or at least give them to Grandpa and the tribe elders. They'll know what to do."

"And then what? Just go back to our normal lives and pretend like nothing happened? That may be easy for you and your imminent fortunes once your dad sells all the houses he's building, but what about me! I just go back to our broken-down mobile home and hope the police never connect me to the biker gang or the other things the creature did? I could go to jail! How would that be fair?"

After several seconds, Richard said, "Listen, cuz. I can't change what happened in the past—and neither can you. The only thing we can do is to change our future by doing the right thing now. I truly believe that giving up these abilities is the best for both of us. You cannot fully control the beast once it takes over you. What if you accidentally hurt or kill your mom—or Chenowa? Are you willing to take that risk?"

"I would never do that!" Ahote shouted. "I can pretty much control the creature. Those guys the other night were just a couple of thugs. If it was someone I really cared about, I'd never hurt them. No, I'm afraid I'm hanging onto this sucker. But if you feel that you're too much of a wimp to handle the one you have, I'd be happy to take it off your hands for you. I'll even make a deal with you. If you hand over the necklace, I'll let you go. I will never bug you—or your family and friends—ever again. Consider it a gesture of good faith. I'll give you my word." He glanced toward Chenowa. "Or even better—I'll let you have it, bro! Granted, it's not as powerful as the one I have, but it's still pretty awesome. Even a total loser like Richard actually put up a decent fight while wearing it. You'd be stronger, faster, and more agile than you could ever imagine possible, and the two of us would be unstoppable together!"

Richard replied in a lower volume, saying, "Hector, give the phone to Ahote."

Hector slowly unplugged the speaker from the phone, cautiously walked over to Ahote, and handed him the device.

"Okay, cuz. It's just you and me now. So what do you have to say to me that you couldn't with your lackey listening in?"

"Don't get Chenowa wrapped up in this thing," Richard said. "He's a good person, and I'm sure he wants nothing to do with whatever egomaniacal plans you might have—if you were somehow able to get a hold of my necklace."

"How the heck would you know what he would or wouldn't be interested in? Here's a novel idea… let's let Chenowa decide for himself? You hand over the necklace and let him try it out for a while. If he decides he doesn't want it, I'll just keep it. It would be nice to have a backup. Maybe I'll try wearing both of them at the same time! Have no idea what might happen, but I'd be interested in finding out. Enough of this talking on the phone nonsense. Are you going to hand over the necklace voluntarily—or am I going to have to take it by force!"

"I'm not going to let you have the necklace!" Richard said. "And I'm sure as hell not going to hand it over to you. I'm going to make one last request in hopes that you still have some sense left in you. Let's both agree to give up the necklaces and call a truce so we can go back to our normal lives again."

"Or what?"

"Or I promise it will end badly."

"Are you insane? You dare to threaten me when you're too cowardly to even meet me in person!" Ahote's face was crimson with rage.

Richard's goal was to get Ahote so upset that he would be momentarily distracted from someone casually walking up behind him.

After handing the phone to Ahote, Hector inconspicuously walked back around and slowly drew a pair of large sturdy scissors from the back of his jeans. If it looked like Ahote was not going to voluntarily hand over the artifact, Hector would try to sneak up behind his foe, cut the leather strap that held the necklace together, and run away with it. Richard had previously transferred his super speed to Hector, so he could move with lightning reflexes and escape if he needed to.

The black hoodie that completely covered the back of the necklace was not part of their plan.

This will not be easy, Hector thought. For him to execute the maneuver, he would need to yank the hoodie down with one hand and try to navigate the scissors underneath the leather strap without stabbing Ahote in the neck. With zero chance of a sneak attack, he'd have to move as quickly as he could and hope that the initial shock of the unexpected action would buy him the time to cut the necklace.

Glancing over to Chenowa, Hector could see sweat forming on his brow. Hector had seen the scissors and could blow the entire thing if he wanted to. Richard assured them that Chenowa was on their side in this endeavor, but this was a massive betrayal of his brother who had just promised him unimaginable powers if he decided to go along with his plan. Only time would tell what would happen.

Chenowa stood silent and motionless as his older brother screamed into the phone, waving his other arm around like a crazed chimpanzee.

Suddenly, the break that Hector had been waiting for appeared. One of Ahote's movements shifted his hoodie back slightly on his shoulders, and the material dipped down about an inch. It was just enough for Hector to see the back of the necklace. There would still be little—if any—chance of surprising him, but at least he'd be grabbing at the actual necklace with his left hand instead of the hood. Realizing he might not have the opportunity for more than a few seconds, he thought, *Go!*

In an instant, Hector closed the six-foot gap between them, and his left hand shot out like a bullet toward the thin piece of leather on the back of Ahote's neck. He could almost feel his fingers grasping it when a voice rang out in his ears.

"Ahote!"

Crap! Hector thought. *Chenowa must have had a last-second change of heart, and he just let his brother know that something's happening. Keep going. You might still be able to pull this off!* Grasping at the strap, Hector managed to get his pinkie and ring fingers beneath the leather.

Ahote's neck jerked to the left in response to his brother's warning.

Seeing his window of opportunity slamming shut, Chenowa attempted to get one of the blades under the strap. Focusing his actions with every ounce of concentration, the metal blade just touched the leather when something hit his left shoulder, knocking him completely off his feet and sending the scissors flying through the air.

Ahote twisted toward his foe and hit him with the back of his elbow. Even in human form, Ahote possessed extraordinary strength.

Hector's shoulder throbbed like it had been hit with a baseball bat.

Ahote's eyes glared with crazed fury, and the veins on his forehead now pulsated like subcutaneous worms. He held Richard's cell phone up to his face and screamed, "You coward! You tried to pull some kind of sneaky crap like that on me? Well, you better say goodbye to your little friend here because I'm about to tear him limb from limb!" Ahote lurched his head backward and pushed out his chest, releasing a scream that froze Hector's veins with terror. Just as Richard had described, he could see the black stones and the wolves' teeth strung along the artifact painfully sucked into Ahote's neck.

Realizing the hoodie would only impede his transformation, Ahote grasped behind his shoulder, bent forward, and pulled it over his head. He struggled with the sweatshirt for a few moments, and when the cloth finally fell to the ground, what stood back up again was no longer human. Black hair covered his torso and face, and claws were forming where the fingernails had been a moment earlier.

Realizing that it would only be a matter of seconds before the transformation was complete, Hector got to his feet and turned to Chenowa. "Run as fast as you possibly can!" Turning back to his foe, Hector could now see the wrenching contortions of his face, arms, and legs as bones grew and distorted, transforming Ahote into the horrible wolflike creature that stood before him. Sensing that the metamorphosis was almost finished, Hector began running toward the path. Just before leaving the clearing, he stopped and glanced back. To his amazement, the beast had not started chasing him.

Behind the menacing creature, Chenowa was still standing in the clearing, and he was only about twenty yards from the horrific beast.

Oh, hell! Hector thought. *This is bad. This dude is a goner unless I do something.* In addition to his enhanced speed, he had one more weapon in his arsenal. He reached down, grabbed a rock, and threw it as hard as he could at the creature, hitting it in the back.

The beast whipped around, faced Hector, and showed off his horrible fangs, which dripped with froth. The creature appeared to be torn between its two potential victims. Chenowa would be an easier kill; he was closer and was apparently paralyzed by fear.

The beast might need some extra motivation to pursue me instead. "Hey! Over here, you stinky fleabag!" Hector shouted. "Come on, you mangy Lassie wannabe! Try to catch me, you worthless mutt— or would you rather hang out with your other dog friends, sniffing each other's butts!"

The beast let out a roar that shook the ground, turned toward Hector, and leaped with demonic red eyes staring right through him.

Realizing that he had successfully gotten the creature's attention, Hector could only pray that the super speed would hold out long enough to make it back to the others. Turning toward the trail, he headed west, running even faster than before. Trees and shrubbery flew past him in a blur as he carefully navigated the rocks and any other obstacles that could potentially trip him up. He could hear the creature tearing through branches and foliage like dried twigs, and he used the sounds of its snarls and growls to estimate the distance behind him. On two occasions, he actually had to slow down a bit to make sure that he didn't lose Ahote during the pursuit. Every moment was absolute terror, but he kept reassuring himself. *You got this! You got this!* When he reached the second clearing, the others would be waiting for him.

Finally, after what seemed like forever, Hector burst into the open area.

When Richard saw Hector, the realization that his friend had not been killed by this crazy scheme was a relief.

Hector darted off behind a large tree.

Moments later, the beast smashed through the branches and screeched to a halt twenty yards in front of Richard. The beast's expression changed, and a sound caught his attention. Glancing behind and to his left, the beast turned and leaped backward as a huge redwood came smashing down with a colossal impact that shook the entire area and cut off the path.

The mighty tree had been cut with a chainsaw, but something powerful must have provided one hell of a shove to knock it the rest of the way over.

Richard was wearing a black and red leather jacket, jeans, and running shoes.

The creature dug in and prepared to leap toward its target.

Richard used every ounce of discipline and self-control to keep his wits about him. For their plan to work, everything would need to go perfectly—and he'd only get one shot at it. He had already passed on his speed, strength, and abilities of the feather, and he only had catlike reflexes and agility to help him. If the creature somehow got a hold of him, it would be over before he could even call out for help.

Launching off coiled hind legs, the creature shot out toward Richard. Its white-fanged, frothy maw opened wide, but a seagull hit it square in the face, immediately diverting its attention. The bird started pecking at the creature's eye with its sharp yellow beak.

Infuriated, the creature jerked its head and mouth toward the bird, and with a horrible snap, it brought its jaws down in a plume of feathers.

When the lifeless seagull fell to the ground, two more swooped down and used their feet and beaks to attack the creature's head.

Roaring in frustration, the beast swung its claws through the air for several seconds and knocked them out of the air.

Richard had moved behind the creature and was holding some sort of rope. There was a large loop with a knot where the two pieces intersected.

Insane with rage, the monster leaped toward Richard with teeth and claws bared.

At the last possible moment, Richard calculating the trajectory of his target, leaped up, completed a twisting front flip over the top of the monster, and allowed the rope to hang down as the creature's head shot through it. Once his feet were back on the ground, Richard tightened the slipknot, turned, and started running to the south as fast as possible. If their calculations were correct, he only needed to make it about thirty feet, but he needed to do so before the creature caught up to him—or it was game over!

Spinning around, the beast lunged toward Richard, quickly narrowing the distance between them. The creature was just bringing down a mighty swing of its claw that would have torn the entire length of Richard's back when something snapped tight across its neck, yanking the creature up and back. The forward momentum was so great that the pullback from the rope, which was firmly encircling its neck, caused the creature's entire body to fly up from beneath it. All four limbs were airborne before it smashed to the ground on its back.

Shocked, enraged, and gasping for breath, it tried unsuccessfully to loosen the noose with its claws.

Another figure blasted its way through the bushes about forty feet away and charged straight toward the creature. The figure was about six feet tall and his stocky build was made stockier by layers of protective clothing. He was wearing a black leather motorcycle jacket, shoulder pads, a football helmet, and several other pads and guards on his arms and legs. The figure was also carrying a large metal pipe like a baseball bat. On one end, layers of duct tape provided a firm grip, and at the far end, two large steel nuts formed an intimidating mace-like weapon.

The beast was still clawing at the rope around its throat.

The figure shouted, "Let's do this, Scooby. You mess with my friends, you mess with me! It's clobbering time!"

The creature leaped out to attack and was yanked into a standing position by the tether around its neck. That was the opening Tommy needed, and he swung the pipe with all his might, smashing the creature just below its hip joint. The thigh bone snapped, and the beast roared in pain and fury. The creature swung its powerful left paw in retaliation, tearing off some of the protective padding on Tommy's right arm and slicing through most of the leather.

Tommy struck straight out with the pipe in a spear-like fashion, aiming for the diaphragm. The blow caused the monster to take another step back, allowing Tommy to land a third blow to the side of his midsection, just below the ribcage.

The beast scurried back in pain. With some slack in the noose, the creature quickly chomped its great jaws down on it, expecting to cut through the rope easily, but it was no ordinary twine. It was synthetic and tough as nails. Though the material was fraying, the beast continued to furiously grind the material across its molars in hopes of freeing itself.

Tommy froze in terror. The fight had gone his way thus far, but if the beast managed to free itself, things could change very quickly. His window of opportunity was closing as the beast tore at the rope, and he charged forward and swung the pipe as hard as he possibly could. Just before the blow impacted, the creature finally cut through the tether and jerked away from the pipe. It could not avoid the impact completely, but it managed to get its forearm in front of its head.

Another roar of pain and fury cried out as beast pulled back its injured paw and backed away from Tommy. The cliff was only about twenty feet behind it. Growing more confident in his abilities, Tommy charged forward a third time to finish this thing off once and for all, but he underestimated the creature's speed.

Freed from the rope, the beast leaped to its right with its good leg and with its only functional claw and brought down a smashing blow to Tommy's helmet and shoulder pads. Were it not for the added protection, the blow would have killed him. Instead, it only left him dazed and battered. His ears were ringing, and his eyes were blurry, but he got to his feet. He took a couple of steps back to reassess the situation, and something caught his attention over the creature's shoulder.

Jenny was standing just outside the tree line. She had gone completely against the plan they had so meticulously worked out. She was supposed stay hidden for the entirety of the battle.

Tommy was not the only person who noticed Jenny's appearance. Hector and Richard immediately saw her as well, and they momentarily froze in fear, unsure what to do about it.

Richard was in a complete quandary. He could yell for her to get back, but that would only draw the attention of the beast to her. It appeared to be fixated on Tommy since he still possessed a legitimate danger to it.

Tommy's momentary pause and the angle of his gaze must have caught the attention of the creature, and it quickly turned its head to the left.

Jenny stared back with a look of absolute terror in her eyes.

The beast spun around to survey its situation, and realizing that Jenny was clearly its most vulnerable foe, it turned and leaped in her direction.

Richard immediately began running as fast as he could, but without his enhanced speed, he feared that—even in its injured state—he would not be able to reach the beast in time.

Jenny was still paralyzed with fear, and she could only stare at the hairy monster that was scurrying toward her. The one person who did have super speed was Hector, and a moment after Richard began running, he could see Hector sprinting toward Jenny. He was actually farther away than Richard, but he was coming from a different angle and was running directly toward the point where Jenny and the monster would meet.

Richard was trying to catch the beast from behind.

Hector sprinted past Tommy, and Richard grazed his left fingers across the back of his friend's right hand—recapturing his bear strength—and grasped the pipe. *Ahote just made this personal, and it is my fight now!*

Richard noticed that Hector's trajectory was wrong. He would actually end up behind the beast. He thought about calling out to him until he noticed the eight or ten feet of rope that still trailed behind the creature. The beast had managed to chew through its tether, but the noose was still around its neck. Richard could see what Hector was trying to do. It was a brilliant tactic—if he could pull it off. It would require perfect timing, and he'd only have one chance to get it right. Gaining on the creature, but knowing he would not reach it in time, Richard could only look on and hope that this strategy paid off.

The creature was only a dozen feet from Jenny and would be on top of her in a moment.

Hector flew behind it, reached out, and grabbed the end of the rope with his right hand. He then reached across his body and just grasped the rope with his left as it snapped taut. The momentum of his 110-pound body traveling at close to forty miles per hour yanked hard and jerked the beast back and to its left.

With only one good hind leg, the creature was pulled onto its side. It rolled over onto all fours. With its injured arm and leg on opposite sides, the creature could maintain balance fairly well, and it turned around.

Hector had been pulled completely off his feet by the maneuver and was scrambling to regain his footing.

The monster lurched toward Hector with its mighty jaws opening wide, and it was just about to bring its fangs down until Hector managed to dive to his right and take off running toward Richard.

Richard momentarily grasped Hector's arm as he ran past, reclaiming his deer speed and returning him to almost his full abilities. Only the feather still resided with Jenny.

"Now it's just you and me!" Richard quickly positioned himself between the creature and Jenny. He had some added protection with his leather jacket and a more reliable weapon with the pipe, but his head and lower body were still vulnerable.

The beast moved back slightly, realizing the cliff was less than a dozen feed behind it. The beast crouched down in preparation for a leaping attack.

Richard would be able to dodge out of the way, but that would still leave Jenny right in its path—so that was not an option. Richard swung wildly with the pipe in a wide arc at the level of the creature's head. He was not trying the hit the beast with the swing, but he wanted to get it to back up and momentarily call off its attack. He swung again, and the monster inched slightly backward. A third swing backed the beast up several more inches.

When it was only a few feet from the edge, the creature retaliated. Using all its strength to push off its one good leg, the creature leaped toward Richard with claws and fangs shooting out at him like daggers. Having just swung the pipe across his body, Richard knew that he would not be able to swing it back in time to connect. Instead, he opted to drop the pipe. Realizing the tiny window of opportunity that presented itself, he crouched down and drove forward with all his might, managing to get himself under the head and shoulders of the beast.

His shoulder hit right below the monster's hairy sternum. The blow stopped the creature's momentum and stood it upright. If the beast had had two good legs to push back with, it would have probably knocked Richard onto his back—and that would have been the end of him. Fortunately, it did not, and in a split-second decision that Richard knew could be his last, he gave one last powerful lunge forward, sending them both right over the edge!

Everything slowed as Richard peered down toward the rocks below. He heard Jenny's scream behind him as she realized that he and his cousin were on this ride together. Richard knew it would not end well for either of them, but at least he would have delivered on his promise to himself that he would keep his friends safe. To his surprise, he began thinking about the story his grandfather had told him about the Spirit Walker—how he did battle with a horrible beast and, in the end, both died in basically this exact manner.

Perhaps it had been his destiny the entire time. *If you chose to take the mantle of the Spirit Walker, you ultimately doomed yourself to this fate.* The thought actually comforted him as the rocks slowly grew closer. It was certainly not the time or the way he would have liked to go out, but he made the choice to protect those he cared about—and he was not going to allow himself to regret it now. Richard simply accepted that the last thing he would hear would be the ever-loudening screams of Jenny crying out after him.

Wait. Ever-loudening screams? That doesn't sound right. If I'm falling away from her, the sound of her voice should be getting quieter—not louder—yet the sound is definitely increasing in volume. How is that possible?

Richard glanced up to the top of the ridge, and to his utter amazement, Jenny was staring right back at him. She must have dived off the cliff after them! She was reaching for one of his ankles, but it was flailing just out of her reach. Realizing what was happening, Richard stretched his leg out, and with one last strain from Jenny, she barely brushed the side of his leg with her fingertip. That was apparently all it took to transfer back the feather-falling ability. With only a thought, Richard felt his body jolt up like someone had just opened a parachute.

Jenny fell past him, but with a lightning-fast extension of his arm, he reached Jenny's hand, grasping her wrists—just as they had after driving the motorcycle off the cliff. With their falling speed reduced drastically, Richard glanced at the monster. It stared back up, but this time it was his cousins eyes looking back, and within the gaze, he saw sadness and regret instead of rage and hatred.

A sickening thud echoed back at Richard and Jenny as the beast finally hit the rocks. Richard and Jenny touched down on the rocks a few seconds later. Richard quickly climbed over a few large boulders, and the great hairy beast was twitching slightly. As Richard put his hand on the creature, the hair on its shoulder fell out, leaving Richard with a handful of the coarse black fur. He was transforming back into Ahote. As the face of his cousin became recognizable, he strained to talk over the blood that was running down the side of his mouth. Forming words looked like agony, but sensing that time was of the essence, Richard leaned down and placed his ear a couple of inches from Ahote's mouth.

"Tell Chenowa I'm sorry. Tell him I'm sorry for everything."

No further sound could be heard except for the water gently swirling around the base of the boulders. Turning his head back to face him, Richard's cousin looked straight up into the twilight sky, the moon, the stars, and the swirling clouds above them. There was a peace in Ahote's eyes unlike any Richard had seen. A drop of water hit Ahote's cheekbone, and Richard glanced up, thinking that it was starting to rain—only to realize that it was one of his own tears streaming down his face.

CHAPTER 20

Richard somberly stared into the flames of the bonfire that burned only a few feet in front of him. There was a much larger one about fifty yards away, and the members of his tribe chanted around it, beat their ceremonial drums, and carried out the dance of mourning that was traditional for his people after the passing of one of its members.

Richard had been with the rest of his tribe for several hours, but he needed to be on his own for a while. He had been at the gravesite as they laid Ahote to rest in the cemetery used by his tribe for as long as any of them could remember. As was the tradition of his people, his cousin was buried in his ceremonial Native American clothes, and his family placed in the casket with him several of his favorite books, his CD collection, and the bow and arrow he'd used to go hunting with his father.

It was an especially somber ceremony. Funerals were never cheery events, but to be having one for someone so young made it especially tragic. Richard could still vividly hear the cries of his aunt as she wailed out in agony, leaning on Chenowa, who was now the man of his family. His grandfather had provided a very powerful speech to commemorate the life of his grandson, and he encouraged everyone to show strength since Ahote was at one with the spirits of their people. Richard could not remember the specific words, and the feeling of despair still weighed on him greatly. Had he done everything he could to keep it from coming to this?

Hearing a sound from behind him, Richard glanced back.

Tommy, Jenny, and Hector were slowly walking toward him. They had been with him all day, and Richard would forever remember their act of friendship. He had always wanted to show his friends around the reservation and provide them with a glimpse of his life before he moved to the burbs, but he had hoped to do so under very different circumstances. Though he had walked over to the smaller fire to be alone, he was glad that the others were with him.

There was one more piece of business that needed to be taken care of, and it felt right that all four of them were there to do it. Reaching into his pocket, he pulled out a length of leather with a collection of black orbs and wolves' teeth strung along its length. He had removed it from Ahote at the bottom of the cliff before climbing back up and contacting the authorities.

"After I destroy this necklace, I'm throwing mine in right after it," Richard whispered as he gently pulled his necklace from underneath his shirt. He could sense that the others, Hector specifically, were dying to do something to try to persuade him to reconsider, but to his amazement, none of them said a thing. "It's just too powerful a thing to have out there, and I don't think I have the maturity to handle it. I just want to go back to the way things used to be."

Glancing to his right and left, he saw reassuring looks returned by his friends, and after taking a deep breath, Richard tossed the wolf-tooth necklace into the center of the fire. For a few moments, nothing happened. Richard had accepted that the artifact would just burn up, which would be the end of it.

Icy winds from the west suddenly chilled all four of them to the core, and dark clouds formed above them. A crack of thunder shot out from nothingness, and from the flames, black smoke started materializing. At first, it swirled like a tornado, and it grew twenty feet tall. The dark fog started to take on an almost humanoid appearance, with armlike appendages growing out of its sides and a head-like protuberance forming at the top.

Richard, Hector, Jenny, and Tommy froze, terrified of what was floating in front of them.

Richard thought, *What the hell is this thing? Can it hurt us or kill us? How do you combat something that appears to be made of smoke?*

Long clawed fingers and a canine face formed within the swirling soot, and a bright red glow shot out from what would have been the creature's eyes.

Richard was trying to call out for help when the flames of the bonfire shot twenty-five feet into the air, completely encompassing the phantom form. The heat from the blaze knocked everyone to the ground, and a powerful roar was immediately drowned out as a second crack of thunder shook all to their core. As soon as the sound of the thunder faded, the group looked back at the flames, which had returned to their previous size. Whatever had been threatening them a moment ago appeared to be gone.

Trying to make sense of what just happened, Richard looked to his friends for reassurance. They were all looking at the necklace. In between the bear claw and the deer antler, the dark red rock, which he had barely acknowledged earlier, glowed bright red. A feeling unlike anything he had ever experienced came over him. Glancing back to the fire, he had a thought in his mind, and within an instant, the flames began swirling into a tornado that was about three feet high. The tube of flames tilted to the right and to the left—just as Richard wanted it to. Then, just like that, the fire tornado was gone. Richard's friends were all staring blankly at the burning logs in front of them.

Richard said, "So I guess I can control fire with this sucker too? Pretty trippy, eh?"

After several seconds of silence, Hector said, "So you still gonna destroy the necklace? It seems like we owe it to science or something to at least test the thing out to see what it can actually do."

A sly smirk crept across Richard's face. "Yeah, I suppose you're right. Doesn't seem right to torch it now. After all, there are four different colored rocks on the necklace. I guess it wouldn't hurt to at least take them for a test-drive or something."

Printed in the United States
By Bookmasters